Welcome to Bellefield …
and Tales from Within

Anthony Roche

Welcome to Bellefield and Tales from Within

Copyright © 2024 by Anthony Roche
All rights reserved. This book or any portion thereof
may not be reproduced or used in any manner whatsoever without the express
written permission of the publisher except for the use of brief quotations in a
book review

The memories depicted throughout this book, those of chasing players for autographs in and around Bellefield, will always be special to me. But no memory will ever be as special as those of my mum, Barbara Roche, who sadly passed away during the writing of the book.

This book is dedicated to her.

The memories we share with loved ones can't be taken away, so this book goes out to everyone who has lost a loved one. Never forget those great times you shared together, treasure the memories you once shared.

R.I.P. Mum.

ACKNOWLEDGEMENTS:

A full list of those who have helped me write this book would run page after page and bankrupt my publisher. I'll do my best to keep this short.

Firstly, I would like to thank everyone who appears in the book. These are real people, with real passions. In the same way that football without fans is nothing, this book, without the memories, humour, and selflessness of the people in it, would lose all meaning. Therefore, my great thanks go to: *my family, Billy Edwards, and Darren Griffiths*.

A special thanks goes to Neil Parker for taking this journey with me, appearing in the book, and being there every step of the way. We became best mates aged five and our mutual love of Everton Football Club has been the foundation of this friendship ever since. To this day we still go to the match together.

The interview section, which appears in the latter half of the book, was a joy to edit. So many ex-players, coaches, and support staff offered up their time, sharing their wisdom, and their experiences, of Bellefield. To every one of them, I offer my sincere thanks.

I'd also like to offer a special thank you to Tommy Wheeldon for taking the time to introduce the book in the foreword.

When it came to putting the book together, I couldn't have done it without the help of some extremely talented people. Instrumental in formatting the work and getting it ready for publication was Terry Melia, a great author in his own right.

David Hitchen ran our advertising across social media, plus a hundred other tasks in the background.

Meanwhile, Steve Fairhurst, Managing Director of Branded Items Group, produced another fantastic front (and back!) cover, utilising images kindly sanctioned by The Liverpool Echo and Mirrorpix.

Proofreading and editing were done by Chandana Das and Billy Edwards. Thank you to both for being part of the team. Further thanks of a technical nature go to the talented members of Liverpool Laid Back Writers Group, run by the ever-helpful Mark Horne. The feedback offered during our sessions was insightful and precise.

Thank you so much.

Gary Bird proved an inspiration throughout. If those mentioned in this acknowledgements section ever took to the field as a football team, Gary would be its captain. Gary is the heartbeat of the operation, always there with encouragement whenever needed.

A thank you also goes to Mersey Windows of Cherry Lane, Walton, who have always kindly advertised my books across their showrooms. Mersey Windows hosts a team of top-class Evertonians, delivering top-class windows and doors across the Merseyside area.

For those unaware of the Everton Heritage Society, I strongly recommend checking out their website and the important work they do for former Everton Players. Richie Graham and Bren Connelly were a great help with their input with autographs and help with photos for the book.

Last, but by no means least, I would like to thank Everton Football Club for its assistance and its co-operation towards putting together this book. Darren Griffiths, Media and Publications manager, was enormously helpful, acting as my main point of contact with the club, offering advice, providing contacts, and then, after all that, taking time out of his busy schedule to personally show me around the club's new training ground, Finch Farm.

I would like to say goodbye to Carl Mills, Joey Parker, John Murphy and Eillen Kearns and to Scooby who all passed away during my writing of this book.

To those not already named, know that your influence has been appreciated and I am every bit as grateful.

I genuinely hope you enjoy the read.

COYB!

FOREWORD TOMMY WHEELDON

The days of getting autographs outside Bellefield I can relate to. I myself had that same passion and undying love for Everton Football Club, as Rochey, Parker, Cooper, and Skinny Maca, as I had lived similar adventures eleven years earlier with my mates from Huyton.

These were the playing days of the Holy Trinity: Ball, Kendall, Harvey. And, as Brian Labone the captain at that time once famously said, "The only three-man team to ever win the League Championship".

My connection with the author Anthony Roche came as he needed to contact the former Swindon Town manager Tommy Wright, a good friend of his who he had lost contact with.

I played the middle man and in our following conversations I found out he was one of the little scally kids that called me Alan Sunderland when I was at Bellefield, getting match tickets off my former team-mate Stephen McMahon in 1980. Small world that's all I'm saying.

That first phone call between us on that Sunday morning was as you can imagine, lengthy. We discussed everything about Everton, shenanigans home and away with our mates in 1970 and 1985, - some great stories by the way. Our topic of conversation eventually got around to us both seeking autographs from our heroes outside the gates of Bellefield.

I then revealed to Anthony that I had turned my dreams into reality by signing professional forms with our boyhood idols in 1977.

This was on the same day Billy Bingham, the Everton manager at the time had signed Duncan Mackenzie and Bruce Rioch, the author's first heroes, alongside Parker's love for Big Bob Latchford.

Both of us, Rochey, with Parker, Cooper, and Skinny

Maca, and me, Tommy Wheeldon, with my mates had waited outside the gates of Bellefield to get autographs from our heroes and it was now my good fortune to walk through those big blue gates as a professional football player for Everton Football Club.

Bellefield was incredible and way ahead of its time. The place, the smell, the ambience, and the history of it all was just mind blowing. To mix and train with players like Andy King, Mick Lyons and Martin Dobson, who I had previously watched and followed, just took my breath away.

I always remember Duncan Mackenzie saying "It is the state-of-the-art sports complex, considering I have just been at Leeds United, who were Champions of England and Anderlecht, who were a top European outfit, this was quite amazing".

The atmosphere and tales around Bellefield will be covered in great detail by Anthony (the author) in this wonderfully written, nostalgic book.

This book is a must for Evertonian's of all eras, as well as the genuine football fan throughout the globe.

TABLE OF CONTENTS:

CHAPTER 1- A BRIEF HISTORY OF BELLEFIELD

CHAPTER 2- TICKET TO RIDE

CHAPTER 3- CAPTAIN FANASTIC

CHAPTER 4- SCOTLAND THE BRAVE

CHAPTER 5- A SCHOOL DAY AT BELLEFIELD

CHAPTER 6- BIG BOB'S HAT-TRICK

CHAPTER 7- THE SCOUSE INVASION

CHAPTER 8- THE LUCK OF THE IRISH

CHAPTER 9- THE LIKELY LADS

CHAPTER 10- THE YOUNG STRIKERS

CHAPTER 11- GIVE PEACE A CHANCE

CHAPTER 12- OH, I DO LIKE TO BE BESIDE THE SEASIDE

CHAPTER 13- CHRISTMAS WISHES

CHAPTER 14- HAPPY NEW YEAR 1981

CHAPTER 15- HAPPY NEW YEAR BILL SHANKLY

CHAPTER 16- IF YOU KNOW YOUR HISTORY

CHAPTER 17- ENGLAND COME TO BELLEFIELD

CHAPTER 18- ROYALTY RETURNS

CHAPTER 19- END OF THE 80-81 SEASON

CHAPTER 20- THE MAGNIFICENT SEVEN

CHAPTER 21- TALES FROM WITHIN

CHAPTER 22- A NEW BEGINNING

Courtesy of Liverpool Echo and Mirrorpix.com

WELCOME TO BELLEFIELD

NIL SATIS NISI OPTIMUM

CHAPTER 1   A BRIEF HISTORY OF BELLEFIELD

Bellefield is the place where it starts for a lot of young Evertonians. It's a place where they meet Everton players face to face, collecting autographs and building up friendships with them. It's a place where memories are forever cemented into their Everton souls.

Bellefield, situated in West Derby, Liverpool, had been the post war 2 training base for Everton football club since 1946.

It was purchased from their landlords in 1965 and officially opened on the 12th of July.

The Brazil 1966 World Cup national team, with the likes of Jairzinho, Edu, Zito, and Pele, who some consider the greatest footballer that has ever lived. All graced the Bellefield pitches when they used it for their 1966 World Cup campaign.

When Brazil used it as their base some fans said it moulded them into the team they became and set them up to go on and win the 1970 World Cup finals in Mexico.

Many supporters would argue that that 1970 Brazil team was the best footballing team to ever win the World Cup. And, it all started to manifest on the pitches of Bellefield in 1966. Some say Brazil took with them some of the spirit from the Everton 1966 winning, F.A Cup team into their 1970 World Cup campaign, as that Everton final team never ever gave up. It was a team that never stopped fighting or believing in themselves.

During Everton's 1985 campaign, supporters watched Everton play and would say that it was like watching the 1970 Brazil World Cup winning team. At times they were unstoppable; it was often suggested that the pitches on Bellefield had rubbed a bit of that Brazilian team's magic into their football boots.

Two English World Cup winners also trained on these pitches on a daily basic they donned the famous royal blue jersey. Alan Ball and Ray Wilson.

Neville Southall graced the goalposts at Bellefield, for an amazing seventeen years. Wayne Rooney was another player that trained there, all of those players to Evertonians were like gods.

Even our bitter rival's former manager Bill Shankly would get his boots on and train with the Everton youngsters when he retired from football.

It was a second home to another fella that the Evertonians nicknamed 'Pele,' the legendary Colin Harvey, who was part of the Holy Trinity. Alongside Alan Ball and the greatest manager in the history of Everton Football Club, Howard Kendall, who, as a player and a manager had more spells at Bellefield than Merlin the great wizard. The list goes on and on.

On Tuesday 9th of October, 2007, Bellefield held its last senior first team training session. It was soon to be demolished to make way for houses.

Meanwhile Everton moved with the times and relocated to their new home Finch Farm.

Bellefield was years ahead of it time not only as a training base but as a place where players and fans mixed and chatted and became friends.

Those days football was for the working class now it's run as business now. It's all changed now and may I say not for the better.

Today's footballers get paid far too much money and some act like they're some kind of God.

They ignore the young kids and walk past them with their headphones on, not looking up at the everyday football supporter.

Some people blame their agents, saying they're told not to sign anything, but at the end of the day surely if a player feels strongly about not ignoring fans, then they should stop and chat and sign autograph books, because without football fans, football is nothing. Surely, it's not too much to ask for these highly paid footballers to take a few minutes out of their day to chat to the ordinary fans.

I must stress it's not all footballers that act in this manner. Lots of footballers take time out to put smiles on a lot of kids' faces and do a lot in the community. But, even if it's only 1% of footballers then it's 1% too many. It's actually a lot more than 1% and the days of getting autographs and being mates with the team like Rochey, Parker, Cooper, and Skinny Maca were have long gone, which in reality, is very sad.

Joe Royle aged just 16, became the youngest player to wear the famous royal blue jersey for the Everton first team in 1966. Just a few years before he made his debut, he would be standing outside Bellefield, collecting the players autographs with all the other fans. He went on to win the League title as a player with Everton and won the F.A. Cup with Everton as a manager. Sadly, that won't ever happen again as the days of mixing and chatting to the players have long gone.

In 1992, when the Premier League was founded, it was supposed to be good for the game. All it did was take away the working man's game and turn it into a financial business dividing the clubs from the fan base.

The bigwigs are more interested in the money than their own fan base. Without football supporters, football wouldn't exist; the bread and butter of the game are often overlooked and money has long become the focal point. The working man's game has long disappeared.

At most football grounds in this day and age, kids hold up banners asking for their favourite player's jerseys. Some supporters think this is embarrassing and, it has become a vocal talking point at the match and after the match in the local pubs.

It's the only time the young supporters can get the player's attention, as every time their favourite players run past them, the banners go up.

That debate has two sides that could be contested forever.

One thing that has to change is the gap between the football clubs and the fan base.

This book is a story about young Evertonians collecting autographs and making memories at Bellefield, they will never forget.

CHAPTER 2   TICKET TO RIDE

"Hey! Where you three going, Rochey?" yells Skinny Maca.

"We're going to Bellefield," Rochey, yells back.

"Are you coming with us?" questions Parker.

"I've only got 20 pence, is that enough?" asks Skinny Maca.

"That's well enough! It's only six pence on the bus," says Cooper.

"Whereabouts, is it? Me mam doesn't like it if I go past the shops. She likes to know where I am at all times," says Skinny Maca.

"Oh, shut up, we're going into senior school after the summer holidays. Plus, first, we're going to the joke shop in West Derby Village and Bellefield's not far from there," retorts Rochey.

"Yeah, plus tomorrow we'll be going to Goodison Park, just the four of us, with no adults," says Parker.

"Oh, alright then, let's go. Why are we going to the joke shop first?" says Skinny Maca.

"Soft lad Cooper is buying stink bombs to take into Canny High when he starts big school in September," laughs Rochey.

"Yeah, and you're buying the Wrigley chewing gum snapper," shoots back Cooper.

"Yeah, so what's your point? I'm just giving them a shock, you're stinking the whole school out," says Rochey.

"Just giving them a shock? The gum snappers nearly take your fingers off," replies Cooper.

"I think that's why he's buying them," says Skinny Maca.

"Shut up, Mummy's boy, and get on the bus!" shrieks Cooper.

Summertime is approaching. The 'Canny Farm Four', as Rochey, Parker, Cooper, and Skinny Maca call themselves, are off to

Everton's training ground to fill their autograph books and chat to any of the players they possibly can. To those four lads, they're not just footballers; to them, they're gods.

The four lads have just finished junior school. It's 1980. The sun is shining on this warm August morning. The four 11-year-olds are spending the summer holidays trying to fill their autograph books before they start senior school.

In the previous season, Everton had finished 19th in the league, but, in these kids' eyes, that didn't matter. The players are still the best thing since sliced bread.

Monday 18th of August, 1980. Two days previously, Everton had started the new season at Roker Park, the home ground of Sunderland A.F.C., who had done a number on Everton, beating them 3-1 with a certain player in their line-up by the name of Sam Allardyce, someone who would annoy a lot of Evertonians again years later.

The Canny Farm Four arrive at Bellefield and see a few familiar faces, and a few new ones hanging around the gates of the Everton Bellefield training ground.

Three 14-year-old girls who have stalked the players for the past two seasons are standing in the corner giggling, talking about Saturday's game: There are also a few older lads on their bikes waiting to catch a glimpse of their heroes. One of the older lads, Mark Kidda, is riding up and down the narrow road that leads to the entrance of Bellefield, doing wheelies on his Raleigh Chopper bike much to the annoyance of the girls.

Rochey and Parker who are wearing adidas tracksuits climb onto the 5-foot wall outside the training ground and then pull up Skinny Maca, who is too small to climb the wall from a standing jump.

"Welcome to Bellefield, Maca," beams Parker.

"I'm not sitting on the wall, I'm going straight in," says Cooper.

"Good luck with that one," smirks Rochey.

"Keep an eye out for that Sid fella," yells Parker.

"Well, Cooper, we'll definitely have to watch out for him now! That Sid fella will have probably heard you yelling his name," tuts Rochey.

"I would be more worried about the dog than Sid. At least Sid smiles when he's kicking us out," pipes up Parker.

"I'm not arsed about the dog," replies Cooper, as he starts walking towards the front entrance of Bellefield, 400 metres away, like he owns the tarmac that his Power Tunis trainers walk on. He only gets 20 metres down the road when, out of nowhere, Yogi the guard dog flies down the road, nipping at the arse end of the retreating Cooper's black Farah trousers.

Rochey, Parker, and Skinny Maca piss themselves laughing, from the safety of their seats on top of the 5-foot wall.

Cooper screams for help, whilst the older lads, led by Mark Kidda, mount their bikes ready to pedal away. The three girls tut and shake their heads at Cooper's antics.

"I did warn you," laughs Parker.

"Yeah, but when does he ever listen?" sniggers Rochey.

"Did you see that? That dog bit me on the arse, look at the teeth marks," screams Cooper, pulling down his trousers.

"We know!" laughs Skinny Maca. "We had a great view up here on the wall."

Sid walks out of the house at the bottom of the entrance.

"That dog is mad, mate," yells Cooper.

"Read the sign on the gates! Keep out! Beware of the dog, it says!" replies Sid.

"We're only here for autographs! The dogs that guarded the prisoners in the two World Wars weren't as vicious as Yogi," says Cooper.

"Well, maybe that will teach you not to enter private land. And if you have any complaints, take it up with Dougie Rose; it's his dog," replies Sid.

"We're more worried for Yogi. He might need a tetanus jab after biting Cooper's arse," laughs Skinny Maca.

"Shut up, knobhead," snarls Cooper, as Sid whistles Yogi, giving him a dog biscuit.

"Look! Someone's coming out with blonde hair" shouts Parker.

"It's Steve McMahon with that blonde wedge, getting in his car," says Rochey, excitedly.

"He's with someone else. It looks like Alan Sunderland from Arsenal, with that perm haircut" yells Cooper.

"We must have signed him today," says Mark Kidda, on his Chopper bike.

"Alan, Alan Sunderland," sing the four lads, as Steve McMahon stops outside the exit gates in his Datsun Cherry.

"Are you Alan Sunderland?" asks Cooper.

"Have you signed for us from Arsenal?" butts in Skinny Maca.

Steve McMahon in his Everton tracksuit looks at the four lads, shaking his head, laughing.

"Alan Sunderland? This man sitting next to me is better than Alan bleeding Sunderland," says Steve McMahon.

"Better than Alan Sunderland? Why, has he scored in an F.A. Cup Final?" asks Parker.

"No, but he signed for Everton on the same day as Duncan McKenzie," replies Steve McMahon.

"What's your name, mate? Can you jump over a Mini?" asks Rochey.

"Do you play for Everton now?" interrupts Skinny Maca.

"Has that dog ever bitten your arse?" asks Cooper, rubbing the top of his leg.

"My name is Tommy Wheeldon. I don't play for Everton now. I played 1976 to 1978 and no, the dog has never bitten my backside. I was too fast for him. My nickname wasn't lightning for nothing," laughs Tommy.

"Who do you play for now?" asks Cooper.

"Southport," replies Tommy.

"Southport! Who are they?" asks Cooper.

"Drink your milk in school and find out," laughs Tommy.

"What are you doing here at Bellefield?" asks Parker.

"Nosey kids, you lot, ain't yers?" laughs Steve McMahon.

"I just came to see Steve, to get some tickets for tomorrow's game at Goodison against Leicester City," says Tommy.

"Have you got any spare tickets for us, Steve?" asks Skinny Maca.

"I've just given the last of my allocation to Tommy. Sorry lads," says Steve McMahon.

"It's okay, Stephen, we'll bunk in anyway," replies Cooper.

"Yeah, 'cos there's no way I'm wasting my pocket money on tomorrow's match after that performance on Saturday," quips Rochey.

Steve McMahon shakes his head as he signs the autograph books for the lads on the Chopper bikes. The girls look and admire him as if he's one of the Beatles.

"By the way, Steve, Happy Birthday on Wednesday," says Skinny Maca.

"How did you know it was my birthday?" asks Steve McMahon.

"We're Scouse Evertonians, Steve. We know everything," laughs Cooper.

As Steve McMahon drives off, Tommy gives the lads the thumbs up from his passenger seat.

"Tommy! Looks like Alan Sunderland, Tommy!" shout the four lads.

Tommy Wheeldon would go on to play for Torquay United after he left Southport. He later coached at Swindon Town when Steve McMahon was the first team manager. Tommy also coached at Exeter City. Later he coached Calgary Storm in Canada for 15 years. Tommy said his best two years in football were spent at Everton from 1976 to 1978. His biggest regret was that he couldn't jump over a Mini.

Meanwhile the lads are buzzing. They've just had their books signed by Steve McMahon. They look up to see two young lads walk out of Bellefield towards them.

"Hey, mate, do you play for Everton?" yells Cooper.

"Yeah," replies one of the lads.

"What's your names? I don't recognise either of you," asks Skinny Maca.

"I'm Brian Borrows and this is Dean Kelly," replies Brian Borrows proudly in his navy-blue Everton tracksuit.

"Have you played for the first team?" asks Parker.

"No not yet, but we will do," says Brian Borrows.

"Well, that'll do for me. Sign my autograph book to Rochey please Brian," replies Rochey.

"Are there any other players on the way out?" asks Cooper.

Yes, Bob Latchford is on his way out," replies a smiling Dean Kelly.

"Nice one. Big Bob is my hero," beams Parker.

"Can you sign my book to Rochey as well Dean?" asks Rochey.

"Yeah, no problem," replies Dean Kelly.

The two players sign the lads' books and head towards the on Eaton Road.

Brian Borrows was a local Scouse lad who was a right-sided full back. He went on to make his Everton debut that season and played 29 matches before being sold to Bolton Wanderers. He later played for Coventry City and gained one international cap for the England B team.

Dean Kelly lived in the Anfield area and was from a family of Everton fanatics. He was a midfielder for Everton. He never did make his debut for the first team, and later the young Scouse lad moved across the pond to play in America in the major indoor soccer leagues, scoring lots of goals along the way.

"Hey, look, there's Bob Latchford getting in his car!" points out Skinny Maca.

"Oh, my word, Bob Latchford, I love him!" shouts Parker.

"I'm going to get him to sign my right foot so his magic rubs off on me," says Cooper.

"Here he is. He's driving down now in his Talbot Alpine," yells Skinny Maca.

The four lads, the three giggling girls, the older lads on the bikes, are full of anticipation as big Bob Latchford drives towards them.

"Get your pens out, lads!" shouts Parker.

The lads move towards Big Bob's car as he drives beside them, but he doesn't stop and signals right as he speeds away from Bellefield.

"What's that all about? Why didn't he stop?" says Cooper.

"All I saw was the *Daily Mail* on the back seat of his car," mutters Rochey.

"That's annoying. I only came here to get his autograph," says Skinny Maca.

"He must be busy. I bet he had a press date with the Liverpool Pink Echo so couldn't stop," says Parker, trying to hide his disappointment.

"Big Bob Latchford walks on water, that's a joke," snipes Rochey.

"He can walk on water! He's the best Everton player I have ever seen. Even my dad says he's brilliant. Big Bob is my hero," retorts Parker.

"Yeah, well, my dad said you should never meet your heroes in real life as you will only be disappointed, and he wasn't far wrong," replies Rochey.

"Yes, but technically you didn't get to meet your hero as he didn't stop. And didn't both of your dads go to the same school and both play for the Sacred Heart school team?" points out Skinny Maca.

"Yeah, they did. Parker's dad, Joey, was the captain but what has that got to do with Big Bob not stopping?" questions Rochey.

"Nothing, I just thought that it's odd how your dads both played in the same school team, and you two both played in the same school team, yet Big Bob didn't stop," sniggers Skinny Maca.

Both Rochey and Parker give Skinny Maca a stare that could cut him into two.

"Come on, let's go home. We can catch Big Bob in a couple of days. He was most probably just rushing home to get some rest. He has a big match tomorrow night, and 'cos he didn't stop, I'm bunking in the ground tomorrow, 'cos I'm not paying for his win bonus out of my pocket," says Cooper.

"Yeah, let's all bunk in the ground tomorrow night and save our money for George's chippy," says Rochey.

The lads all look at Rochey, nodding in agreement, as they make their way home.

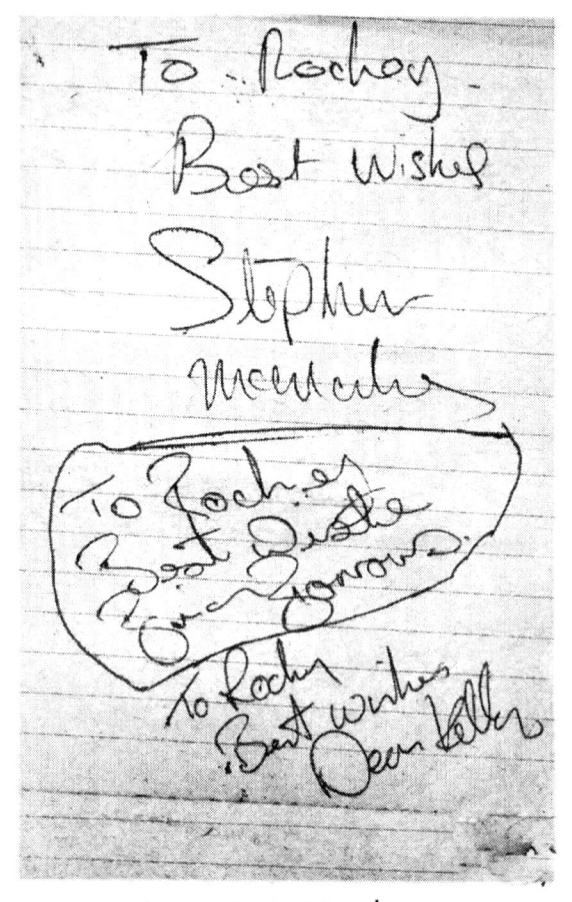

STEVE McMAHON
BRIAN BORROWS
DEAN KELLY

CHAPTER 3   CAPTAIN FANTASTIC

It's Thursday 21st of August, 1980, two days after Everton's first win of the season against Leicester City, who they defeated at Goodison Park, the only goal coming from Peter Eastoe in a 1-0 win.

The four lads, Rochey, Parker, Cooper, and Skinny Maca are heading back to Bellefield to fill up their autograph books, only this time they're on bikes.

Liverpool at this time was a poor city. No-one had any money. The city was on its arse because a certain woman named Margaret didn't like the fact that the city was Labour.

It had always been that way, and would never change, so she cut the city off from anything that could be of benefit.

However, these four lads didn't have a care in the world as they rode their bikes out of Canny Farm, pulling wheelies. They passed the local shops in Cantril Farm and whizzed past their mate, Sean Quinn, who, at 10-years of age, was a school year younger than the four lads'.

Parker was setting the pace in pole position on his Raleigh racer bike, followed by Rochey who was doing wheelies on his black Raleigh Commando. Skinny Maca was cruising behind Rochey on his Tomahawk, whilst Cooper was lagging behind on his Raleigh Grifter, sucking on his orange frozy, a frozen carton drink.

"Rochey! Wait up!" shouts Sean Quinn.

"We can't stop. We're on a mission. What do you want?" asks Rochey.

"Where are you going?" asks Sean Quinn.

"We're going to Bellefield for autographs," replies Rochey.

"If I give you all a lolly ice stick to put in your spokes, can I come with yers?" asks Sean.

"Of course, it'll be boss 'cos I have got all my bread clips hooked onto my brake wires," beams Skinny Maca.

"It's not fully finished until you have a frozy carton stuck onto the back bar by the wheel. The empty carton makes my Grifter sound like a motor-bike," boasts Cooper.

The lads pedal off with the bikes roaring from the lolly-ice sticks stuck in the spokes, whilst Cooper thinks he really is on a motorbike as they cycle past the army barracks towards Bellefield.

The time is 11:30am and the sun is shining as the lads lean their bikes against the walls at the entrance of Bellefield. Cooper is being daring as he does a wheelie towards the front entrance. Out of nowhere, Yogi the dog chases Cooper, nipping at his ankles as he pedals desperately away.

"That dog never gives up," moans Cooper.

"Shut up moaning and get up here on the wall with us," says Sean Quinn, as he holds out his hand to lift Cooper up onto the wall.

"Nice one Quinny lad, I didn't think you would've wanted to come today with your Mick being a pro at Wigan Athletic," retorts Cooper.

"Are you kidding? This is Everton, the team that I love. Our Michael is only 18. Yeah, he's scoring goals, week in, week out, but this is Everton," says Sean.

"Didn't your Mick start off with Derby County, Sean?" queries Skinny Maca.

"Yeah, but even Derby ain't a patch on Everton," says Sean.

"Anyway, that's enough about their Mick. Look down there! Billy Wright is getting in his car with our own Mick, Captain Fantastic Mick Lyons," says Parker.

"Well, if that really is Mick Lyons we best get down from this wall," says Skinny Maca.

"Why would we get down from this wall?" asks Rochey.

"Why? Because he might have seen Cooper riding his bike down the entrance and Gordon Lee might have sent him out to get us," replies Skinny Maca.

"So why would Gordon Lee send Mick Lyons out to get us soft-lad?" asks Parker.

"Why? Why do you think soft-ollies? Gordon Lee runs the club and my dad says Mick Lyons would run through brick walls for Everton," argues Skinny Maca.

"Well, he won't be running through brick walls today," says Rochey.

"How do you know he won't?" questions Skinny Maca.

"How do I know? Well, for starters he's just got into Billy Wright's Ford Capri 3000, so it would be hard running through brick walls while he's sitting in the passenger seat," replies Rochey.

"Shut up, now. Billy is driving down. Let's get their autographs!" says Parker.

Billy Wright smiling wearing his Everton tracksuit alongside Everton captain Mick Lyons, stops his car next to the lads to sign their autograph books.

"Can you sign my book, Billy?" asks Cooper.

"Hello Mick, can you sign mine to Rochey?" asks Rochey.

Mick Lyons looks up and smiles at the lads.

"It was a great result on Tuesday against Leicester City, Mick," says Cooper, as Lyons signs his book.

"A clean sheet as well, Mick," says Parker, as his book is signed.

"Hey, Mick, is it true that you would run through brick walls for Everton?" mumbles Skinny Maca.

Mick Lyons looks up at the lads. "I think anybody that is lucky enough to play for Everton Football Club would run through brick walls for them because the club is so special."

"Is right, Mick, lad," replies Sean, giving Mick Lyons the thumbs up as Billy Wright drives away.

"He's boss! My dad told me he dived under Norman 'bite yer legs' Hunter's boots to score a goal from six yards out, with his head! That day we played Leeds United," says Skinny Maca.

"He's proper hardcore is Mick Lyons. Loves Everton, just like we do," says Parker.

"He's a proper Scouser him mate," yells Cooper.

"Billy Wright is a proper Scouser as well," says Skinny Maca.

"I know he is. Scouse Billy, they call him," laughs Cooper.

"He's built like a brick shit-house. Before he signed for Everton, he was the doorman in the Conti nightclub," says Skinny Maca.

"Yeah, Billy Bouncer," laughs Cooper.

"Make sure he never hears you say that, otherwise you'll be spitting out teeth," says Parker.

"Talking about teeth, did you see Mick Lyons' teeth when he smiled? I thought it was Donny Osmond for a sec," laughs Rochey.

"Oh, yeah, Mr. Puppy Love, himself," laughs Sean.

"How did you know Donny Osmond sang Puppy Love?" asks Rochey.

"Well, for starters, our Mick has all the Osmond's records and plays them all the time in his bedroom," says Sean.

"Is that why his hair is so long? Does he think he's the long-haired lover from Liverpool?" asks Skinny Maca.

"No, he's got long hair cos he's thinking of getting a perm," replies Sean.

"A perm? Hmm, no wonder he's playing for Wigan," laughs

Rochey.

The lads are just about to pedal home on their bikes, when they hear the roar of a car engine coming out of Bellefield. Everton defender Mark Higgins is looking like a rally driver with driving gloves on in his RS2000 Ford Escort as he stops to sign all the lads' books.

"That's some more new signatures for our collection, Let's get off now. We can come back next week," says Parker, as the lads make their way back to Canny Farm.

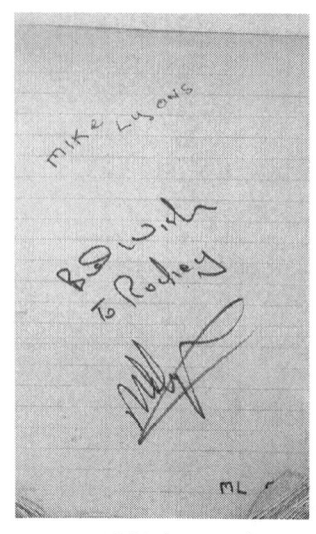

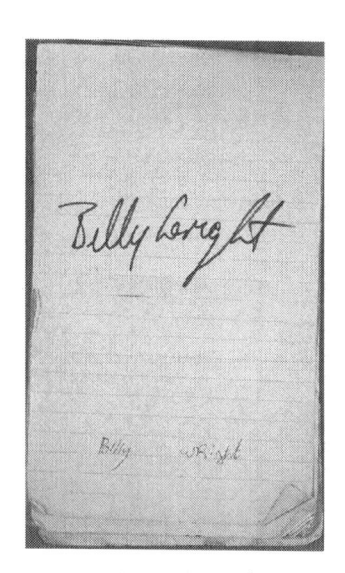

MICK LYONS   BILLY WRIGHT

MARK HIGGINS

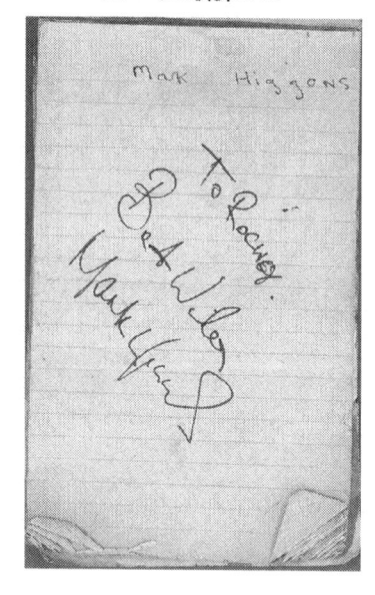

CHAPTER 4   SCOTLAND THE BRAVE

It's Thursday, 28th of August, 1980, and the school summer holidays are coming to an end. Two days previously, the lads had seen Everton beat Blackpool 3-0 in the first leg of their League Cup tie.

The Everton goals came via Peter Eastoe in the 4th minute, Big Bob Latchford in the 67th minute, and the young Scottish winger, Joe McBride, rounding the scoring off in the 89th minute.

Blackpool's manager that night was none other than the famous World Cup winner, and Everton legend, Alan Ball.

Outside Bellefield, the four lads, Rochey, Parker, Cooper, and Skinny Maca wait patiently for the players to come out, so they can get more autographs in their books. Over in the corner, the three girls are back again, giggling.

"Hey, girls, do you just come here to giggle?" asks Cooper.

"Do you just come here because you fancy all the young players in the team?" enquires Skinny Maca.

"What's yer names?" asks Parker.

"What's with all the questions? I'm Sue Jones, and this is my cousin, Marie Jones, and this is our other mate, Sue Lloyd," replies Sue Jones.

"We don't fancy all the young players, only a few of them," laughs Marie Jones.

"Well, that's you all getting told," laughs Rochey.

"Did you all go to the game on Tuesday?" asks Sue Lloyd.

"Of course we did! We all bunked in," boasts Cooper, trying to impress.

"Did you see Joe McBride's goal?" asks Sue Jones.

"Yeah, of course we did, that's why today we're getting as many Scottish autographs as possible," says Skinny Maca.

The lads and the girls look down the road, awaiting any

movement that might signal a player's arrival. First out is Trevor Ross driving a Volvo GLE.

"Here comes Trevor," yells Parker.

"Get yer pens ready, lads," says Rochey.

"Hurry up! Get ready! Here's our first Scottish player, Trevor Ross," yells Cooper.

"He's not actually Scottish," says Skinny Maca.

"Shut up, soft lad" He's as Scottish as can be. He played for the Scotland Under-21's national football team in 1977," replies Cooper.

"Yeah, I know that, but he also played for the England Youth team. He was born in Ashton-under-Lyne near Manchester. He played for Scotland through his dad, Willie Ross," says Skinny Maca.

"Well, that will do for me. Hey, Trevor, can you sign my book, please?" asks Rochey, as Trevor Ross pulls up.

The girls giggle amongst themselves as Trevor Ross drives away.

"Look who's coming out? It looks like Barry Manilow?" yells Skinny Maca.

"Barry Manilow! Why would he be at Bellefield?" snaps Cooper.

"We might have signed him from Copacabana," says Rochey.

"I can't smile without you, Skinny, especially as it's Asa Hartford," smirks Parker.

"Well, at least he's Scottish so we can get him to sign our book," replies Skinny Maca.

Asa Hartford drives down in his Rover 3500 and stops to sign the books.

"Can you sign my book, Barry?" grins Cooper.

Asa Hartford signs Cooper's book, with his golf clubs resting on his back seat before driving away looking confused.

"He must be going to play golf," says Parker.

"What makes you think that?" asks Cooper.

"The golf clubs on his back seat were a big giveaway," smirks Skinny Maca.

The lads are on a high and the day gets even better as Parker spots Graeme Sharp, Joe McBride, and another young lad, walking out of Bellefield towards them.

"Three Jocks ahead! Get your pens out, lads," shouts Skinny Maca.

"We have to get Joe's autograph! He scored on Tuesday," says Parker.

"Joe, can you sign this book, please?" asks Rochey.

"Aye, did you enjoy the match the other night, lads?" asks Joe McBride, looking fresh in his Everton tracksuit.

"Yeah, Joe, that was a great goal," replies Parker.

"It was even better as we all bunked in," states Cooper.

Joe McBride looks at Sharpie, smiles and winks.

"Well, that's my goal bonus gone with them bunking in the match, Sharpie."

"Never mind, Joe. I bet you'll score lots more goals this season," says Skinny Maca.

"Will you sign my book please, Graeme?" asks Rochey.

"Hey, Graeme, before you signed for Everton, were you in that band, the Bay City Rollers? You look the spitting image of one of them," asks Cooper.

Graeme Sharp looks shocked as Joe McBride and the young lad next to him start laughing.

Rochey, Parker, and Skinny Maca all look at Cooper with open mouths as they shake their heads at him.

"No, mate. They're all from Edinburgh, and I'm from Glasgow," replies Graeme Sharp.

"I thought you were from Dunfermline," says Cooper.

"Don't you mean Dumbarton, the team we signed him from?" queries Skinny Maca.

"No, I thought we signed him from Shang-A-Lang. I thought he was in the Bay City Rollers and that they sang a song about his football team," replies Cooper.

"Shut up soft ollies. I bet he can't even sing," says Rochey.

"Who's your mate, Joe? Does he play for Everton?" mumbles Skinny Maca.

"Yeah, his name is Kevin. He's one of our apprentices," replies Joe McBride.

"Hey, lad, are you Scottish?" Cooper asks the young apprentice.

"No, aye, man," replies the young apprentice in a thick Geordie accent. The lads all look at each other, puzzled.

"What did he just say?" grins Skinny Maca.

"I'm not sure. Did he say something about his nan? But I'm certain he's not Scottish," replies Rochey.

"I think he's a Geordie," whispers Parker.

Rochey smiles at the young apprentice as he says, "We're only getting Scottish autographs today, mate. We'll get you to sign our book next time."

The three Everton players sign Sue Jones' and her mates'

books and pose for pics with them, before walking out of the Bellefield training ground. As they walk towards Eaton Road, just before they move out of sight, Cooper shouts, "Graeme, bye, bye, baby, baby goodbye." Sharpie looks back laughing, shaking his head.

The lads missed out on a top autograph that day as the young lad who was with Joe McBride and Graeme Sharp was none other than Kevin Richardson who, later in his career, would become an Everton legend.

"Oh, my word, get onto who's just got into his car!" yells Skinny Maca.

"It's Big Bob Latchford," screams Parker.

"Yeah, but he's not Scottish. We're only getting Scottish autographs today," says Rochey.

"That doesn't matter. He scored on Tuesday. Big Bob, is my hero. I'm getting his autograph," snaps Parker.

As Bob Latchford drives towards the lads in his Talbot Alpine, their smiles are as wide as the Mersey Tunnel.

Sue Jones puts on some lippy as Big Bob approaches but the smiles are soon wiped off the lads' faces as Big Bob whizzes past them, right out of the gates, not stopping until he gets to the junction at the end of Bellefield Drive.

"Well, that's a surprise, Big Bob not stopping again," bleats Skinny Maca.

"He didn't stop because he must have seen Sue Jones put her red lippy on," snaps Parker.

"Don't be silly. He didn't stop because he never does," replies Rochey.

"He will stop maybe not today, maybe he was just too busy but he will stop one day," replies Parker, close to tears.

"He's not Scottish anyway and today's Scottish autographs only," pipes up Skinny Maca.

"Scottish only today, hey. Come on then. Let's go to Bill Shankly's house and ask him to sign our books," says Rochey.

"How? We don't even know where he lives!" replies Skinny Maca.

"Yes, we do. He lives just up there around the corner," replies Rochey.

"Number 30, Bellefield Avenue," butts in Cooper.

"How do you two know that?" replies Skinny Maca.

"Mick Kearns told us. He said Bill Shankly trains with the team he runs, Allerford. That's why me, Rochey, and Parker have signed for Allerford," replies Cooper.

"That's brilliant. Why are we waiting here then? Let's go!" shrieks Skinny Maca.

"Okay, calm down. I have unfinished business here first," replies Cooper.

"What unfinished business are you on about?" queries Skinny Maca.

"Watch and learn Skinny! Watch and learn!" replies Cooper.

Parker looks at Rochey "This should be good. What's he doing?"

Rochey shrugs his shoulders. He's just as confused as Skinny Maca.

Cooper walks over to the three young girls, smiling like he's just won a raffle. He stands opposite Sue Jones and says "Hey Sue, don't waste that lipstick. I've got the perfect kissing lips for you to practice on."

"No, thank you. I want to kiss a boy my own age, not a little boy trying to act like a man," snaps Sue Jones.

"Hey, Sue, I'm a big boy, with man lips," replies Cooper.

"Take your man lips and practice kissing your pillow," replies Sue Jones, as she giggles with her mates.

"Watch and learn, hey Coops? Watch and learn!" laughs Rochey.

"She must be a lesbo," replies Cooper.

"Yeah, either that or it just might be that she just doesn't like little boys. Now hurry up! Let's go to Shankly's house!" laughs Rochey.

"Oh, alright, turn it in. I had to try," says Cooper.

The lads walk up the street towards Bill Shankly's house onto Bellefield Avenue.

"So, who's going to knock?" asks Skinny Maca.

"We'll all knock at his house. It's only Bill Shankly," replies Cooper.

"Only, Bill Shankly? To millions of Liverpool fans, he's the Messiah," replies Skinny Maca.

"Well, we're Evertonians so to us he's just another Scottish fella giving us his autograph," says Parker.

The lads slow the pace down as they reach the front path of Bill Shankly's house. The big white walls at the front of the house are immaculately clean.

"Is this really a good idea?" questions Skinny Maca.

"Of course it's a good idea. Get out of my way! I'll knock," says Cooper, knocking on the front window.

"What're you doing soft lad? Why didn't you knock on the door, or ring the bell?" snaps Rochey.

"It's okay. He'll hear me knocking on the window as he's most probably in the living room, watching the TV," replies Cooper.

"Here's someone coming to the door," whispers Skinny

Maca.

"It's Nessie, Shankly's wife, so you'd better all be on your best behaviour," barks Rochey.

Nessie Shankly opens the front door, looks at the four young lads, and greets them with a big warm smile.

"Hello, love, is Billy in?" asks Cooper.

The three lads look at Cooper and can't believe what he has just said.

Rochey kicks Cooper in the shins, pushing him back as he moves forward to talk to Mrs Shankly.

"Hello Mrs Shankly. Can we talk to Mr Shankly, please, to get his autograph?" says Rochey.

Nessie Shankly smiles at the lads. "I'll just go and get him," she says as she turns to go back into the house.

As Bill Shankly walks out the front door, the heavens open as the rain falls down heavily. Bill Shankly opens a big umbrella and tells the four lads to stand under it.

"Aye, boys, what can I do for yers?" asks Bill Shankly.

"Can we have your autograph, please, Mr Shankly?" asks a nervous Rochey.

"Aye, no problem, laddie. Just give me a minute."

"Thanks, Bill. It's Scottish autograph day today," says Cooper.

"Scottish autograph day?" replies Bill Shankly, confused.

"Take no notice of him, Mr Shankly. He thinks everybody is Scottish," pipes up Skinny Maca.

Bill Shankly, shaking his head, turns and goes back into his house, leaving the lads at the door.

Rochey looks at Cooper in disbelief and snaps, "I can't

believe you just said that."

"Me too. And stop calling him Bill!" mutters Parker.

"What shall I call him then? Shall I call him Bob?"

"No, call him Mr Shankly. He's most probably gone back in to call the police," quivers Skinny Maca.

"Let's get off then," replies Cooper.

"Let's get off? Don't be stupid! Do you think he would leave us with his umbrella if he'd gone to call the police? And why would you call him Bob?" asks Rochey.

"Why? Because the other team, from down the road, who play in red, have a manager whose name is Bob," replies Cooper.

The three lads look at Cooper, shaking their heads, as Bill Shankly returns holding four cards displaying a picture of him in a Liverpool tracksuit, holding the F.A. Cup.

"Aye, boys, who do you want me to sign these to?" asks Bill Shankly.

The four lads look at each other.

"Mr Shankly, we're Everton supporters. Can we just have your autograph in our autograph books, please?" stutters Rochey.

"Yeah, we are collecting Scottish autographs today, Bill, not postcards," says Cooper.

Bill Shankly looks at the four boys with a stare that could cut Mother Earth into two. The four boys gaze at Mr Shankly, not daring to move. Skinny Maca's bottom lip begins to quiver, Rochey stands in disbelief at what Cooper said. Parker is motionless, while Cooper smiles at Mr Shankly as the raindrops bounce off his cheeks.

"Scottish autographs?" asks a confused Bill Shankly.

"What he's trying to say, Mr Shankly, is today we are collecting the autographs off the Everton Scottish players," replies Parker.

"We've come to your house because we signed for the Allerford Junior Football Team. Mick Kearns, our manager, told us how you join in with the training on Barnfield Drive pitches," says Rochey.

"Allerford, hey? You lot must be all good footballers, as Big Bob Pendleton only signs the best," replies Bill Shankly.

"We play in green and yellow Mr Shankly. If we played in blue we would be even better," says a smiling Parker.

"Mick told us you've been sponsoring the kit since 1978. He told us that you buy each player a tracksuit and a sports bag," adds Cooper.

"That's the reason we've knocked today for your autograph Mr Shankly because you support grassroots football," says Rochey.

"Is it true that you talk tactics after each training session, with Big Bob outside the railway house, Mr Shankly?" inquires Skinny Maca.

"Aye, Bob is a good man. He puts a lot into helping to develop kids from good footballers into brilliant footballers," replies Bill Shankly.

The lads all get their autograph books signed and tell Bill Shankly to enjoy his day. As he says good-bye the rain stops and a rainbow appears in the sky above Bill Shankly's House.

(*The Barnfield pitches have since been renamed The Bill Shankly playing fields.*)

The lads would knock and chat to him quite a lot after this first meeting. Bill and Nessie always greeted the lads with a smile and Bill loved talking about football. He enjoyed his training sessions with Allerford. He would also pop into Bellefield to join in with the Everton training and would often join in kickabouts fouling the Everton players with a smile on his face.

Graeme Sharp tells the story of when he first signed for

Everton. He was sitting on the treatment table and, out of nowhere, Bill Shankly appeared at the door and asked Sharpie what was up with him. Trying to not stutter, as he was in awe of the great man, he replied, "I've got a calf strain. My muscle is tight."

Bill looked towards Sharpie saying, "Well laddie, it's Tuesday today so by the weekend you should be playing again. Now, if you excuse me, I have a game that I have to join in."

Sharpie had to pinch himself as he couldn't believe that the legendary former Liverpool manager had taken time to chat to him. He was even more astonished that Bill Shankly was at Bellefield, training with the Everton team!

The four lads were walking towards Liverpool's training ground, Melwood, to get the bus home. As they passed the big red double gates at Melwood, they spotted Kenny Dalglish and David Fairclough, walking towards a coach, decked in red, that would take them to Anfield for their dinner.

"Hey, look, it's Dalglish" Let's get his autograph," yells Cooper.

"Don't be stupid, he plays for the red shite," snaps Parker.

"So! that doesn't matter! He's Scottish! He can sign my book next to Shankly," says Rochey.

The four lads bolt through the red gates, ignoring the groundsman's shouts to get out. The lad's approach Dalglish and Fairclough to get their books signed.

"Kenny, can you sign my book, mate?" asks Cooper.

Kenny Dalglish signs Cooper's book and hands it to David Fairclough, but Cooper snatches it out of Fairclough's hand.

"It's okay, Davie, I don't need your autograph. You lived in our street. I lived 10 doors away from you. Plus, we're only getting Scottish autographs today," says Cooper.

"I know you did, Lee. I watched you and Rochey play in the Junior Cup Final for The Spinney a few months back. I gave you both your medals," replies David Fairclough, with his bright ginger curly hair, shining in the sun.

"You gave us winners medals, Davie. We were gutted! We thought we would get a famous Everton player giving us our medals, and we got you, a fella that used to live in the same street as us," says Cooper.

"Aww, sorry about that, Lee. How's your dad anyway?"

"He's okay, Davie," replies Cooper.

Kenny Dalglish has a wee smile on his face as Rochey hands him his autograph book. "Hiya Kenny. Can you sign that above Bill Shankly's name, please?" asks Rochey.

"Billy Shankly and Kenny Dalglish on the same page. Two Jocks! That's brilliant!" pipes up Skinny Maca.

"It's not that brilliant if they sign it as Jock," laughs Cooper.

Dalglish signs Rochey's autograph book and grins as he asks, "Shall I give it to Davie to sign as well, 'cos I have been in his house, I know he lives at number 10, in your street?"

"No, thank you Kenny. He played in the same street team as my cousin and I haven't got my cousin's autograph in my autograph book. Plus, he should have lived in number 12," replies Rochey, as he looks up at Davie Fairclough and winks at him.

"Yeah, number 12 same number you wear for Liverpool, like your nickname says, Super Sub," laughs Cooper.

Parker and Skinny Maca follow suit and get Kenny Dalglish's autograph without getting Fairclough's signature.

"Are you two done now?" Rochey asks Parker and Skinny Maca.

"Yeah, why?" queries Skinny Maca.

"Why? Because the groundsmen are coming over, so let's leg it," says Cooper.

The four lads get on their toes and leg it out of the gates, putting two fingers up to the groundsmen as they run past, with Cooper shouting, "Behave, fatties! you'll never catch us!"

David Fairclough turns to Kenny Dalglish as they board the coach, saying, "Kenny, you can take the kid out of Canny Farm but you can't take Canny Farm out of the kid."

"Aye, I know. I have been in your street. They said the same about you, Davie," smirks Kenny Dalglish, as he sits in his seat on the coach.

The four lads catch the 12C bus, that has just stopped, and the lads all scramble up the stairs. Cooper swings around the bar floating into his seat.

The 12C bus driving through Cantril Farm comes to a standstill as a mob of about 60 youths aged between 15 to 21, are marching in the middle of the road chanting, "SRS, SRS, SRS!"

"What's going on? Who are they?" mutters Skinny Maca.

"They're the SRS. They're the hard-cases of Canny Farm. They march through Canny Farm taking on anybody that stands in their way," replies Rochey.

"Why are they wearing kilts? Why would hard-cases march through Canny Farm wearing their sisters' skirts?" laughs Cooper.

"Shut up, knobhead. If they hear you, they will storm the bus," hisses Parker.

"How will they hear me? They're too busy chanting SRS and holding down their skirts in case they blow up," laughs Cooper.

"What does SRS stand for? Is it the Scottish Republican Squad, with them wearing kilts? Hey can we get off the bus and get them to sign our autograph books seeing as it's Scottish autograph day?" asks Skinny Maca.

"Don't be stupid! SRS stands for the Steerscroft Riot Squad. They would most probably burn our autograph books and stab us with our pens. I'm staying on the bus! I'm going nowhere!" says

Rochey.

"Well, I hope they hurry up. I'm going to our Danny's later to watch the Wanderers on his new video player," mutters Skinny Maca.

"No way! What type has he got? Has he got a VHS or a Beta-Max?" asks Parker.

"He's got a VHS. The Beta-Max ones are crap. All the Russians have them," replies Skinny Maca.

"Well, I hope the hard-cases wearing skirts pick up the pace because we've got football practice at half three," says Cooper.

Look, they have turned into Woodfarm! The bus can move now," says Parker.

"We can go to football practice now. I bagsy being Joe McBride!" yells Cooper.

"In that case, I'm Graeme Sharp," barks Skinny Maca

"Who are you going to be?" Rochey asks Parker.

"I'm going to be Bob Latchford," smirks Parker.

"He's not Scottish," says Cooper.

"That's okay, cos I'm not Scottish either," says Parker, as they all get off the bus to get changed into their kits.

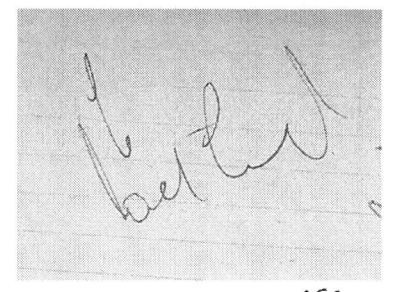

ASA
HARTFORD

TREVOR
ROSS

JOE
McBRIDE

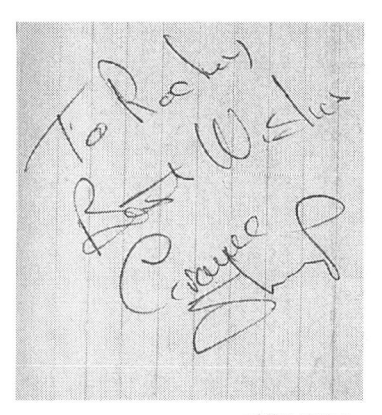

GRAEME
SHARP

KENNY
DALGLISH

BILL
SHANKLY

CHAPTER 5   A SCHOOL DAY AT BELLEFIELD

It's Monday, 8th of September, and the lads started their new schools Saint Dominic's and Cantril High, less than five days ago. It's 8:45 on this cold September morning as Parker passes Rochey's house on his way to their new school.

Two days earlier Everton beat Wolverhampton Wanderers 2-0 at Goodison Park, courtesy of goals from Peter Eastoe in the 16th minute, with Billy Wright wrapping it up in the 66th minute. Playing for Wolves that day were two future Everton players who would go on to win the League championship with Everton. One went by the name of Andy Gray who won the league title with Everton in 84/85. The other player was Wayne Clark who featured as a substitute that day. He became part of Everton's 86/87 title winning team.

"Hey, soft ollies, wait up" Have you got your autograph book on yer?" shouts Rochey, as Parker passes his front door.

"Yeah, why? Hurry up! We're going to be late!" shouts back Parker.

"Never mind being late! why don't we bunk off school and go to Bellefield?" utters Rochey.

"How can I bunk off school? My mum is a dinner lady there."

"What lessons have you got this morning? I've got French with Miss Walsh just before dinner. My first two lessons are Science with that teacher that's built like a bouncer, Mr White, I won't be missed."

"I've got the same, but I'm in French with Miss Powley just before dinner, and my first two lessons are Science with Mr Hedges."

"We'll be back for dinner time. The players get out about 12 o'clock. I only want to get the autographs of the scorers from Saturday's game, Peter Eastoe and Billy Wright. Then we can jump the bus back. Your mum won't even notice."

"Come on, then. But we'd best be back for dinner time!"

replies Parker.

The lads walk down the back path away, from the school, where they bump into Sandra Hampson, who is two years older than Rochey and Parker.

"Hey, Sandra, will you do us a favour? Will you write us both a sick note saying we weren't in this morning 'cos we had a dentist appointment?" asks Rochey.

"Get lost! You only started school last week," comes back the reply.

"Aww, don't be sly, San. I'll give you Everton's match programme from Saturday if you do," utters Rochey, dangling the match programme in her face.

Impressed by the match programme, Sandra Hampson starts writing the sicknotes for Rochey and Parker.

"What's your teacher's name?" asks Sandra.

"My teacher is that little fella who takes the metalwork class, Mr Docherty. And Parker's is Miss Wynn."

Sandra takes the Everton match programme from Rochey as she hands over the sick notes. Rochey and Parker proceed to skip down the back path, happy as a pair of Larrys. They start the hour walk to Bellefield to get their autograph books signed.

The walk to Bellefield wasn't without its trials as the lads watched out for the bizzies, and the local School Board. They took every back street available to them on the journey.

The lads get to Bellefield at 10am. They have a long wait for the players to come out, so they sit on the wall to keep safe from Yogi, the guard dog.

An older-looking lad is standing outside the Bellefield gates. He nods at Rochey and Parker, asking them why they're not in school.

"What's it got to do with you, mate?" snaps Rochey.

"Yeah, who do you think you are, mate? The School Board?" snarls Parker.

"Alright, lads, calm down, I'm just like you two, just here for the autographs. My name is Franny Robb."

"I'm Rochey. He's Parker. Have you left school, or don't you wear a uniform in your school?"

"I go to St. Aloysius in Huyton. We wear a school uniform but I've been suspended. That's why I've come here like this wearing my Lois jeans and my Fred Perry t-shirt. What about you two?"

"We go to St. Dominics. We've got free lessons this morning," replies Rochey.

"Free lessons! Really? In the second week of a new school year?" laughs Franny Robb.

"Yeah. Does a bear shit in the woods?" replies Rochey.

"What's bears shitting in the woods got to do with us not sagging school?" asks Parker.

Rochey gives Parker a stare that could kill.

"Who mentioned us sagging school? It's a saying, like 'is the Pope a Catholic?' I think you need to get back to school to get educated," snaps Rochey.

"Calm down, will yer. He's not the school board. Hey, lad, we're not sagging, alright!" shrieks Parker.

"Okay, I believe yers. Millions wouldn't," smirks Franny Robb.

"How come they suspended you? We only went back to school last week? How old are you?" asks Parker.

"I was fighting over football with some lad in my school. I'm 15. This is my last year in school."

"Last year! We're only five days into our first year!" replies

Rochey.

"Well, you both need to get back to school to get a good education."

"We get our education here, at Bellefield, and at Goodison Park watching Everton," says Parker.

"Well, next time you're at Goodison Park, go to turnstile 59. It's the Upper Bullens. My dad is Eddie Robb. He works behind the turnstile. One of you pays and one bunk in behind him. My dad just turns a blind eye," replies Franny Robb.

"Thanks for letting us know about your dad, Franny. He sounds like a great fella, but there are four of us that go to the match. We just bunk in the Gwladys Street End. I don't think I'd enjoy sitting down. I love standing up, singing with the lads," says Parker.

"Yeah, thanks Franny. Your dad is a man of the people. Our two other mates go to the match with us, Cooper and Skinny Maca. We're the Canny Farm Four," says Rochey.

"Where are they now?" asks Franny Robb.

"Really! What are you, mate a bizzie? What's with all the questions?" snaps Parker.

"They're in school. They don't go to the same school as us. They go to Canny High. They didn't have free lessons today, like us," replies Rochey, quick as a flash.

The lads hear the West Derby Church bells ring out as the clock strikes Twelve.

"They'd best hurry up. We have to get back to school for our dinner," moans Parker.

"Oh, shut up, stop moaning. We're only here for Peter Eastoe and Billy Wright," snaps Rochey.

"Don't worry, lad. My dad is picking me up at 12:30. I'll get him to drop you off if you want," says Franny Robb.

"Aww, nice one, Franny. That would be boss. As long as he's

not picking you up on a Chopper bike," jokes Rochey.

"I don't care even if it's a Chopper bike. As long as we get back to school, I'll get on the handlebars," laughs Parker.

"Don't worry. He drives a car. It will take five minutes," replies Franny Robb.

"I can see movement. That's Billy Wright getting into his Ford Capri!" yells Parker.

"Okay, calm down, before you shit your undies," laughs Rochey.

Billy Wright drives up towards the Big Blue Gates, stopping to sign the lads' autograph books.

"Hey, Billy, didn't you get a shower?" asks Rochey.

"Of course I got a shower. It's muddy on the pitches. Why are you asking that?" asks Billy Wright, sniffing up.

"I'm asking because when we have football practice, in school, Parker is always first out the changing rooms to get his dinner and he never gets a shower," replies Rochey.

"Why are you not in school today?" asks Billy Wright.

"He's suspended," says Parker, pointing at Franny Robb.

"And what about you two? You're both wearing your school uniform," asks Billy Wright.

"Hey, Billy, that was a great goal you scored on Saturday against Wolves!" replies Parker, swiftly changing the subject.

"Yeah, it wasn't bad. A half volley from twelve yards out," smiles Billy.

"That's your first in a league game for nineteen months, isn't it, Billy? Well, besides the own-goal you scored on the first day of the season at Roker Park, against Sunderland," smirks Rochey.

"Yeah, but own goals don't count," laughs Billy Wright.

"The last goal you scored before Saturday's goal was against Bristol City on the 10th of February, at Goodison Park in a 4-1 home win," reels off Parker.

"Was it that long ago?" asks Billy Wright.

"Yeah. The only other goals you've scored were against Manchester City on Boxing Day in 1978, and against Chelsea in the April of 1978 on your third appearance for the first team," replies Parker.

"Well, that's good to know. You lads take care!" says Billy Wright, as he drives away.

"My word, I thought he would never go. He was like a bizzie with all the school questions," growls Rochey.

"I know. We only wanted his autograph," replies Parker.

Franny Robb looks at Rochey and Parker in amazement, shaking his head laughing.

The lads only have to wait a few more minutes and another Ford Capri drives out towards them. Rochey and Parker stand in front of the car so they can get another autograph.

"Hello, mate. Can you sign my book? What's your name?" asks Rochey.

"It's Paul Lodge! He's a Scouser. He's one of us," says Franny Robb.

"Paul Lodge? Didn't you make your first team debut last season against Middlesbrough on the 22nd of March, at Ayresome Park?" asks Parker.

"No. I was an unused substitute that day. I haven't made my debut yet," replies Paul Lodge.

"Why doesn't that count? You were on the team sheet! You had a first team shirt on! That's crap, that," utters Rochey.

"You have to be on the pitch to make your debut," replies Paul Lodge.

"We got beat 2-1 anyway, so it was best you didn't get on. There wouldn't have been a win bonus that day. Just keep playing as you have been. You'll make your debut before you know it," says Parker, encouragingly.

Driving off, Paul Lodge smiles and beeps the car horn as he heads towards Eaton Road.

"You two really do know your stuff about Everton. You weren't kidding! You must be the cleverest in that school of yours," laughs Franny Robb.

"Never mind that, that's Peter Eastoe getting into his Citroen Athena!" yells Rochey.

"He's giving someone a lift! Who is it?" asks Parker.

"It's John Barton, the full back," replies Franny Robb.

"Oh, yeah, we signed him from that non-league team, Worcester City, last year. He's from Birmingham," says Parker.

"Well, that makes sense, Eastoe giving him a lift, 'cos Eastoe is from Dordon, near Tamworth, in Staffordshire. He goes past Birmingham. He must be giving him a lift," replies Rochey.

"Are you sure you're both only eleven years of age?" laughs Franny Robb, shaking his head.

Peter Eastoe stops his car and winds his window down, smiling at the lads as he munches on a peach. "Hello lads, no school today?"

"Yeah, of course we have, Peter. But It's 12:20 it's dinner time! Can you sign my autograph book and pass it to John as well, please?" asks Rochey.

"It was a great goal you scored on Saturday, Peter. Set us up for a great win," says Parker.

"Thanks, son," replies Peter Eastoe, as he passes the autograph book and pen back.

"Are you enjoying that peach, Peter?" asks Rochey.

"Yeah. I always have a peach before a game. You lads' take care. And don't be late for school after dinner," says Peter Eastoe, as he drives away with his passenger, John Barton, who waves at the lads with a smirk on his face.

"Peter the Peach, hey. I bet he peels oranges in his coat pocket," laughs Rochey.

Franny Robb's dad turns up bang on 12:30 and, as good as his word, Franny gets his dad to drop Rochey and Parker off outside St. Dominic's school gates.

They say their goodbyes, then both leg it to the dinner hall where they're met with a glare from Parker's mum, Beryl, who is tapping her watch, shaking her head, saying,

"What time do you call this? Dinner time is nearly over. Where have you been?"

"We've just had French, Mum. That was our last lesson."

"Your last lesson was over 40 minutes ago!" replies Parker's mum.

"Beryl, je suis Rochey. Mon professeur est Mademoiselle Walsh, qui nous a garde tard en classe," says Rochey.

"Neil, what has soft-lad just said to me?" asks Parker's mum.

"He's just said to you, in French, 'Beryl, I am Rochey. My teacher is Miss Walsh, who kept us late in the classroom'."

"Hey, he's good. And so are you, understanding French like that. Both of you sit down and I'll bring you both extra chips," says Parker's mum, as she disappears into the school kitchen.

"Well, that was a close call," says Parker.

"I know. Wasn't it lucky that was the only French we learned last year on that induction?" laughs Rochey.

"Yeah. That, and the fact we both rehearsed it while we were getting a lift helped," laughs Parker.

"I told you we would be back in time. It was worth it getting our books signed. Now all you have to do is hand in that sick-note to your form teacher after dinner," laughs Rochey.

Parker's mum brings out two plates of chips, pie and gravy. The smell of the gravy fills the room as Parker's mum puts the dinners down.

"Is that Bisto gravy, Beryl?" asks Rochey.

"Yes, now eat it all up."

"That Bisto is the best," says Rochey.

"I love Bisto gravy. I'm just waiting for the two Bisto kids to pop up and sing the Bisto song," replies Parker.

"Nar, never in a month of Sundays," laughs Rochey.

The two lads, still on a high, start chanting, "Everton, Everton, Everton," as they munch on their school dinner.

BILLY
WRIGHT

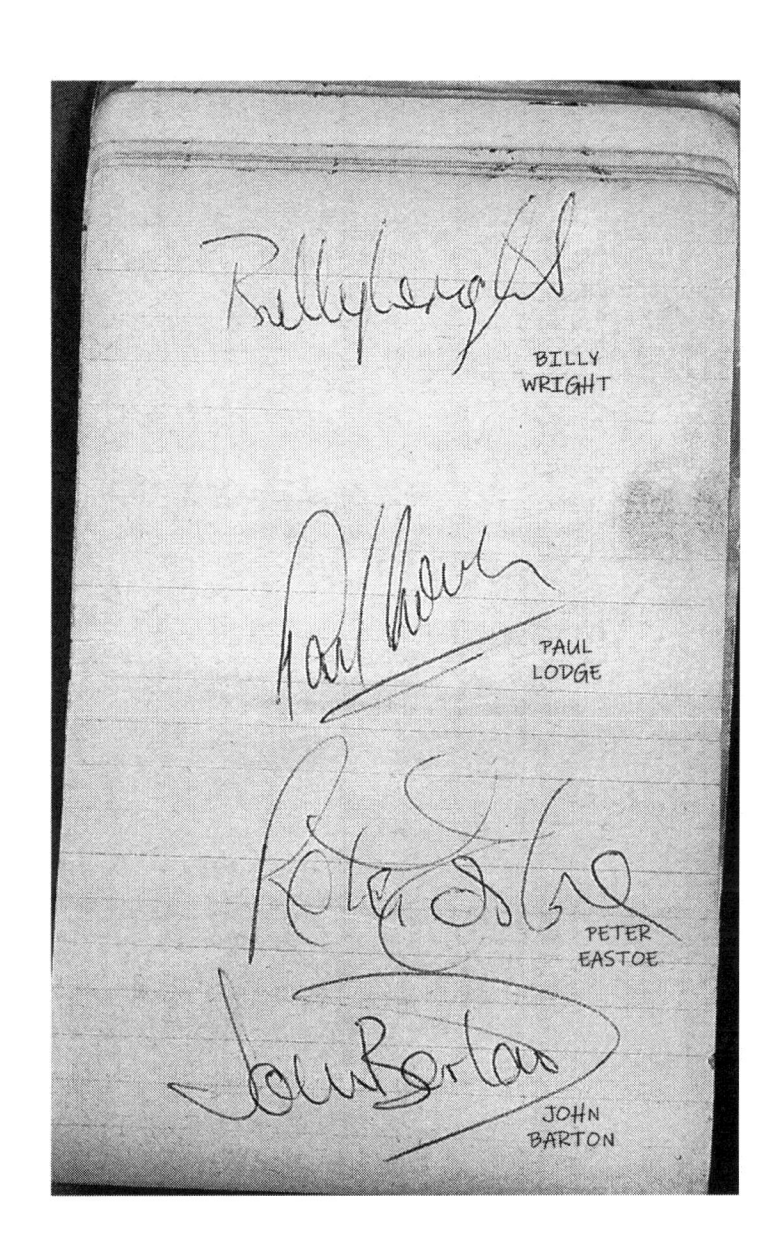

PAUL
LODGE

PETER
EASTOE

JOHN
BARTON

CHAPTER 6   BIG BOB'S HAT-TRICK

It's 5pm, on a cold September afternoon. Rochey, Parker, Cooper, and Skinny Maca are smiling while walking out of Goodison Park. They have just watched Everton beat Crystal Palace 5-0. (Managed by Terry Venables.)

The atmosphere inside the ground during the second half was electric as Big Bob Latchford opened up the scoring in the 49th minute to make it 1-0. Within ten minutes he'd netted two more making it a hat-trick.

In the 69th minute, a John Gidman penalty made it 4-0, with Peter Eastoe rounding off the scoring in the 78th minute, making it 5-0.

The lads are walking towards the bus stop with big smiles on their faces.

"That's why we love Everton," beams Rochey.

"I know. A 5-0 win, with a Bob Latchford Hat-trick. What more could you ask for?" grins Parker.

"I love looking up at the big floodlights when we score and all the fans are going wild, singing and dancing," says Skinny Maca.

"Me too. That's what Everton are all about. Gordon Lee can eat his roast dinner with a smile on his face now," replies Rochey.

"I'm going to play for Everton when I'm older and have the fans chanting my name when I score in front of the Gwladys Street End," declares Cooper.

"We can all play for Everton if we keep playing football and learn from the Everton players, week in, week out," says Parker.

"That's sorted then. We're all going to play for Everton. So, we don't really need to go to school, so we can bunk off school one day this week and get some autographs," prompts Rochey.

"No, don't be daft, you need an education. Look at Steve Heighway. He went to university and played for Liverpool," pipes up Skinny Maca.

"Well, you don't have to worry about that, cos there is no chance of you ever going to university. You're still learning your 2 times tables in school," laughs Rochey.

The lads jump on the bus singing Everton songs, dancing as they walk up the stairs of the double decker bus.

Tuesday 23rd of September, 1980. It's ten in the morning as Cooper and Skinny Maca stand outside Saint Dominic's school gates, waiting to catch sight of Rochey and Parker.

"It's freezing standing here," whines Skinny Maca.

"Oh, shut up moaning. Put my jacket on. Just keep an eye out for them," replies Cooper, handing Skinny Maca his jacket.

"There they are!" yells Skinny Maca.

"Where?" asks Cooper, as he looks over towards the school's drama hall.

"Over there!" points out Skinny Maca.

"Hey, Rochey, Parker! Over here!" Cooper yells, as Skinny Maca whistles to get their attention.

Rochey and Parker spot them and walk towards the school exit gates accompanied by Anthony Carty, David Nuttall and Ray Duffy.

"What are you two doing here?" asks Parker.

"The school was broken into last night. They smashed all our classroom windows and said it was unfit to teach in, so they have sent us home," smirks Skinny Maca.

"We're going to Bellefield. Are you coming?" asks Cooper.

"How can we soft lad? We haven't been sent home," replies Rochey.

"Well, I can see that your school windows are all boarded up. Do you ever see daylight in your class?" smirks Skinny Maca.

"Just bunk off. We're going to get Big Bob Latchford's autograph," boasts Cooper.

"Latchford's autograph? Count me in then," says Parker.

"He never stops to sign our books, so why do you think today will be any different?" asks Rochey.

"He will today. We've got a plan up our sleeve," says Skinny Maca.

"Count me in then," utters Anthony Carty.

"I will bunk off if you go to Melwood as well, so I can get Liverpool autographs," pipes up David Nuttall.

"I will cover for all of yers. We 've art next lesson, until dinner time," says Ray Duffy.

"Bleeding heck, our art lesson will have none of us in it," laughs Parker.

"Never mind the art lesson, I'm more bothered that we have to go to Melwood," moans Rochey.

"Forget about Melwood, just make sure we duck down with our school blazers over our heads as we sprint across this playground, so none of the teachers see us bunking off," says Anthony Carty.

"Let's go then. Just leg it, and don't look back," yells Rochey.

The lads sprint across the school playground trying not to be seen as they duck behind the bushes dropping out of sight of any teachers that could potentially spoil their escape.

The walk to Bellefield was an eventful one as the lads kept off the main roads, taking all the back streets to avoid the School Board that patrolled the city. Rochey took great pleasure showing David Nuttall the autographs that he got from Bill Shankly and Kenny Dalglish. His autograph book goes everywhere with him.

The lads get to Bellefield at 11:05am Standing outside the

training ground is a young lad no more than nine years of age. He has a skinhead and has a royal blue Everton jersey on and is freezing his balls off.

"Hello, mate, have any of the players come out yet?" queries Skinny Maca. The young lad shakes his head and looks down towards the floor.

"Ain't you cold? You've only got an Everton jersey on," points out Cooper.

"Yeah," replies the young lad, who again puts his head down looking towards the floor.

"What school do you go to?" asks Cooper.

"Stop with all the questions! Can't you see you're intimidating the young lad?" snaps Rochey.

"I know. Leave the poor lad alone," utters Parker.

"What's your name, mate?" asks Cooper.

Rochey gives Cooper a stare.

"I'm only asking him his name. We're all Evertonians here," snaps Cooper.

"My name is Jeff, Jeff Ollerhead."

"Hollow head? Cooper could definitely be your cousin with a name like that. He's a hollow head as well. He's definitely got nothing in between his ears," laughs David Nuttall.

"How come you're not in school, mate?" asks Skinny Maca.

"I'm off school today. I was boxing last night for Sandbrook ABA Boxing Club."

"Sandbrook! Where is that? Where have you come from today?" asks Anthony Carty.

"It's on the Wirral. I'm from over the water. I go to Sacred Heart school in Moreton."

"You've travelled far to come here today. How old are you? What made you come here today? How come you're boxing at your age?" asks Cooper.

"Did Cooper come up for air then, asking the kid all those questions?" asks Rochey, as he looks at the other lads, shaking his head. "This kid must think he's on a quiz show with all these questions."

Jeff smiles at the lads. "I came here on the train, then jumped the bus. I'm nine. I'm here because I love Everton. I boxed last night. Grandad runs the boxing club and I've been boxing since I was six."

"A boxer or not, you look like you're freezing. Put my jacket on," says Skinny Maca, as he hands Jeff his jacket.

The lads wait patiently for the players to come out.

"Look! Someone's coming out carrying a guitar case," says Anthony Carty.

"He looks like Brian May," says Rochey.

"Who's Brian May? He doesn't play for Everton," retorts Anthony Carty.

"He's the lead guitarist in that rock band, Queen, I thought you knew your music? Didn't you say you wanted work as a DJ when you left school?" laughs Rochey.

"Well, whoever it is, he's rocking down here now," says Parker.

"It's John Gidman," pipes up Skinny Maca.

"Make sure he doesn't just drive past us. He's a proper Scouser. He's from Garston, and he's played for England against Luxembourg," yells Cooper.

"Yeah, that was when we didn't qualify for the finals in Argentina, so don't mention it," whispers Rochey.

John Gidman drives slowly towards the exit gates. As he gets near the lads, he stops his car, winds down his car window, and smiles at them, with curly hair blowing everywhere.

"Hello, lads, no school today?"

"No, Giddy, we're off today," replies Anthony Carty.

"Do you always wear your school uniform on your days off?" asks John Gidman.

"It's the school boilers," pipes up Rochey.

"Yeah, Giddy, boiler's gone again," smirks Anthony Carty.

"Can you sign this for me, John?" asks Parker, as he passes a piece of paper and a black bic pen through his car window.

John Gidman signs all the autograph books with a big Scouse smile and beeps as he drives off.

"Look who's on his way out! It's only Peter Eastoe!" yells Skinny Maca.

"Okay, calm down. The way you're shouting, I was thinking it was Bob Latchford," snaps Parker.

Peter Eastoe drives down slowly, smiling at the lads as he reaches them. He pulls up in his Citroen Athena and winds his window down.

"No school today, lads? We don't usually get fans here on school days."

"No, Peter, the school boilers have burst. We all got sent home," replies Cooper.

"Yeah, so we have come to our second home, Peter," smirks Skinny Maca.

"Well, I could believe that. you're never away from here," laughs Peter Eastoe. He signs all the books and drives off.

The lads are getting restless. They're waiting for the best thing since sliced bread to come out; the man mountain himself, Big Bob Latchford.

"Here's someone," says Ant Carty.

The lads all wait patiently with their autograph books. The car drives up towards them.

"Who is it?" pipes Skinny Maca.

"Looks like Martin Hodge, the goalkeeper," says young Jeff Ollerhead. Martin Hodge pulls up, smiling at the lads as he signs their books.

"Nice one, Martin. Top Scouser," says Ant Carty.

"Scouser? We signed him from Plymouth Argyle," says Cooper.

"So, what! Christopher Columbus discovered America but he wasn't American; he was Italian," snaps Ant Carty.

"He actually didn't set foot in America," says Parker.

"According to our history books he did," replies Anthony Carty.

"Does it matter? In school, on the school dinner menu, it says chips, pie and gravy costs fifty pence, but Parker's mam only charges me twenty pence," laughs Rochey.

The lads all start laughing as Martin Hodge looks on bewildered.

"Where are you from, Martin?" asks Rochey.

"I was born in Southport," replies Martin Hodge.

"So, a posh Scouser then, Martin," laughs Skinny Maca.

"No, he's not even a Scouser. He's a woolly back," pipes up Cooper.

The lads all look at Cooper as Martin Hodge drives off smiling, shaking his head.

"Look at that. Martin Hodge has signed my book twice in two different colour pens," says Rochey to Skinny Maca and Cooper.

"That's brilliant. Two for the price of one," smirks Skinny Maca.

"Yeah, you buy one, you get one free," laughs Cooper.

"Look, look! It's Big Bobby Latchford coming out," cries out Skinny Maca, as Latchford walks out through the Bellefield doors towards his Talbot Alpine.

"What's the plan to make him stop his car?" asks Ant Carty.

"He won't stop. He never does," says Rochey.

"Yes, he will. Cooper has a plan," growls Parker.

"Well, I haven't actually got a plan. I just said that to get you all here," whispers Cooper.

"Well, you best come up with a plan! I've just bunked art to get his autograph," snaps Parker.

With wide eyes and a shrug of his shoulders, Cooper looks towards Rochey.

"You're crap at drawing anyway, so does it matter that you're missing art lesson?" jokes Rochey, as he tries to defuse the situation.

"Yes, of course it matters. I'm not bad at drawing."

"Well, what I'm saying is you're no Pablo Picasso or Vincent Van Gogh, are you? You can't draw or paint for toffee," laughs Rochey.

"I support the Toffees and love Big Bob, so Cooper had best have a plan because Bob Latchford is driving down now," screeches Parker.

There is silence in the air. The leaves on the surrounding trees blow down towards the tarmac.

Big Bobby Latchford edges closer and closer towards the lads.

Cooper looks around at the lads, praying that Bob Latchford stops.

"He's not going to stop," pipes up Skinny Maca.

"Yes, he will," whispers young Jeff Ollerhead, as he walks into the middle of the tarmac and pretends to slip on the fallen leaves, ten metres from Bob Latchford's Talbot Alpine.

"Are you okay, son?" asks Bob Latchford, as he stops his car next to the lads.

"Yes, I'm okay, Sir. I just skidded on the slippery tarmac," replies young Jeff Ollerhead, as he looks towards Cooper, smiling.

"Can you sign this please, Bob?" asks Parker, pushing his autograph book inside Latchford's car window, not for one second taking his eyes off him, with a smile on his face that could have lit up the sky.

Cooper breathes a sigh of relief.

"That was a superb hat-trick you scored on Saturday, Bob," says Skinny Maca, as he gets his autograph.

"Bob scores goals for fun. He's the best in the world," retorts Parker, with his eyes still glued to Bob Latchford's every move.

"Can you score your signature on my book Bob," smiles Rochey, as he hands Bob his autograph book.

Bob Latchford signs all the autograph books passed across from the lads. He gives little Jeff Ollerhead the thumbs up as he drives away.

Cooper smiles at Parker, saying, "I love it when a plan comes together."

That was the one and only time Bob Latchford stopped for the lads. But that was all the lads needed to forge a lasting memory.

Big Bob was one of the greatest centre-forwards to have worn the famous royal blue number 9 Everton shirt. He graced the green turf year in, year out, at Goodison Park, scoring lots of goals both there and all around the world.

Parker winks at Cooper as he dances away from Bellefield, singing:

"Bobby Latchford walks on water. Na..na na..na.. na ...Na na na na.

"We love you Bob," shouts Parker.

Bob Latchford beeps his horn and gives Parker a thumbs up out of his car window as he drives towards Eaton Road. The lads all go crazy and start chanting:

'Oh, his name is Bobby Latchford,

He's the leader of our team,

The finest centre-forward that the world has ever,

When Ronny takes a corner, he knocks it in the goal,

And as for Kevin Keegan, you can stick him up yer hole,

Na, Na, Na, Naaaa………………………….'

Not amused, Liverpudlian, David Nutall walks away muttering something under his breath.

Skinny Maca bounces down the road and starts singing to the tune of 'One Day at a Time, Sweet Jesus.'

'One goal at a time, Bob Latchford,

That's all we're asking of you,

If you hit the bar,

We all go aaaah. One goal at a time.'

Rochey, laughing, shakes his head, looks straight at Skinny Maca and says, "Have you been robbing your grandad's music hymn sheets again?"

"No, I just sang that because you sang that old song with

Keegan's name in it," points out Skinny Maca.

"You're not even a Catholic."

"I know. But I still believe in God. I believe he created life, the earth and the oceans."

"Maca, I thought the oceans were created by leaving the tap on in the house," pipes up Cooper.

The lads all look at Cooper in astonishment, shaking their heads at what he has just said.

With this young Jeff Ollerhead bids the lads farewell and goes for his bus to make his long journey home.

"Right, it's 12:30. Let's get to Melwood and catch the Liverpool players to get their autographs," says David Nutall.

"Nah, jib that. It's pink custard today in school," says Ant Carty.

"Yeah. And Parker's mum gives you extra portions. We can go to Melwood on another day," laughs Rochey.

"Do you think we could go for our dinner? I love pink custard," asks Cooper.

"Don't be stupid. You don't go to our school. You don't even wear a uniform in your school," says Ant Carty.

"We could say we're sixth-form students. They don't wear a uniform in your school. We could have the pink custard, then disappear," mocks Skinny Maca.

"Are you having a laugh? You're both three foot-tall and look about ten years of age. The teachers in our school ain't thick like the teachers in your school," replies David Nutall.

The lads walk to the bus stop to get the bus back to school.

"Here's our bus. Let's get on it," shouts Parker.

"That young kid! What's his name? that Jeff Ollerhead? He's

just disappeared. I thought he was getting the bus home? He's nowhere to be seen," mutters Skinny Maca.

"That's because he's a magician," answers Rochey.

"How is he a magician?" inquires Skinny Maca.

"How is he a magician? Well, for starters, he's just made your jacket disappear," laughs Rochey.

"He hasn't made my jacket disappear, I didn't go to school this morning with one, I borrowed Cooper's outside your school gates," smirks Skinny Maca, as he gets on the bus.

Cooper dumbfounded at what he's just heard looks at Skinny Maca in disbelieve.

JOHN
GIDMAN

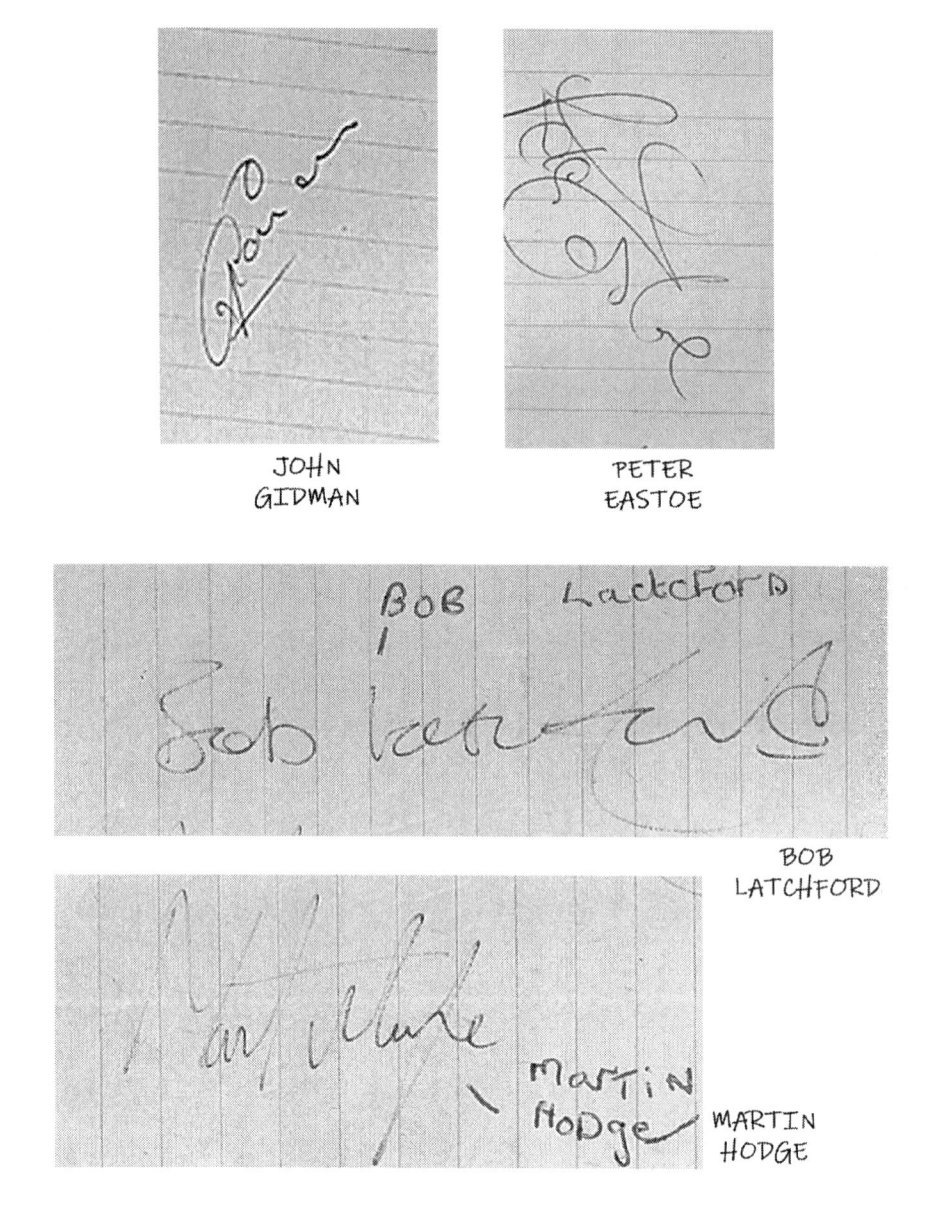

PETER
EASTOE

BOB
LATCHFORD

MARTIN
HODGE

CHAPTER 7   THE SCOUSE INVASION

The long nights of winter are finally here! It's 7 o'clock on a dark, damp, October evening but the weather hasn't managed to dampen the four lads' spirits for one simple reason; this coming Saturday, Everton will play their local rivals, Liverpool, in the first derby of the season at Goodison Park.

The four lads are sitting in Parker's kitchen, drinking bottles of green cream soda, a fizzy drink that Parker's dad, Joey, gets from the Alpine man on a Saturday morning.

"Scousers in the house!" yells Cooper.

"Come on you blue boys," chants Skinny Maca.

"Shut up, yer pair of muppets! You'll wake my dad up. He's in bed. You know he always has a sleep when he gets home from work," scoffs Parker.

"Are you both thick? Has that fizz gone to your heads? You do know if you wake his dad up, we'll get kicked out of here, back into the cold, no more green cream soda," snaps Rochey, filling his glass up as he speaks.

"Sorry, it's the biggest game of the season on Saturday. I just got a bit excited," replies Cooper.

The lads hear a noise from the stairs. They've only gone and woken Joey, Parker's dad.

Joey walks into the kitchen where the lads are sitting. "What's with all the noise? I was fast asleep! You've woken me up!"

"Sorry Joey, it was that muppet," replies Rochey, pointing at Cooper.

"Never mind sorry, yer can all piss off now. I've got a date with Elvis, so you can get your coats and do one."

"Does Beryl know you've got a date with Elvis?" smirks Cooper.

"Don't be cheeky softarse! Beryl's at the bingo. And don't

be playing football outside the door Neil! Go and play on the field. All you ever do is hit the window with the ball," complains Joey.

"It's two extra goals for hitting the window," Skinny Maca, says smirking.

Joey glares at Skinny Maca as he walks out of the kitchen into the living room and within seconds, Viva Las Vegas is blasting out the speakers. The vinyl Elvis record on his record player is doing the business.

"Not only has Joey got a date, but he's in Las Vegas as well," laughs Skinny Maca.

"Yeah, well, while me dad has a date with Elvis in Las Vegas, we've a date with this ball outside. Let's go!" says Parker, picking up the orange trophy football on his way out.

"Let's knock at Paul's. He can be our goalkeeper for headers and volleys," says Rochey.

"Don't be stupid, Paul's twenty-seven years old and married, with a two-year-old," replies Parker.

"Yeah, but he's also your next-door neighbour, who just happens to support the red shite, so if we hit his window with the ball, it's laughing," says Rochey.

"No, it's too late to knock. Plus, Collette won't let him out," replies Parker.

"It's only 7 o' clock. He's a grown man," snorts Rochey.

"I know that, but he'll be getting Esmy to sleep. He hasn't got the freedom we have. Let's go play outside the Harvester pub," replies Parker.

The four lads walk towards the Harvester pub, kicking the ball at every lamppost along the way.

A few years down the line, when the lads will be no more than 15 years of age, Parker's next door neighbour Paul Evans, then aged 31 will be the lads' Sunday afternoon goalkeeper, where they will take on grown men twice their age. Rochey will nickname him 'Hans Grandad' as he'll be miles older than them. The lads will love having him play in goal for them, as no one will score past him and Paul will love playing football with the lad in return he'll see their skill and passion for the game, that had been in them from such an early age.

When Parker is eighteen years old, he'll be banging the goals in, week in, week out, for the Croxteth Legion in the Liverpool Sunday Premier league. He'll often ask Paul to play in goal for them when their regular goalkeeper is injured. Parker and Rochey will return that favour a few years down the line, making guest appearances for Paul's Sunday League team, Barnfield, who play in the Liverpool Business Houses League.

The Derby match at Goodison Park on October 18th finished Everton 2 Liverpool 2. The official attendance that day was 52,565.

In the Everton starting eleven that day, five Scousers started the match; full backs John Gidman and John Bailey; centre-halves, Captain Marvel Mick Lyons and Billy Wright; and Stephen McMahon in centre midfield.

The red half of the city had four Scousers in their starting eleven including Phil Thompson and Sammy Lee, the latter of whom scored that day would later become assistant manager at Everton.

In reality, Sammy was in a no-win, situation! The Everton faithful didn't want him there as he was an ex-Liverpool player, and the Liverpool die-hard supporters thought he had sold them out by coaching on the blue side.

In all fairness, he was a top coach that had worked with the England national team, though some wondered whether it was wise for him to come to Everton as part of the coaching staff. Only Sammy Lee can answer that one.

Also, in the Liverpool team that day were David Johnson and Terry McDermott. Johnson started his career at Everton before moving to Liverpool via Ipswich Town. When he left Liverpool in

1982, he re-joined Everton for two seasons between 1982-84 where he played 40 games, scoring four goals, before then moving onto Manchester City.

The four lads walk out of the stadium happy. They hadn't been beaten by their arch rivals. But if truth be told, they're also a bit upset, as Everton were leading 2-0 after twenty-one minutes, only for Liverpool to pull two goals back to snatch a draw. They took comfort in the fact that, before the start of play Everton were sitting 4th in the league table whilst Liverpool was sitting 2nd. After the game Everton had stayed in 4th place whilst Liverpool had dropped down a place to 3rd in the league.

"It's teacher training day on Tuesday, so shall we go to Bellefield to get the autographs of the Scousers that played today?" asks Rochey.

The other three lads nod as they walk towards the bus-stop, munching on their chips that they have just got from George's chippy on Priory Road.

On Tuesday 21st f October, 1980, the four lads were joined by Carl Mills, a big Evertonian.

Walking alongside him is John Saidie, a supporter of the red shite. With him are Sean Quinn, Joey Hunt, Lee Grant and Stephen Grant.

"Scouser day today!" says Cooper, with a smile as wide as the Mersey Tunnel.

"Scouser day? So, were going to Bellefield and Melwood?" remarks John Saidie, who is a staunch Liverpudlian.

"Yeah, of course that's were going! We can get autographs from both sets of players," replies Coopers.

"I won't be getting Sammy Lee's autograph," says Rochey.

"Why not? he's a Scouser!" asks Lee Grant.

"Why? I'll tell you why! The little knobhead scored against us on Saturday, that's why I won't be getting him to sign his name," snaps Rochey.

"Well, that's a fair point," says John Saidie, with a grin on his face, thinking back to Sammy Lee's goal at the weekend.

The lads are at the gates of Bellefield waiting for the players to come out. John Saidie and Lee Grant are moaning about being Liverpool supporters and having to come to Bellefield first.

The way they see it, the odds were stacked against them 7:2, as young Stephen Grant didn't get a vote because he's only seven. He's only here because his older brother Lee Grant is baby-sitting him for the day.

"Shut up. Quit yer moaning you two," moans Rochey.

"I'm not moaning! I'm just making a point," says John Saidie.

"Well, it sounds to me like you are. We'll go to Melwood after here. There're loads of time to get to both training grounds today," remarks Rochey.

"I wouldn't mind but, Saidie, you play for Liverpool Schoolboys. So, you train at Melwood twice a week," says Carl Mills.

"Yeah, and you get to change in the Melwood changing rooms while we're outside in the cold here waiting for the players to come out," butts in Sean Quinn.

(Sean Quinn signed apprentice forms for Liverpool in 1986, he had every team in the English football league fighting for his signature.)

"I know all that. But we train at night time, and I don't get to see the first team players like Kenny Dalglish, Souness, and Terry McDermott," replies John Saidie.

"So, you get to play for Liverpool schoolboys under the floodlights for the second-best team in the city, and you're still moaning?" smirks Rochey.

"Shut up now! There's Mick Lyons coming out with Billy Wright!" yells Parker.

"Get your pens and books out lads'! Today's Scouse autograph day!" says Skinny Maca, excitedly.

John Saidie, a year older than Rochey and the other lads, would later be a regular visitor at Bellefield. He would play for Everton schoolboys, though at that time, he and Rochey's older brother, Brian, were the two best twelve-year-old footballers in the Cantril Farm Junior Sunday Football League. As luck would have it, Rochey's older brother was due to have a trial for Everton on his 16th birthday, but broke his ankle, the day before his big chance. He came off a BMX bike on the track in Cantril Farm.

John Saidie and Brian Roche never did reach their full potential as footballers. Paths took them in different directions and, like so many other kids with bags of skill and talent both fell at the final hurdle. In today's game lots of professional football clubs have football academies. Maybe if they had had them in the 1980's they would have been guided, protected, and nurtured to help them achieve their dream of becoming professional footballers.

A few lads from the Cantril Farm Junior Football League did get to fulfil their dream David Fairclough (Liverpool) Mick Quinn (Newcastle United) Ian Bishop (Manchester City) Paul Fitzpatrick (Leicester City) and Billy Mercer (Chesterfield) these are just a few. But for every player that did make it as a professional footballer there are kids that were just as talented who didn't get there. Some took the wrong path in life and were let down by the system. Some didn't get spotted by the scouting system for one reason or another. Some didn't get the luck that they needed to make the breakthrough. This is why all the top football league clubs today have football academies.

Billy Wright drives towards the lads with Mick Lyons alongside him.

"Hello, Billy, can you sign my book please? It's Scouse signing day today," says Cooper.

"Are you two always side by side?" laughs Skinny Maca.

"Yeah, nobody gets past us two, in the centre of defence," laughs Billy Wright.

"Sammy Lee and Kenny Dalglish did on Saturday," mutters John Saidie, under his breath. Carl Mills and Sean Quinn, stare at him growling.

"I'm not surprised that no-one gets past you two. You're both built like brick shithouses," laughs Cooper.

"Well, you got the shit bit right," mutters John Saidie, again under his breath, this time a little louder.

All the lads give him the eye, hoping that these two great Everton giants didn't hear him. Billy Wright and Mick Lyons look at each other in disbelief. The lads aren't sure if the look is due to Cooper's comments about them both being built like brick shithouses or Saidie's comment about them being shit.

Parker quickly changes the subject:

"Hey, Billy, my neighbour, Ike Flexen, said you know his niece, Val Flexen, that you both lived in Norris Green?"

"Yeah, I know Val. She's a blast from the past. Val Flexen, Little Curly Wurly."

"He told me that you were her first proper boyfriend," smirks Parker.

"We were just kids, even younger than you lot. We were only about six or seven. We just used to listen to records together," laughs Billy, as he hands the books over to Mick Lyons to sign.

Rochey winks at Parker who then nudges the other lads. They all stand as one, facing Billy Wright and start singing: "I'm not in love, so don't forget it, it's just a silly phase I'm going through, I call her Curly, Curly Wurly, she's just a girl that loves me too."

Mick Lyons can't contain his laughter, as he signs the autograph books. Billy Wright drives away, tears in his eyes from laughing so hard. l Mick Lyons, a huge smile across his face is howling as the tears roll down his face, too.

"There's that Donny Osmond smile again," laughs Sean Quinn.

"Hey, that's John Bailey, who's walking out," yells skinny Maca.

"That's good. At least he can't drive past us," smirks Parker.

"No, but he might run past us," laughs Carl Mills.

John Bailey walks towards the lads with a smirk on his face.

"Hello, lads, who's book I'm I signing first?" asks John Bailey.

"Hello John, can you sign my book please?" asks Rochey.

"Of course I can, son. Give us your book."

"Can you sign mine as well?" asks Cooper, excitedly.

"I'll sign all your books. Not to worry. Don't fuss. I'm in no rush. The pub I'm going to, The Halton Castle doesn't open till midday," smirks John Bailey.

"Where's your car, Bails?" asks Parker.

"Left it at home. I'm going for a hard-earned pint today, lads."

"We love your Ford Capri 2000, Bails. Cooper thinks you look like Doyle from The Professionals when you drive it," laughs Skinny Maca.

"I'll give Giddy a lift in it then next time, 'cos then we can be Bodey and Doyle," laughs Bails.

The lads all get their autograph books signed as John Bailey stands and chats football with them before he heads off towards The Halton Castle.

In today's football, the supporters are lucky if they get to make eye contact with their heroes, never mind experience an autograph and a chat as though they were old friends.

In today's football, a lot of players think they're royalty, or rock stars. That's not to say all footballers show such behaviour; some have genuine love for their fan base. In reality, they get paid far too much money. What they should remember is, kids look up to them and they need to set a good example.

How can someone be a true hero if you don't get to meet them and chat to them like a normal human being? This is why, these days, back in the 80's were so special to these lads. They got to meet their heroes, and those heroes treated the lads like old friends. They always had time for the lads, always had a smile, whether if they played for Everton or Liverpool. These legendary players had time for all of the supporters. There were no airs or graces about them. They were all down to earth, with a genuine love for the fan base.

Football clubs have widened the gap between themselves and the everyday football supporter who, in reality, are the bread and butter of the club. Without football supporters, there is no football club.

"That's three down, two to go! Come on down John Gidman and Stephen McMahon!" yells Skinny Maca.

John Gidman and Stephen McMahon shortly follow and sign the books for all the lads. They stop and have a chat before driving off to enjoy the rest of the day.

"Right, that's the Everton Scouse lads done. Let's get to Melwood now," yells John Saidie.

The lads walk down to Liverpool's training ground, Melwood, and as they approach the big red gates, they spot nineteen-year-old ticket tout, Melvo, aka Joey Egghead, who lives on their manor.

"Hello, young Rochey. I heard on the grapevine that you've been chatting up my bird, Julie Hamo," says Joey Egghead, straight-faced.

"Me? I don't think so, Joey, she's eighteen, I'm eleven. But I do think she fancies me," laughs Rochey.

"She only has eyes for me, young Rochey," replies Joey

Egghead.

"It's not her eyes I look at," mutters Rochey, under his breath.

"What was that you just said, young Rochey?" asks Joey Egghead.

"I said, what are you doing here?" replies Rochey.

"I'm just here to see a couple of the reserve players, to get tickets off them for Saturday's match," replies Joey Egghead.

"Do you get free tickets off the players, Joey?" asks Lee Grant.

"No, don't be soft, young Granty. These players ask me for top dollar."

"Do they call you Joey Egghead 'cos you're bald, Joey?" asks Cooper.

"No, don't be stupid soft lad, it's because me and Joey Jones have the same smile."

The big red gates open as the Liverpool players make their way to the coach from the Melwood changing room. The lads are on their toes, ready to leg it for some autographs. Joey Egghead breezes in like he owns the place, cool as you like. John Saidie and Lee Grant shoot off towards the players like greyhounds chasing the hare in the 12:15 at Monmore.

Rochey, who is not impressed, leans on the gates with no intention of getting any autographs.

"Can I get some autographs in your book?" asks Ste Grant.

"Why? You don't like football, Ste," replies Rochey.

"I know that. But it's good to be part of the gang."

Rochey hands Ste Grant his autograph book. Ste legs it to catch up with the other lads.

"Look after that autograph book, Ste! It's priceless!" yells Rochey.

All the lads walk out of Melwood with big smiles on their faces.

"Here's your book Rochey," says Ste Grant.

"Thanks Ste. Who did you get to sign it?" asks Rochey.

"I don't know. I don't even like football. I haven't got a clue who signed it. I just smiled at them and said 'sign that for me mate.'"

John Saidie looks at Rochey's autograph book.

"Oh, my word. He's only gone and got you the best midfielders in the world for your book: Kenny Dalglish, Graeme Souness, Jimmy Case and Ray Kennedy."

"Ste, why did you get Kenny Dalglish's autograph? He scored against us on Saturday!" grumbles Rochey.

"I don't know. They all seemed like nice people. They all smiled at me."

"Oh, stop moaning! He's just got legends to sign your book! Let's go and get the bus home," says John Saidie.

The lads all walk to the bus stop and, as they're waiting, Joey Egghead pulls up in his sky-blue VW Beetle.

"Rochey, do you and the gang want a lift home?"

"There's ten of us. Will we all fit in, Joey?"

"Yeah, just all squeeze in, all aboard the Skylark!" yells Joey Egghead, as the lads squeeze in the back of the car.

"You must make a few quid, having a car like this Joey, ticket sales must be good," says Skinny Maca, as he pops his head through from the crowded back seat.

"Ticket sales have been brilliant since we won the European Cup in 1977. People from all over the world want to watch Liverpool now. We just charge them ten times the cost price," laughs Joey Egghead.

"One born every minute, Joey. but you wouldn't get away with that, selling to Everton fans!" says Parker.

"Why is that Mr Parker?" asks Joey Egghead, with a smirk.

"Why? Because all Evertonians are proper Scousers. We don't pay daft prices. If we haven't got a ticket, we just bunk in."

"I didn't know I was giving a lift to the ten Wise Men," laughs Joey. "I'll stay clear of the Everton matches then otherwise I'll be skint then I'll have to sell my car, and get a pedal bike."

"The Reds are the best. They will always make you money. This time next year you'll be driving a Rolls Royce. How fast does the Skylark go, Joey?" asks John Saidie.

"It doesn't go as fast as you, Saidie, when you're running down the wing with the ball, playing for Liverpool schoolboys. But it hit 93 mph downhill when I was coming home from Oxford."

"Can you make it go 94 mph today, so we get home quicker. So, I don't have to hear all this crap about Liverpool?" says Rochey.

"I second that," says Parker.

Cooper starts to bang on the car roof panels singing *'Everton, Everton, Everton.'* All the lads join in with him except John Saidie. The car is swaying side to side' Joey Egghead beeps his car horn and shouts out the car window. *'All aboard the Skylark, Evertonians in the house.'*

In the 80's there was still a rivalry between the two sets of fans, but it was a friendly rivalry. They were mates who went to Bellefield and Melwood together and, though there was always banter between both sets of fans it was never nasty. The city at the time, regardless of who they supported always stuck together

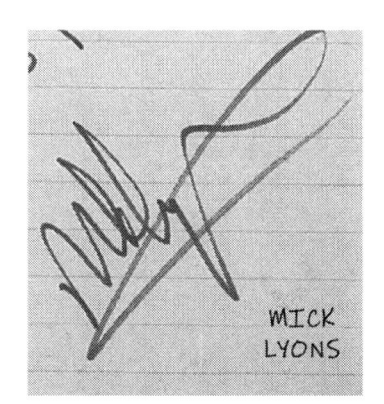

MICK LYONS

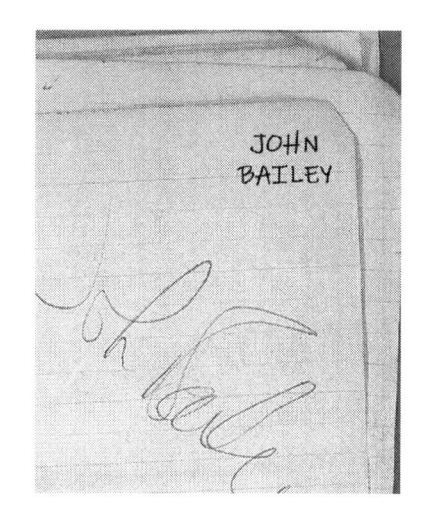

JOHN BAILEY

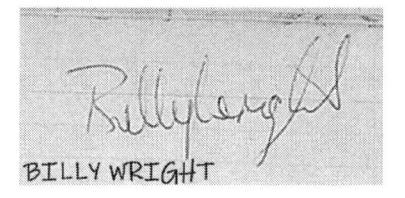

BILLY WRIGHT

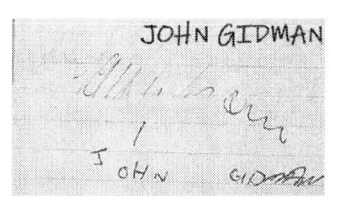

JOHN GIDMAN

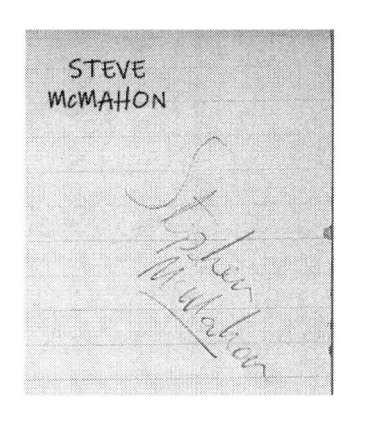

STEVE McMAHON

RAY KENNEDY

KENNY DALGLISH

JIMMY CASE

GRAEME SOUNESS

CHAPTER 8   THE LUCK OF THE IRISH

Tuesday 18th of November, 1980. The four lads, (Rochey, Parker, Skinny Maca, and Cooper,) have decided to use their day off school wisely as it's teacher training day and have headed off to Bellefield to get more autographs. The previous Saturday, Everton had beaten Sunderland 2-1 with goals from Eamonn O' Keefe and Asa Hartford. As the lads make their way, they bump into eleven-year-old Bob Dring who has got his air rifle strapped over his shoulder, his Jack Russell walking alongside him.

"Hello, Bobby boy," says Rochey.

"My name is Brian," replies Bob Dring.

"Why do they call you Bob then?" asks a confused Parker.

"It's because Rochey's older brother is called Brian, and as we live in the same street, he decided that there wasn't room for two Brians, so they gave me the name Bob."

"Hmm, wise decision. Bob Dring sounds better than Brian Dring," butts in Skinny Maca.

"I like my real name, Brian."

"Well, on that note, Bobby boy, we're going to Bellefield to get some autographs. Do you fancy coming with us?" asks Rochey.

"No, ta, I'm going hunting."

"Can I ask you something, Bob? Why in the middle of winter, and today of all days with it being foggy and cold; why are you only wearing a t-shirt?" asks Parker.

"I'm not cold. Plus, if I wear a coat, it stops how quick I can get my rifle out, and it slows me down when I'm chasing my prey."

The four lads say their goodbyes to Bob and carry on with their journey to Bellefield.

"He must have been cold," says Parker.

"I think he thinks he's that kid from the Ready Brek advert, with that orange glow warming him up," laughs Rochey.

"I not sure about the orange glow, but he's got red hair, Bobby Ginger," says Skinny Maca.

"Don't let him hear you call him ginger. He can throw those French arrows that he makes over a block of hi-rise flats," replies Rochey.

"It'll be okay saying it today. He'll never see me through all this fog," laughs Skinny Maca.

The fog is getting thicker and thicker as the lads reach the gates of the Everton training ground, they notice a young lad aged about 12 wearing a green top, leaning against the gates. The lads can just about make him out within the fog that has surrounded the Bellefield training ground.

"With all this fog, it's the best time to sneak in to watch the players as that mad dog won't be able to see us," says Cooper.

"No, you're right, it won't see us. But it'll be able to smell us," replies Rochey.

"Plus, we won't be able to see it either. We'll be easy prey," says Parker.

"It would be a waste of time anyway. The players won't be training outside in this weather. They'll all be inside in the sports hall," utters Skinny Maca.

Bellefield was a state-of-the-art training ground; years ahead of its time. A lot of football clubs didn't even have a training ground, never mind an indoor sports hall.

"Why is that lad in the corner wearing a green goalkeeper's top?" asks Cooper.

"How do I know?" replies Rochey. "Go and ask him."

"Hey mate, why are you wearing a goalkeeper's jersey?" asks Cooper.

"My name is Lucky. And it's not a goalkeeper jersey, it's a

Republic of Ireland jersey," comes back the response in an Irish accent.

That voice belongs to Lucky Keane, who is twelve years of age and is from the city of Cork, in Eire. Lucky walks towards the lads. They're all admiring his Republic of Ireland jersey. He is over visiting his aunt's house in West Derby, which is a 10-minute walk from Bellefield.

"Are you from Ireland?" inquires Skinny Maca.

"Yes, I'm from Ireland."

"Is Lucky your real name? Why did you get called Lucky?" asks Cooper.

"Yes, that's my real name and yes, I get called Lucky, because everywhere I go, I bring the luck of the Irish with me."

"Did you bring the fog and the cold weather with you too?" laughs Cooper.

"No, I didn't! I'm here to get some autographs from the Irish Everton players, and to bring them luck."

The four lads look at each other. Bemused, they scratch their heads trying to think what Irish players he is talking about.

"We haven't got any Irish players in the first team. The only Irish player we have is Gerry Mullan, who we signed from Ballymena United this October for £30,000. But he hasn't played for the first team yet," says Rochey.

"He's the most expensive player ever signed from the Irish League," butts in Skinny Maca.

"Well, that's fine. He'll do," replies Lucky.

The lads play ('Nearest-Coin-to-The- Wall') as they wait for the players to come out. They're hoping to catch Eamonn O' Keefe, who scored in the 2-1 win against Sunderland at Goodison on Saturday. He is their player of the week. They want him in their autograph books. First out of Bellefield is Everton Goalkeeper, Jim

McDonagh, who stops in his Ford Capri.

"Hello, Jim, can you sign my book please?" asks Rochey, handing him his pen.

"Watch you don't drop that, Jim," laughs Cooper.

"Watch he doesn't drop you!" mutters Parker. "Look at the size of his hands."

Jim McDonagh signs all the books. Lucky gives him a big smile shouting, "Thank you my man in green. May the luck of the Irish be with you!" as Jim McDonagh drives off.

"Look at his signature! Has he signed his name or done a drawing of a Penny Farthing?" moans Rochey.

"Oh, stop moaning. Its's another name in the book," replies Parker.

"You should have told him to get on his bike," laughs Cooper.

Rochey looks at Parker, who shrugs his shoulders back at him, whilst Skinny Maca looks up at the sky bewildered.

"I thought all Scousers were supposed to be funny. That wasn't even the slightest bit funny," pipes up Lucky.

"Yeah, you can get on your bike and leg it as well" replies Cooper.

"How can he get on his bike and leg it at the same time?" asks Skinny Maca.

"I don't know. It's just a saying. Anyway, shut up! Here's another car coming. I can hear it. Get your pens out at the ready," replies Cooper.

Out of the fog appears Eamonn O' Keefe in his Ford Capri.

"Great goal, on Saturday Eamonn," says Rochey, as he hands him his book.

"Thanks, mate. It was good to score," replies Eamonn O' Keefe.

"Where are you from, Eamonn?" asks Cooper.

"I was born in Manchester. That's where I'm from."

"You sound like Bobby Ball, from Cannon and Ball. Rock on Tommy!" laughs Cooper.

Eamonn O'Keefe looks at the lads and Lucky, shaking his head, laughing. He has a little chat with them before saying his goodbyes. Lucky waves to him again, shouting, "Eamonn, you're a corker. May the luck of the Irish be with you," as he disappears into the fog.

"Get on that! Look what Eamonn O'Keefe wrote in my autograph book!" says Rochey, showing the lads and Lucky what he wrote.

The temperature drops to zero. It's really cold as the fog thickens. Visibility is really poor, as Gerry Mullan pulls up in his car.

"Here's the Irish Everton player that you have come to see to sign your book Lucky!" says Skinny Maca.

Lucky walks over to Gerry Mullan and asks him to sign his book. The lads wait patiently as Lucky starts to chat in Gaelic. Rochey stands next to him and hands Gerry Mullan his book and asks him to sign it for him using Lucky's green inked biro. He signs all the books and gives the lads all the thumbs up, before driving off, beeping his horn.

"What were you saying to Gerry Mullan in that Irish language?" asks Cooper.

"I was wishing him the luck of the Irish in Gaelic," comes back the reply.

"We all got the luck of the Irish when he signed our books in your green biro pen," replies Skinny Maca.

"Well, that's me done here. Take care lads," says Lucky, as

he walks into the fog towards Eaton Road. Within seconds he disappears out of sight.

"The luck of the Irish has gone and left the fog here," says Cooper.

"He also left his green pen! Gerry Mullan gave it to me after he signed my book," says Parker.

"Let's go and find him. That's his lucky pen," says Skinny Maca.

"Find him in that fog! You'll be lucky" laughs Rochey. "There's more of a chance of Bob Latchford stopping at the gates for us!"

"Stop having a go at Big Bob. We have got three autographs for our books today. It's too cold here now. Maca's right let's go and find him," snaps Parker.

The four lads' jog down Eaton Road towards West Derby Village. They check every street, every bus that drives past, go into every shop, but Lucky Keane has totally disappeared out of sight.

"How has he just disappeared into thin air?" says Skinny Maca.

"Thin air? It's thick fog," laughs Rochey.

The four lads walk towards the bus stop, talking about Lucky Keane, and get on the 12C back to Cantril Farm.

Jim McDonagh left Everton the following Season signing for Bolton Wanderers. He was born in Rotherham, England, but made his international debut for the Republic of Ireland in 1981, going on to win twenty-five international caps (after he left Everton.) Whilst playing for the Republic of Ireland, Jim McDonagh was known as Seamus McDonagh.

Eamonn O' Keefe, who was born in Manchester, represented the England Semi-Pro team in 1979. During the 1981 season whilst an Everton player he won his first full cap for the Republic of Ireland. After his debut FIFA banned him from representing them again due to the fact that he had played for the (England semi-pro team.)

FIFA lifted that ban in 1983. O' Keefe played as an over-age player in the Republic of Ireland Under 21 team. He played four games for them scoring four goals. In total, he won five caps for the Republic of Ireland senior team, scoring one goal, between 1981 to 1985. He also played for Cork City from 1987 to 1988, where he was later appointed player/manager.

Gerry Mullan, never did make an appearance for the Everton first team. He left Everton in 1981, less than a year later, to sign for the Irish league team Glentoran. He made his international debut for Northern Ireland in 1983, going on to win four international caps.

The four lads still, to this day talk, about Lucky Keane. Was he real! Was he a figment of their imagination? Where did he disappear to? Did he go back to Ireland?

All of these questions are unanswered. Maybe his plan was to simply bring the LUCK OF THE IRISH *with him to Bellefield, which he certainly did that.*

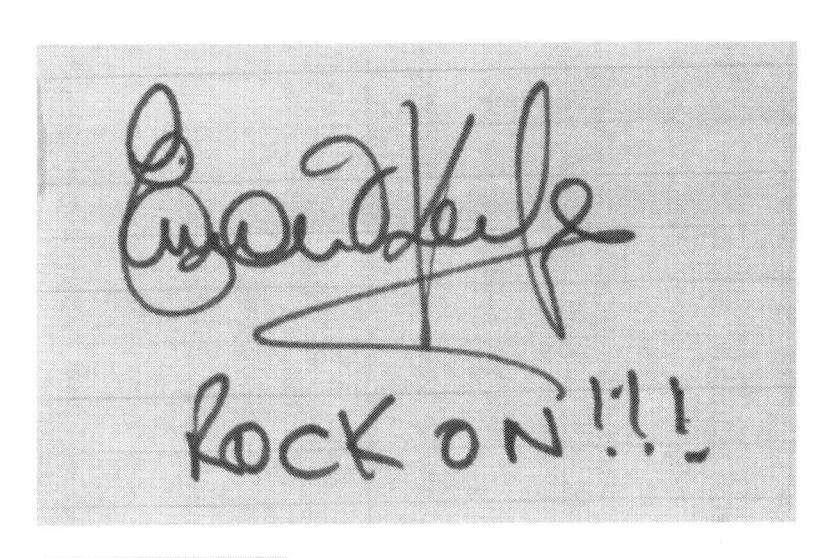

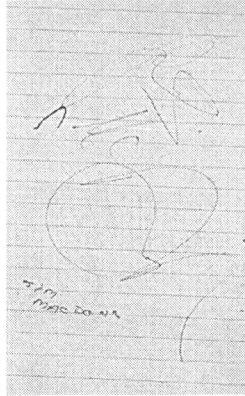

EAMONN O'KEEFE

JIM McDONAGH

GERRY MULLAN

CHAPTER 9   THE LIKELY LADS

The first day of a freezing cold December morning., Rochey, Parker, Skinny Maca and Cooper have faked illness to come to their second home Bellefield.

On Saturday, at Goodison Park, Everton had shared the points with Birmingham City in a hard fought 1-1 draw. The visitors had their striker Frank Worthington, sent off in the 72nd minute. Alan Ainscow, who was to become an Everton player the following season, scored first for the visitors in the 27th minute. Their lead was wiped out in the 44th minute by the Everton forward Eamonn O' Keefe.

In the Birmingham line up that day was former Everton player Colin Todd. Also, in the Birmingham City team that day was Scotland captain Archibald Gemmill, who was better known as 'Archie.' His son, Scot Gemmill, would later play for Everton.

The lads spot two players getting into a Colt Soparro car. "Look, it's David Essex giving that ginger lad from the Partridge family a lift!" yells Cooper.

"Shut up! It's Garry Stanley and Gary Megson," says Parker.

"So? It's Garry and Gary then," laughs Cooper.

"Yeah, soft lad," replies Parker.

"Well, in that case, the Likely Lads had best sign my autograph book," pipes up Rochey.

Garry Stanley full of smiles stops his car. "Hello, lads. Have your schools closed today?"

"No, Garry, this is part of our history lesson; to get famous figures to sign our autographs books, but there's none about so you two will have to do," smirks Cooper.

"In that case, let's get you lads top marks," replies Garry Stanley.

"Why do you two share a car?" asks Cooper.

"We share a bachelor pad together, so it makes sense to car share," replies Garry Stanley.

"We both lived in the Holiday Inn when we first signed, so we needed somewhere we could call home" says Gary Megson.

"I told you, they were the Likely Lads," smirks Rochey.

"I bet none of them can cook. I bet it's a chippy tea every night," laughs Parker.

"Chippy! Not for me! I love seafood with a cup of tea," replies Garry Stanley.

"Yeah, Rochey loves seafood. He sees food and wants it," laughs Parker.

"My favourite food is Italian, with a nice cup of tea," says Gary Megson.

"Cups of tea? I'm having second thoughts now on you both being the Likely Lads," mutters Rochey.

"It's good they show a professional manner when they play for Everton," pipes up Skinny Maca.

"Professional? When did you learn to say big words?" asks Parker.

"He's okay saying big words but I bet you a quid he couldn't spell it," smirks Cooper.

Garry Stanley and Gary Megson both played in Saturday's draw against Birmingham City. Gary Stanley played in the back four alongside Billy Wright. It was not the tallest centre-half partnership but they were solid and complemented each other on the pitch. Gary Megson never stopped running in the Everton midfield.

Rochey hands Gary Megson his autograph book, "Can you sign my book twice please Gary, so I get top marks?" Both players sign the autograph books before driving off as the lads call it a day and make their way back to school."

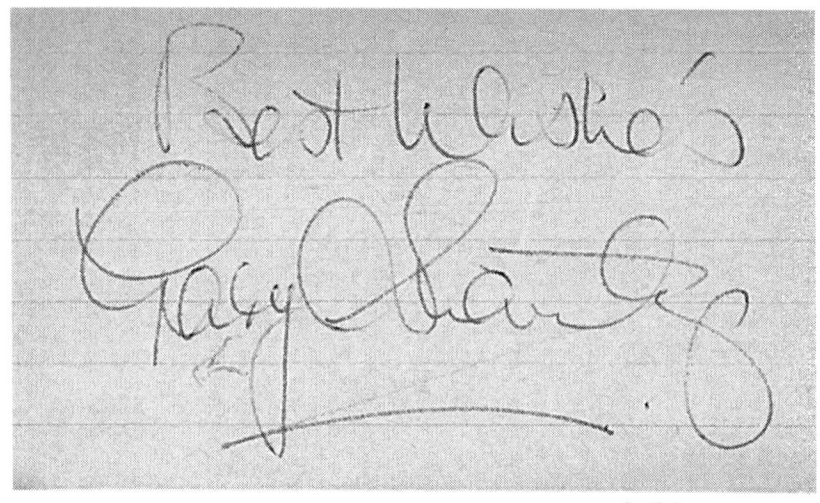

GARRY STANLEY

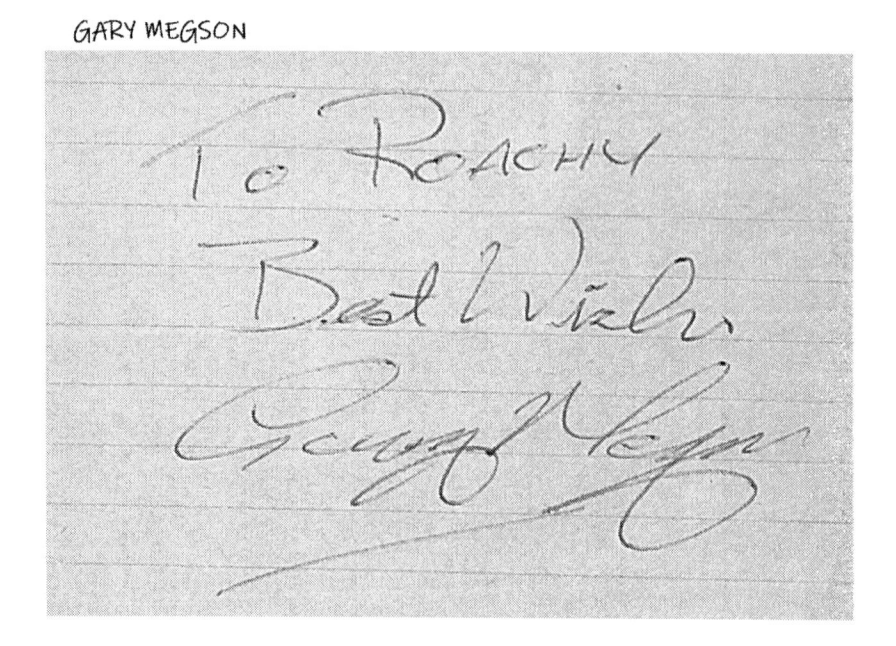

GARY MEGSON

CHAPTER 10   THE YOUNG STRIKERS

Saturday 6TH of December, 1980. A wet winters day. Everton have travelled to play Stoke City at the Victoria Ground. In the 74th minute Stoke City were awarded a penalty which the Everton goalkeeper Jim McDonagh duly saved earning the Blues a point. Joe McBride scored in the 13th minute and Imre Varadi found the back of the net in the 61st minute to also earn Everton a 2-2 draw. In the Stoke City team that day were two players that would leave lasting memories on many Evertonians. Eighteen -year-old teenager Paul Bracewell and nineteen-year-old Adrian Heath, few years down the line.

Monday, 8th of December. The lads have a day off school. It's Christmas shopping day. But instead of going to Gansgear or Goldrush in St John's market, to get their Fred Perry t-shirts, Slazenger jumpers, Fu's Jeans, and their Power Tunis trainers, they're off to Bellefield to get their books signed.

Every time they set off it was a new adventure for these four lads. Every time, they met new people there waiting outside the training ground. spending hours waiting for the Everton players to sign their autograph books. Rain, snow, fog, heatwaves the English weather never stopped them and they loved every minute. There weren't any phones, social media or PlayStation consoles back in 1980, so, the lads created their own fun. They made memories that lasted a lifetime. They bonded with the players.

Everyone was on this journey together. Even at the tender age of E their love for Everton shone brightly. Every one of them born a Evertonian. The four lads reach their destination and straight away see some familiar faces. Bellefield is rammed. Mark Kidda the kid from Park Road is doing wheelies on his bike.

Sue Jones who Copper has a crush on is looking as lovely as ever, says Cooper to the other three lads, who just shake their heads at him. Sue is with her two mates. Franny Robb is also back this time with his mate, who is doing keep ups with his orange trophy football.

"Hello Franny. Who's your mate? Does he work in Billy Smart's circus?" jokes Parker.

"Are we okay for later for a lift off your dad Franny?" asks Rochey.

"This is my mate, Terry Anderson, from the Bully. And no lift today. My dad's not picking me up," laughs Franny.

"Hello lads. Franny just told me that you call yourselves the 'Canny Farm Four'," says Terry Anderson, putting his ball down for a second.

"We might do. What's it got to do with you what we call ourselves, Terry from the Bully?" replies Rochey.

"Calm down, will yer! Terry's a good lad. He's a very good Evertonian, Rochey," says Franny Robb.

"I'm calm Franny. You can tell he's your mate. He's nosey just like you were the first time we met you," snaps Rochey.

"The reason I'm asking is because my auntie- Betty and my cousin, John Saidie, are from Canny Farm," says Terry.

"Well, why didn't you say that in the first place? Saidie is our mate. He was here with us a few weeks back. He's in the gang," says Rochey.

"Yeah, he's one of the lads and a great footballer. But he's not perfect. He's a red nose," says Parker.

Rochey starts chatting to Terry Anderson who, at fifteen years of age is a bit older. But that doesn't stop the two of them from sharing stories about Everton. Once a blue, always a blue. It's one big happy family. The lads spot Imre Varadi and Graeme Sharp walking out of Bellefield. They all get out their pens and autograph books and wait patiently for the two young strikers to walk towards them. "Great goal on Saturday Imre, that got us a well-earned point," says Terry Anderson.

"Thanks mate," replies Imre Varadi.

"Imre, is your dad's first name Ollie? asks Cooper, keeping a straight face.

Imre Varadi smiles at Cooper, whilst all the other lads look away, shaking their heads.

Rochey walks over to Graeme Sharp as the other lad's chat to Varadi.

"Hello, Sharpie. Can you sign my book please?" asks Rochey.

Terry Anderson legs it over to Sharpie all excited.

"Can you sign mine to Terry Anderson from the Bully? And can you sign this one to Georgie Anderson, one top Evertonian?" says Terry Anderson. "Terry from the Bully. Whose Georgie Anderson?" asks Graeme Sharp. "That's my dad, Sharpie. He loves Everton."

Graeme Sharp looks at Imre Varadi and says, "That's why I love this club so much. This is why I never want to leave. From father, to son, to grandson, they're all born Evertonians."

Both players sign the books then chat to the lads and girls for a good ten minutes before walking towards Eaton Road.

"Them two are two great strikers, lads," says Franny Robb.

"No, not just great strikers, Franny, they're two great young strikers," pipes up Parker.

"He's a Sheffield lad, that Varadi. He's made of steel," says Terry Anderson.

"No, he's not Terry. We signed him from Sheffield United, but he's actually a Cockney, born in Paddington," pipes up Rochey.

"He played for Spurs youth team where he won the Southern Counties League Cup," says Parker.

"Then he played for Letchworth in 1978. In 1979 he signed for Sheffield United, playing ten games and scoring four goals before signing for Everton," says Skinny Maca.

Terry Anderson looks at Franny Robb shaking his head. "What they don't know about Everton isn't worth knowing, I learned that the first time I met Rochey and Parker in this same speck. They schooled me. Not that they're ever in school, like," laughs Franny Robb.

Rochey and Parker give Franny Robb a look that could kill

"I will school them. Hey lads, do you see them goals over there on Barnfield playing fields? Five penalties each, and for every penalty you score you get a gobstopper off me," says Terry Anderson.

"Well at five pence a gobstopper that's going to cost you a green one," says Cooper.

"A green one?" asks a confused Terry Anderson.

"Yes, a green one; a crispy one-pound green note. That's it we all score our penalties," replies Cooper.

"I don't intend to spend a penny. Not today anyway. I don't think any of you'll score a single one between the four of you," replies Terry Anderson.

"I'll be the referee. I'll put the ball on the penalty spot," offers Franny Robb.

"I must watch this. I'll check to make sure the goalkeeper stays on his line," says Mark Kidda.

"We'll come over and be cheerleaders," says Sue Jones.

First up to take his five penalties was Parker who took no prisoners leaving Terry Anderson flat footed with each strike. Five out of five for Parker. Up next was Rochey, who wasn't waiting around, sending Terry Anderson the wrong way on all five. Another five out of five. Up next was Cooper, who does a bit of showboating in front of Sue Jones but still manages to score his five too. Skinny Maca steps up next. The first two penalties he shoots wide. The third penalty goes over the bar. The fourth, he kicks the tuft on the penalty spot and the ball gently rolls to Terry Anderson in his goal.

When he steps up for his fifth and final penalty, he miskicks it but to the astonishment of all watching, it spoons into the top right-hand corner of the goal.

Rochey, Parker, and Cooper run over to him, lifting him up and celebrate like he had just scored the winner in the World Cup Final.

They all have a little game of football for the next hour not realising that all the players have driven out of Bellefield.

They were having so much fun playing football, they didn't even notice. After the penalties, Terry Anderson goes to the sweetshop and returns with sixteen gobstoppers, shaking his head at the lads as he hands them out, not quite believing four eleven-year-old kids scored all those penalties against him.

Rochey and Parker each share their gob stoppers with Franny Robb, Mark Kidda and Sue Jones. Cooper doesn't share his, as his go straight into his pockets.

Not even the fluttering of Sue Jones eyelashes can get him to share. It's long been known that Cooper can peel an orange in his pocket without even looking. The four lads all wink at each other and stick a gobstopper into their mouths looking at Terry Anderson shouting, "I'm glad you schooled us Terry from the Bully," with smiles that could light up Bellefield on a dark winter night.

GRAEME SHARP   IMRE VARADI

CHAPTER 11   GIVE PEACE A CHANCE

Tuesday 9th of December, a cold surreal winters morning, is a day Rochey, Parker, Skinny Maca, Cooper, Anthony Carty, Carl Mills and Brian Sinnott will never forget. It was the morning that they found out John Lennon had been fatally shot. Shocked and distraught, they had gathered at the local sweetshop.

"Look, there's some of the Huyton lads, Mills and Sinnott outside the sweet shop," says Anthony Carty, one of Rochey's classmates.

"So, this is Christmas, and what have you done? War is over, if you want it," says Cooper.

"Why are you two over this side? Have all the Huyton shops run out of sweets?" asks Parker.

"No. Sinnott came to mine this morning, told me about John Lennon. So, we came over here to see if any of you knew," replies Mills.

"I can't believe it. John Lennon was one of us," utters Rochey.

"Working- class hero," says Cooper.

"Why would someone do something like that?" mutters Skinny Maca.

"All he was saying was give peace a chance," replies Cooper.

"Why is Cooper answering with John Lennon songs? He doesn't seem right. Is he okay?" asks Brian Sinnott.

"He's in shock," replies Rochey.

"I'm in shock. I can't go to school," says Brian Sinnott.

"He was great yesterday when we went to Bellefield," says Parker.

"Let's go to Bellefield today to get some autographs, see if we can forget about John Lennon for a bit," says Millsy.

The lads take it upon themselves to bunk school and head to Bellefield to help take their minds off the upsetting news.

John Lennon's death was a shock to the world. A Scouser who shook the world with his lyrics. Hearing this news that day devastated everyone in the city of Liverpool. John Lennon died far too young. No matter if you were a red or blue that day, they were united as one. If someone hurts one of us, we stick together as a city. The City of Liverpool is known for its football, music, and club scene, amongst many other things and today the whole city of Liverpool joined together mourning one of their own. John Lennon was one of four lads from Liverpool that set the world alight with his music.

The lads stand and wait outside Bellefield in silence as they wait to collect their autographs. Grey skies have descended down onto the city.

The players drove out one by one, signing the autograph books for the lads, but there was no banter like every other time.

Today even the players were in shock. The lads got their books signed and left Bellefield.

There was a silence all the way back to Canny Farm.

John Lennon was a man of peace, a peace activist and now this terrible thing had happened to him.

Over the Christmas period of 1980, at both Goodison Park and at Anfield, SoThis Is Christmas, and Give Peace A Chance were played before every match on each occasion, the fans from both blue and red sides of the city sang the words hand in hand, united as one, to show the world that John Lennon was a Scouser, a breed so different from any other.

John Lennon was a working-class hero who had done well for himself but had never forgotten his roots. Scousers at Goodison Park and Anfield were sending out a message at their football stadiums after John Lennon's death: 'Give Peace a Chance.' It's been said time and time before, but Scousers really do stick together during bad times. The city is renowned for its football and its music.

local boys and girls have achieved success across many fields, bought glory to the city and in doing so have lit up the city. But on this day, the 9th of December, 1980, the city is in mourning for one of its much-loved sons.

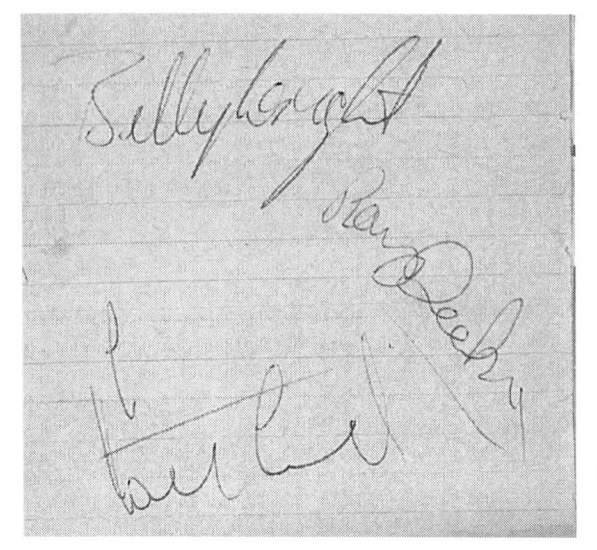

BILLY WRIGHT

RAY DEAKIN

ASA HARTFORD

JOHN BARTON

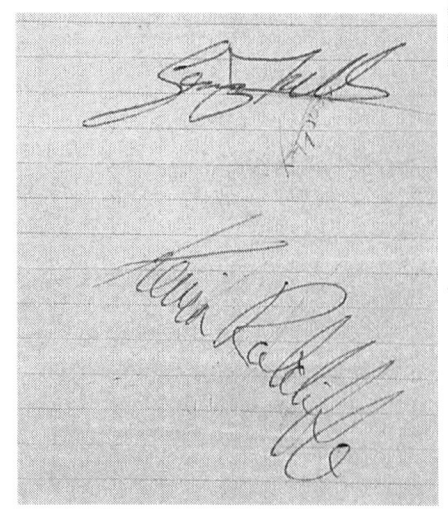

GERRY MULLAN

KEVIN RATCLIFFE

CHAPTER 12 OH, I DO LIKE TO BE BESIDE BY THE SEASIDE

It's Tuesday, 16th of December, 1980, Christmas is just around the corner, school will soon be closed for the Christmas break. In Rochey's and Parker's households, Santa wears blue, and blue only. On the Saturday just gone, Everton beat Brighton Hove Albion 4-3 at Goodison Park. It was an exhilarating match that could have gone either way.

Peter Eastoe scored in the 8th minute to start the ball rolling with Steve McMahon scoring Everton's second in the 20th minute. Peter Eastoe added his second, Everton's third in the 68th minute. Imre Varadi snatched victory for Everton in the 82nd minute.

Everton won't play again until the 26th of December, Boxing Day when they will take on Manchester City at Goodison Park.

Rochey and Parker are on their way to Bellefield. Again, they have bunked off school. They're going to miss double French and double History, but they're not bothered. They've every intention of going back for the afternoon football practice one lesson that they wouldn't ever miss.

Rochey tells Parker not to worry about bunking off school because learning the French language is pointless because they're never going to live in France, as the standard of French football is bad, and that going to Bellefield is a history lesson in itself.

Parker agrees and points out in forty years' time the autographs in their autograph books will be historical.

In theory, they'll be creating their own history.

First out to stop and sign their autographs books is John Bailey. He's in his Ford Capri with a big smile on his face.

"Hello, lads. No school today? I see you're both wearing your school uniform."

"Of course we have school, Bails. We've both been the dentist," replies Rochey.

"You've both been the dentist in your school uniform?"

"Yeah, Bails, we're going to school this afternoon. We've got football," says Parker.

"Can you sign my book? Can you sign it best wishes to Billy. That's my dad, Bails? He'll be made up, he told me that in October, when we played Brighton, that he, Gerry Bowness, and Tricky, who are all brick-layers, downed their tools at ten in the morning, on the building site and drove to Brighton, and that you came out of the players' lounge before the match and gave them three free tickets for the match."

"Did I? Well, that's nice to know. I must have thought they were on their holidays, and we do like a day beside the seaside," laughs John Bailey.

"They certainly did, Bails. Especially with us winning that night 3-1," replies Rochey.

"If this is for your dad, are you going to give him your autograph book?" asks John Bailey.

"No, don't be silly, Bails. This book is more precious than the crown jewels. I will just let him look at it once a week. In fact, just sign 'best wishes."

"Right, lads, you both get back to school and don't be chewing on Kola Cubes and Cough Candy sweets. And brush your teeth three times a day," laughs John Bailey.

"We do Bails. Morning, noon, and night," replies Parker.

"Okay, don't get carried away. I thought you were doing an advert for Colgate then," snaps Rochey.

"I don't use Colgate. I use Crest toothpaste."

"Good. Because for one minute there, I thought that you thought you was in the Colgate advert, and that you were going to burst out singing, 'the cream in your mouth is Colgate,' because that's all that was missing, from the advert."

Rochey and Parker sit back on the wall outside Bellefield as they wait for a couple more players to sign their autograph books before they head back to school. Next out is Peter Eastoe who pulls up shaking his head:

"No school again lads? What's the excuse for missing school today?" asks Peter Eastoe.

"Dentist, Peter," responds Parker.

"The two of you? Together?"

"No, don't be silly. You have to go in one at a time. But anyway, they were two great goals you scored on Saturday, Peter," replies Parker.

Peter Eastoe looks at the two lads shaking his head and smirking as he signs their autograph books before driving off.

"He's like a school-teacher him. He's always quizzing us about school," moans Rochey.

"I know. But he scores goals for fun. And he does play for Everton, so he's allowed," replies Parker.

"Yeah, I suppose you're right," says Rochey, as they wait for the next player to come out.

Next to drive out of Bellefield is Steve McMahon, who stops to sign their autograph books with a big smile on his face.

Joe McBride and Brian Borrows, walk out of Bellefield wearing their Everton tracksuits and stop to chat with Rochey and Parker.

"Hello, Joe. Great win on Saturday! Why are you both walking?" asks Rochey.

"We're going to the shop," replies Joe McBride

"Can you sign our books, Joe?" pipes up Parker.

"Yeah, of course we will," beams Joe McBride, as he signs the books and hands them to Brian Borrows.

The next player out is the man who scored the match winner against Brighton, Imre Varadi. He stops for a chat as he

signs their autograph books

Last out is Trevor Ross, all smiles as he talks about Everton.

Rochey and Parker go back to school happy and 'once again' they have met and chatted to their heroes, who wear the famous royal blue jersey.

There was a great team spirit during those days at Bellefield. All the players stopped to chat with the fans. It was one big happy family.

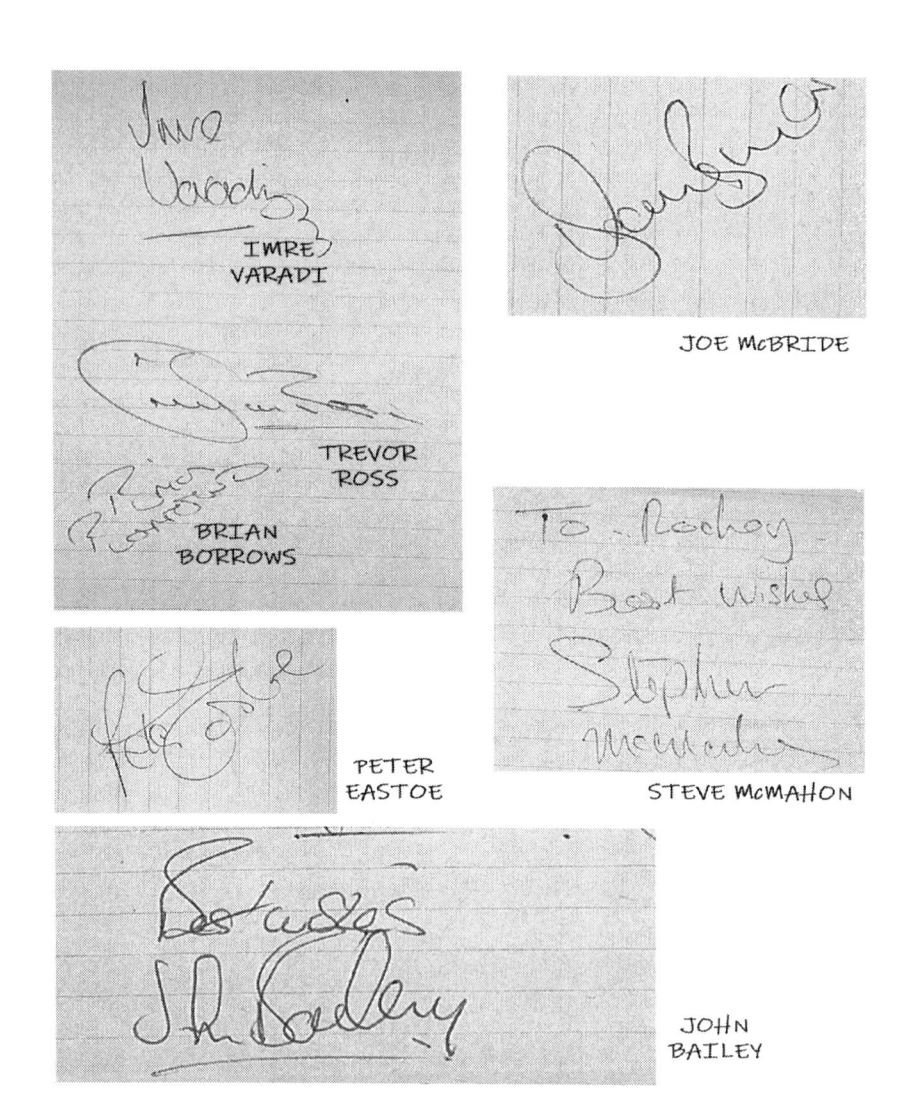

IMRE VARADI

JOE McBRIDE

TREVOR ROSS

BRIAN BORROWS

PETER EASTOE

STEVE McMAHON

JOHN BAILEY

CHAPTER 13   CHRISTMAS WISHES

CHRISTMAS WISHES, WITH MICK LYONS.

It's Monday 22nd of December. On Boxing Day, Everton take on Manchester City at Goodison Park. It's the Christmas holidays, so Rochey, Parker, Cooper and Skinny Maca are joined by Carl Mills and Sean Quinn as they march up to Bellefield with their packed lunches where they aim to get as many Christmas autographs as possible.

Everton are the team that the lads love to follow. They have built up a friendship with the players that has been cemented during their time collecting autographs at Bellefield. They chat to the players, who give them advice in return. All the lads look up to them and treat them as friends. Win, lose, or draw, Rochey, Parker, Cooper, Skinny Maca, and the rest of their blue family, still want to get down to Bellefield to discuss the Everton matches with the players.

Everton go into the Christmas festival sixth in the league table. They have five first-team players that were born in Liverpool. The Scouse back four is led by the club captain Mick Lyons, who plays centre-back. Billy Wright, from Norris Green, stands alongside him at centre-back, with John Gidman at right-back, and John Bailey at left back. In front of them is a young Stephen McMahon, who anchors the midfield.

The lads wait patiently at the entrance gates for the players to come out. No matter what the weather is, the lads will always be there due to their love of football. The bond they share with Everton is the reason they travel to the home matches week in week out.

First to come out is Captain Marvel, Mick Lyons.

"Here's Mick Lyons, walking out!" says Parker.

"I wonder why he's walking?" mutters Skinny Maca.

"He must have left his car at home," utters Cooper.

"He usually gets a lift from Billy Wright," says Rochey.

Mick Lyons walks towards the lads. He reaches the Bellefield entrance gates, happy to sign their books and to chat to them about Everton football club.

"Hello, Mick, why are you walking?" probes Cooper.

"I'm just going for a stroll up to the shops for some shampoo."

"Mick, Happy Christmas! Can you put best wishes on all our autograph books for Christmas?" asks Rochey.

"Yeah, no problem, Happy Christmas lads," replies Mick Lyons, with a huge smile on his face.

"Oh no, I see Donny Osmond's back," mutters Sean Quinn, under his breath.

"Pity he's not with Marie Osmond," mumbles Millsy.

"Why Marie Osmond? That's not really Donny Osmond. It's Mick Lyons," says Cooper.

"I know that softarse! I just like the Puppy Love song they sing together," replies Millsy.

"I thought Donny sang that on his own," butts in Cooper.

"He does, daft arse. But he also sings it with Marie Osmond on the Donny and Marie show," snaps Millsy.

"What? You watch the Donny and Marie show? And you're the cock of the year in our school? Don't let people hear about that! They'll think you've gone soft," jokes Rochey.

"Hey! I listen to Bob Dylan and Neil Young soft-lad," snaps Millsy.

"I have never heard Bob Dylan sing Puppy Love," says Rochey, smirking.

"Shut up! I just like that song. It's our Jimmy who watches it.

He thinks he's their younger brother, Jimmy Osmond, the long-haired lover from Liverpool," replies Millsy.

Mick Lyons keeps a straight face trying not to laugh, as he takes all their autograph books. Meanwhile the lads discuss the Donny and Marie Show between themselves. He signs all the books and gives the lads a thumbs up as he walks towards West Derby.

Mick Lyons, was born on 8th of December 1951. He was an Everton captain who led by example. Mick was a Scouse lad who was educated at the all-boys De La Salle School in Croxteth. It was a school renowned for its football teams.

Mick was an Evertonian and would stand on the terraces at Goodison Park as a young lad, cheering them on. His dream as a fan from an early age was to play for Everton. That dream came true when he signed for them as a striker.

Whilst training at Bellefield, the Everton coaching staff spotted his potential and he was soon shaped into a no-nonsense centre-back. Despite this change of position, he never lost is goal scoring ability as over the years he popped up regularly on the Everton score sheet, scoring some important along the way, especially if Everton were a goal down.

Mick signed for Everton as a professional footballer in 1970 after serving his time at the club as an apprentice. He stayed at the club until 1982.

Mick Lyons won two England B caps during his time at Everton. He will always be remembered as a footballer that never gave less than one hundred per cent every time, he went out onto the football pitch.

No matter what level he was playing at, he was a captain that led by example and he would never let his team down.

He was as brave as a lion and always played the game with a smile on his face. Or as Quinny always said, 'with that Donny Osmond smile.'

CHRISTMAS WISHES WITH KEVIN RATCLIFFE.

"Hey, look, it's Eddie Shoestring getting into his Datsun 120Y Coupe," smirks Parker.

"Why would a TV detective be at Bellefield?" asks Cooper.

"I don't know. Maybe one of the players has pinched Mick Lyons shampoo. Or someone might have nicked a meat pie out of the canteen and he's here to investigate. It's definitely Eddie Shoestring! Look at his moustache!" replies Parker.

"If someone has nicked a meat pie, then Billy Wright must be the chief suspect," pipes up Sean Quinn.

"Not necessary. Your Mick could have played here during the week for Wigan. I heard he's fond of pies. He could have eaten all the pies," laughs Rochey.

"No, it definitely wasn't their Mick. He lives next door to me. He's on a seafood diet. Every time I see him, he's eating food," laughs Millsy.

"He's on the same diet as Rochey then," laughs Parker.

"It's not even Eddie Shoestring! It's that young Welsh lad, Kevin Ratcliffe. He's played a few games for the first team. He actually made his full debut for Wales against Czechoslovakia not so long ago," pipes up Skinny Maca.

"Well, Shoestring or Ratcliffe, he'd best get his bootlaces down here and sign our books," smirks Parker.

Kevin Ratcliffe stops his car next to the lads, wishing them all a happy Christmas as he signs their autograph books.

Kevin Ratcliffe, born in Mancot, North Wales, in on12th November 1960. Kevin began his Everton career as an apprentice in 1977 and made his first team debut against Manchester United, at Old Trafford, on the 12th March 1980.

Kevin remained at Everton from 1977 until 1992 when he moved on to pastures new. He was initially used as a left-back, but he blossomed when he was moved to centre back. His blistering pace was a sight to behold.

When Kevin was a young lad supported Everton his childhood hero being the legendary Alan Ball. The greatest influences on his football career were his father and the legendary figure, Colin Harvey.

Colin was an Everton coach when Kevin first started at the club. The man who made him the Everton captain at the tender age of 23 was Howard Kendall. who was also a legendary figure to have influence over the young Kevin Ratcliffe.

Kevin Ratcliffe went on to become the most successful captain in Everton's history, winning two league championships, The F.A. Cup and The European Cup Winners Cup.

He represented Wales at under 21, youth, and school-boy level. He was capped 59 times by the Welsh national team.

CHRISTMAS WISHES, WITH GARRY STANLEY.

"Player number 3 on his way out. It's Garry Stanley getting into his Colt Soparro," pipes up Skinny Maca.

"It looks more like David Essex, when he sang 'Rock On'," says Sean Quinn.

"I see you've been playing your Mick's records again. Rock on, Quinny," laughs Rochey.

"Rock him on down here, 'cos it's Garry Stanley, not David Essex," says Millsy.

"Do you know his real name isn't even David Essex? It's David Cook, and he actually played for West Ham Juniors," replies Sean Quinn.

"Well, that's okay then, because it's Garry Stanley, who plays for Everton, on his way down to us, not David Cook, of West Ham. And if you ever see Joey Egghead, never mention that David Essex's real name is David Cook," says Parker.

"Why doesn't he like David Essex?" asks Sean Quinn.

"He does like David Essex! Don't you remember he had 'Rock On' blasting out of his car radio when he gave us all a lift home from Melwood the other month? He just doesn't like anyone called David Cook," replies Parker.

"Why?" asks Cooper.

"I don't know," replies Parker.

"I heard it was because Joey was selling his Liverpool matchday tickets at Anfield and that Dave stood in front of Joey in a pair of Alvin Stardust leather black gloves, smashing his hands together, demanding two tickets for cost price. I don't know how true it is, but that's what I heard," says Rochey.

Garry Stanley stops next to the lads for a chat.

"Hello. Happy Christmas, Garry. Can you sign best wishes in all our books?" asks Rochey.

"Yeah, of course I will," replies Garry Stanley.

"Nice one Garry, rock on," smirks Cooper.

Garry Stanley signs all the books and drives a few metres forward before stopping and leans out his car window and shouts, "Happy Christmas, lads. Let's hope it's a happy blue, blue, Christmas!" before driving off.

"I thought he was David Essex, not Elvis Presley, with the 'Blue Christmas' impressions," smirks Millsy.

"He's sharp, that Stanley," grins Skinny Maca.

"I don't know who's worse, Elvis, Essex, Stanley, or Skinny Russ Abbot, Maca," sneers Millsy

"Put them both in the Jailhouse Rock, Millsy," laughs Cooper.

Garry Stanley was born in Burton upon Trent on the 4th March 1954. He signed for Everton in 1979 for £300,000 and left in

1981 for in a deal worth £150,000 with Swansea City. Garry signed as a midfielder but, occasionally he would play centre-back.

His time at Everton wasn't helped by injury but he will always be remembered for getting sent off against their arch rivals Liverpool in 1979. A big brawl started in the centre of the pitch, which resulted in both Garry Stanley and Terry McDermott getting a red card.

A red card usually resulted in one match ban, but the pair of them shook hands in the tunnel and both made arrangements to go to a nightclub together the same evening. They still got a match ban but they were best of mates and laughed it off in the nightclub.

The younger Everton players also recall the time Garry Stanley got the full wrath off Colin Harvey when playing in the reserves. The side where pipped back to 3-3, after being 3-0 up. Garry was just about to get a shower and was asking for shampoo. Colin Harvey wasn't pleased about his attitude as he didn't like that someone was more concerned about their hair than their football, and stormed into the dressing room to give him a telling off as Colin was a born winner and always wanted his teams to be head and shoulders above the rest.

CHRISTMAS WISHES, WITH BRIAN BORROWS.

"Bugs is on his way out," mutters Sean Quinn.

"Why do they call him Bugs?" asks Cooper.

"I don't know. Maybe it's because he's got teeth like Hartley Hare," replies Sean.

"Whose Hartley Hare?" asks a confused Cooper.

"He's the rabbit puppet on 'Pipkins'," comes back the reply.

"Do you still watch that?" questions Skinny Maca.

"Of course I do. It's the second-best program on telly, after The Dukes of Hazzard," retorts Sean.

"What about Grange Hill, with Tucker and Benny? That's the best thing on TV!" pipes up Rochey.

"Don't forget Rocky O' Rourke in a Pair of Jesus Sandals, as well," says Parker.

"I like Tiswas with Sally James, on a Saturday morning, but I watch Pipkins as well during the week at dinner time when I go home for my dinner. It's a boss program with Pig, Topov, Octavia, and the gang," pipes up Millsy.

"I'm getting worried about you now, Millsy. Cock of Huyton watching Donny and Marie, Pipkins. Next, you'll be telling us you watch Playschool, as for Tiswas it's never going to happen in our house when Swap Shop is on the other side" laughs Rochey.

"Shut up, soft-lad 'Tiswas' is better than 'Swap Shop'," snaps Millsy.

"Brian Borrows is walking down here now. Let's get his autograph!" says Parker.

"Is he walking or hopping down? Why isn't he in the car? I'm confused. Is Hartley Hare a hare or a rabbit? It could Bugs for Bugs Bunny" says Cooper.

"It doesn't matter, 'cos he's walking down and he hasn't got teeth like a hare, or a rabbit. His nickname is Bugs because his second name is Burrows. The only other Bugs is you bugging me with all the questions," snaps Parker.

"Well, now all is revealed by Sherlock Parker, can we get his autograph?" utters Rochey.

Brian Borrows walks up to the lads with a big smile on his face.

"Happy Christmas, Brian," says Cooper, followed by Rochey, Parker, Millsy, Skinny Maca, and Sean Quinn.

"Happy Christmas, lads."

"Can you sign our autograph books Bugs?" requests Skinny

Maca.

"Do you think you will make your first team debut this year, Bugs?" asks Cooper.

"I can sign the autograph books for you, but I don't think I'm making my debut this year. We only have nine more days 'till it's 1981 and we play Manchester City at home on Boxing Day. Then, the next day, we're away to Middlesbrough and I'm not in either squad to travel with the first team."

"That's mad. Two games in two days Does the Football League think our parents are made of money?" snaps Parker.

"It doesn't matter to us anyway. We bunk into the match every game," laughs Cooper.

"Don't worry anyway, Bugs. You're a Scouser just like all of us. You'll make your debut soon," says Sean Quinn.

"We're all Evertonians here, Bugs. You'll get to wear that famous royal blue jersey for the first team," says Rochey.

"We all dream of playing for Everton, Bugs. You're living the dream just training with them every day," utters Parker.

"I've watched you play centre-half, and left back, for the reserves, Bugs, so you must be doing something right," pipes up Cooper.

"I'd drive the team coach just to get near the first team," mutters Skinny Maca.

"I don't think the first team would get far with an eleven-year-old lad driving the coach," says Cooper.

"Thank you for signing our autograph books, Bugs. Happy Christmas," says Rochey.

Brian Borrows smiles and waves at the lads as he makes his way home.

Brian Borrows signed professional forms for Everton on the 23rd April, 1980.

He played as an amateur for two seasons before being rewarded with a professional contract.

Brian started out as a centre-forward for his school team before becoming a full back at Everton. Brian was born in Liverpool on the 20th December, 1960.

Bugs didn't make his debut that season, but did the following season. In the next two seasons he made twenty-seven league appearances before leaving to sign for Bolton Wanderers. But it was at Coventry City that he flourished, gaining an England B international cap.

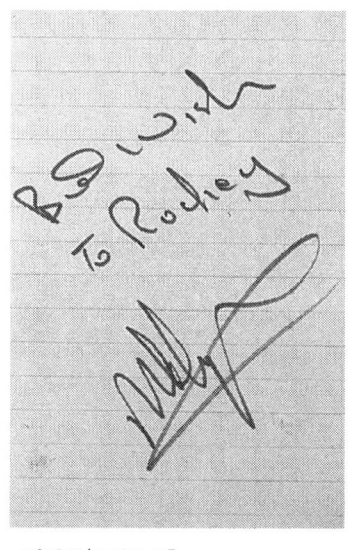

MICK LYONS

KEVIN RATCLIFFE

BRIAN BORROWS

GARRY STANLEY

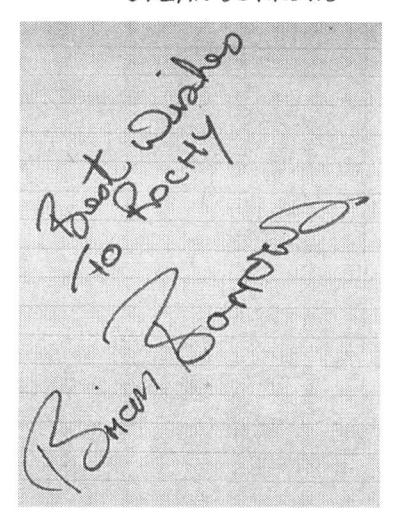

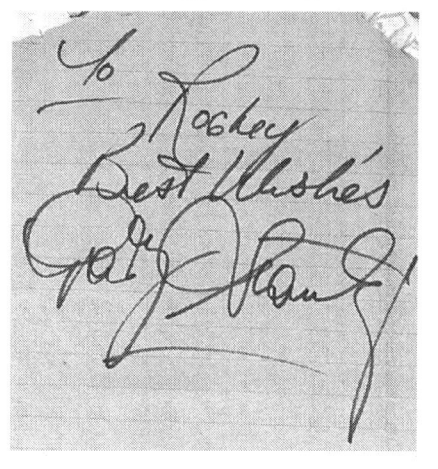

GRAEME
SHARP

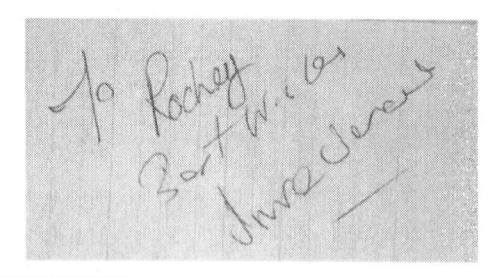

PAUL
LODGE

STEVE
McMAHON

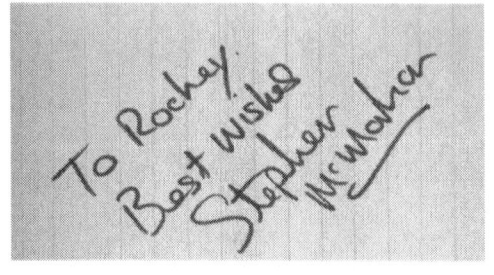

IMRE
VARADI

CHRISTMAS WISHES, WITH STEVE McMAHON.

"Maca's is on his way out!" shouts Cooper.

"No, he's not. He's standing next to me," sneers Rochey.

"That must be my twin," giggles Skinny Maca.

"It's not Skinny Maca. It's Steve McMahon getting into his Cherry Datsun," replies Cooper.

Rochey looks at the other lads shaking his head as a smiling Steve McMahon stops his car at the exit gates.

"Hello lads. it's cold out here. Do you want me to sign your books? Are you all looking forward to Christmas?" asks Steve McMahon.

"We're looking forward more to the Man City game on Boxing Day, Steve," replies Parker.

"So, can you get us a nice win against Man City and then a win the next day against Middlesbrough for us?" pipes up Skinny Maca.

"Yeah, a nice four points for Christmas," says Cooper.

"We'll do our best," says a smiling Steve McMahon, as he signs their autograph books.

"We don't play for our Sunday team, now, 'til after Christmas, Steve. Does the kids under 12 team that you run, in the Halewood and District League, play over Christmas?" asks Parker.

"No, the kids don't play now 'til after Christmas, what team do you all play for?" asks Steve McMahon.

"We play in the Under 12's for Allerford. Except for Sean, who is Under 11," replies Cooper.

"They're the creme de la creme, that team. You must be all good to play for them. I could do with you playing for my team," says Steve McMahon.

"Thanks, Steve, but no thanks. Bob Pendleton runs Allerford. He's a super scout for Everton. We want to play for Everton, just like you," replies Parker.

"You can have Skinny Maca on a free transfer," laughs Cooper.

"That's only if Brandearth Hey under-5's has enough players," smirks Millsy.

"I'll sign for them, Steve," says Skinny Maca.

"I wanted the Allerford lads to sign for my team, to be honest, but you keep shining for Brandearth Hey, mate," replies Steve McMahon.

"Okay, Steve, Happy Christmas," comes back the reply from Skinny Maca.

Steve McMahon wishes all the lads a Happy Christmas as he pulls off with a big smirk on his face.

"He's a proper Scouser. Top lad, that Steve McMahon. He was a ball-boy at Everton when he was our age," says Cooper.

"Yeah, he's not soft. He knows his football. Even he wouldn't sign Skinny Maca," laughs Rochey.

"No, not him, nor his twin," laughs Cooper.

"I haven't got a twin," pipes up a confused Skinny Maca.

"Well, you had a twin when McMahon first came out," smirks Cooper.

Skinny Maca is not amused and gives them all a dirty look.

The lads look at their autographs pleased with themselves as the wait for the next player to come out.

Steve McMahon was born in Liverpool on the 20th August 1961. He signed professional forms in 1979, going on to make one hundred league appearances for the blue side of Merseyside, as a central-midfielder. He captained them on a few occasions. He earned six England under-21 caps and played seventeen times for the full England national team.

CHRISTMAS WISHES, WITH PAUL LODGE.

"Who's this driving out in his Ford Capri?" asks Millsy.

"It's Terry McCann," smirks Rochey.

"Terry McCann!" replies Millsy.

"Yeah, that fella who works for Arthur Daley as his minder," laughs Rochey.

"Leave it out, Arthur Roche. It's Paul Lodge the young Scouse midfielder," butts in Skinny Maca.

"Call me Arthur Roche again and it'll be you who will need Terry McCann as your minder," growls Rochey.

"Okay, calm down. It's Christmas time! We're all mates, here. What happened to the season of goodwill?" says Parker.

"He lost the season of goodwill when he said he'd leave Brandearth Hey for Steve McMahon's team," replies Rochey.

"You lost the season of goodwill, Arthur, when Steve McMahon called me his mate and didn't call you his mate," smirks Skinny Maca.

"Shut up, the pair of yers. Let's get Paul's autograph," says Parker.

Paul Lodge stops his car outside the gates and lowers his car window to sign the autographs for the lads.

"Hello, Paul. Happy Christmas. Can you sign our books with best wishes please?" asks Sean Quinn.

"Yes. Pass all your books to me. I'll sign them all together. Where are you lads from?" asks Paul Lodge.

"We're from the Farm," replies Sean Quinn.

"The Farm?"

"Yes, Canny Farm Where Ginger Fairclough is from. He lives in Rochey and Coopers' Street," replies Sean Quinn.

"That's good, I bet you're all good footballers, being from Canny Farm."

"Yeah. All but Skinny Maca," says Rochey, from the back.

"I'm good as well, Paul. There was talk about me signing for Steve McMahon's kids' team," says Skinny Maca.

"Yeah, Santa was going to get him a game for Christmas," laughs Rochey.

"Well, whatever Santa brings you all for Christmas, have a great one!" replies Paul Lodge, before driving off.

"Another Scouser playing for Everton! how good is that? We should be renamed Everton Scouse," laughs Cooper.

Paul Lodge made his Everton first team debut two months later as a substitute against Aston Villa in a 3-1 defeat.

He loved every second of his time on the pitch as an Everton midfield player. Born in Liverpool on the 13th February, 1961, he signed professional forms in 1979 and stayed on Everton's books till 1983, making twenty-four league appearances, before leaving to sign for Preston North End.

Paul Lodge went on to play in every division of the English Football League, as well as the Football Conference, the Northern Premier League. and the League of Wales.

CHRISTMAS WISHES, WITH IMRE VARADI.

"Here's the goal machine coming out!" says Rochey.

"Is it Bobby Latchford?" yells Parker excitedly.

"No, it's Imre Varadi!"

"He's not the goal machine! How is he the goal machine? Big

Bob is the goal machine," snaps Parker.

"Well, considering Big Bob has been out injured for the last four games, and Varadi has scored in his last two games against Stoke and Brighton, that makes him the goal machine," replies Rochey.

"Big Bob is my hero. He scores goals for fun," tuts Parker.

"Well, it's not Latchford, it's Imre Varadi. Plus, Bobby Latchford never stops for us to sign our books," replies Rochey.

"Yes, he does! We've got his," mutters Parker.

"Once! In all the time we have been here. I've got pics of the Queen on my bank notes. I've seen her more times than Big Bob, and I've never met her either."

"Yes, but you have met Bob. The Queen might rule Britannia but she can't walk on water like Bobby Latchford," replies Parker.

"Will you two shut up! Imre Varadi is ten yards away from us!" snaps Millsy.

"Happy Christmas, Imre! Can you sign our books?" asks Cooper, shoving his book into Imre Varadi's face.

"Two great goals you've scored in the last two games, Imre. You're the goal machine," says a grinning Rochey, as he looks towards Parker.

"Yeah, well done Imre. Just another 104 more league goals to be on par with Big Bobby Latchford," smirks Parker, as Varadi signs his Book.

"Happy Christmas, lads. Take care!" says Imre Vardi, as he makes his way to Eaton Road.

"Let's get one more autograph, then get the bus home and have a game of footie," says Sean Quinn.

"Yeah, I'm up for that. But I'm not going in goal again. The next one out might be Santa," mutters Skinny Maca.

"Well, if it's Santa, and he's wearing a red costume, I won't be getting him to sign my book," snaps Cooper.

The lads all laugh as they wait for the next player to come out.

Imre Varadi was born in London on the 8^{tH} July, 1959.

He signed for Everton in 1979 as a forward.

He left the blues to join Newcastle United in 1981, after playing twenty-six league games scoring, six league goals

Imre Varadi was also the scorer of that famous F.A Cup goal against Liverpool which knocked them out in the 4th round.

CHRISTMAS WISHES, WITH GRAEME SHARP.

"That young Scottish lad is coming out," yells Cooper.

"Who?" asks Millsy.

"That young forward. Sharpie, the Bay City Roller fella, the lad we signed from Dumbarton," replies Cooper.

"Why is he walking out? asks Millsy.

"He must have left his Raleigh Chopper at home," smirks Rochey.

"He scored seventeen league goals in forty league appearances for Dumbarton before Everton signed him. He was only 18," pipes up Skinny Maca.

"Get his autograph! He's sound! He always stops and talks to us," says Parker.

Graeme Sharp walks over to the lads and stops for a chat. He's not put out one bit as he signs all the autograph books.

"Happy Christmas Graeme. Are you looking forward to Christmas?" asks Sean Quinn.

"It's just a quiet one for me," replies Graeme Sharp.

"Will you be playing over Christmas?" asks Cooper.

"I'm not sure, pal. I'll just wait for the manager to pick the squad," replies Graeme Sharp.

"I would play you every game 'cos you're our favourite player," says Skinny Maca.

"Favourite player? I've only played two games for the first team!" laughs Graeme Sharp.

"That doesn't matter! We've seen you play lots for the reserve team. You're brilliant! And you've scored loads for them," replies Skinny Maca.

Graeme Sharp smiles and wishes all the lads a happy Christmas as he makes his way to his lodgings.

"With players like him at Everton it makes you proud to be a supporter," says Parker.

"He's the older brother that I need. Our kid would be gutted if I brought him home with him supporting Liverpool," mutters Cooper.

"Sharpie's not something you win at the fair like a goldfish. Plus, your Deano's younger than you," says Rochey.

"That doesn't matter. He can be our kid's older brother as well," replies Cooper.

"If Cooper doesn't want him as his older brother, he can be mine. I can swap him for Jimmy. He looks like our Jimmy, so no one in the street will twig on," pipes up Millsy.

"So, if you swap him for your Jimmy, does that mean you and Sharpie will be watching Donny and Marie singing Puppy Love?" smirks Rochey.

"I never thought of that. I best keep our Jimmy, in case Sharpie doesn't like Donny and Marie singing," replies Millsy.

"He's a Bay City Roller," smirks Cooper.

"He can't be my older brother. Our Mark would set our dog, Kai, onto him if he got a bigger dinner than him," laughs Sean Quinn.

"Well, he can definitely be my older brother as I don't have one. We could play footie in the garden and he could teach me to be the best," says Skinny Maca.

"It's not 'rent an older brother' day. He can't perform miracles. He's an Everton player! So, you'll just have to put a black wig on your Tracey, call her Graeme, then settle for being a sub for Brandearth Under-5's," laughs Rochey.

"I could swap him for our Ste. I'd even let him read the Christmas edition of the T.V. Times first, so he could watch what he wanted," says Parker.

"He's not up for adoption! But I did feel sorry for him being all alone for Christmas. Do you think we should catch him up and invite him to our house for his Christmas dinner?" debates Rochey.

"Don't be silly. He could be in the Everton squad for the Christmas games. Plus, I go to your house for my Christmas dinner, and he's not getting my roast potatoes," scoffs Millsy.

"Talking about Christmas, let's get home now and get our footie kits on. We can pretend to be Sharpie, scoring the winner against Manchester City on Boxing Day," pipes up Sean Quinn.

"Graeme Sharp is the best! He's just made my Christmas," utters Skinny Maca.

Everton went on to play Manchester City that Boxing Day at Goodison Park. Unfortunately, it wasn't with a Christmas cheer as Everton were beaten 2-0. It didn't get any better the next day, away to Middlesbrough when they returned home after being beaten by a single goal in a 1-0 defeat. But that didn't spoil the lads' Christmas because, no matter what, win, lose, or draw, Everton were the team that they loved and would always love. They're born, not manufactured, Evertonians.

Graeme Sharp went from playing two league games to playing three hundred and twenty-two games and scoring one hundred and eleven league goals during an eleven-year period. With the club having paid only £120,000 for his services. It was money well spent. At the time, some Evertonians said it was the purchase of the century.

Sharpie left in 1991, having played 426 times in all competitions scoring 159 goals, a post-war scoring record. Only Dixie Dean has scored more goals for Everton.

Graeme Sharp will go down in Everton history after his goal in the 1984 F.A. Cup Final, which helped secure Everton's first major trophy since 1970.

Born in Glasgow, Scotland, on 16th of October, 1960, as he represented his home country, Scotland, at both under-21 and senior level, playing twelve times for the senior team. Evertonians looked up to Sharpie. On the pitch, he never gave less than 100%, never shirking a tackle, never giving up on lost causes.

Off the pitch, he was a true gentleman, carrying no airs or graces. As he always had time for the supporters whether it was to sign autographs, or just to chat about his love for Everton.

CHAPTER 14   HAPPY NEW YEAR 1981

A HAPPY NEW YEAR, FROM JOHN BAILEY.

After the disappointing Christmas period, Everton came storming back on the Saturday, beating Arsenal 2-0 in an F.A. Cup 3rd round tie, at Goodison Park, on the 3rd January, 1981. The goals came courtesy of an own goal by Kenny Sansom in the 85th minute, with Mick Lyons who had come off the bench in the 75th minute, wrapping up the game in the dying seconds.

Arsenal had Alan Sunderland playing up front and every time he ran at the Everton defence, the four lads burst into song, chanting, 'There's only one Tommy Wheeldon, one Tommy Wheeldon!' which got them a few peculiar looks from the Everton fans around them.

Tommy Wheeldon was the former Everton player that the four lads met outside Bellefield.

On Tuesday the 6th of January, on a cold frosty morning, Rochey, Parker, Cooper, and Skinny Maca, accompanied by Liverpool supporter John Saidie, bunk off school to visit Bellefield once again.

John Bailey stops outside the Bellefield gates in his Ford Capri.

"Happy New Year, Bails, great result on Saturday beating Arsenal," says Parker.

"Happy New Year lads. That dentist by yours must be making a fortune," replies John Bailey.

"What do you mean by that, Bails?" inquires Skinny Maca.

"Well, let me just say, every time you come here, you're all wearing a school uniform and them two," says Bails pointing at Rochey and Parker, "Are always telling me they're off school, because they've been the dentist."

"Me and Cooper ain't wearing a school uniform," replies Skinny Maca.

"Yeah, we don't wear a uniform for school," pipes up Cooper.

The other lads look at Cooper in disbelief shaking their heads.

"Can you sign our books saying, 'Happy New Year', Bails?" asks Rochey.

"Shall I sign it, 'Happy New Year to the Famous Five'?" smirks John Bailey.

"How can we be the Famous Five? In the Famous Five, two of them were girls. And the other one was a dog," asks a confused Rochey.

"Okay, then, shall I sign it to the 'Just William Gang?"

"Bails, none of us are called William," pipes up Cooper.

"Rochey's dad's name is William. I got him tickets for the Brighton away game a few months ago," replies John Bailey.

"My dad's name is Billy. Can you just sign it to Rochey?" says Rochey.

"Yeah, of course I can," says a smirking John Bailey.

After he signs all the autograph books, John Bailey beeps his horn smiling as he drives away down Sandforth Road, towards Eaton Road.

John Bailey was born in Liverpool on 1st April, 1957, growing up in the Everon district.

He was voted the Everton Supporters' Player of the Year in 79/80 being the only ever-present player that season, playing in all 55 first-team fixtures.

Bails signed for Everton in 1979 as a left-back then departed in 1985, having spent six years at the club managing to muster up 171 league appearances scoring three league goals.

He was a great character to have in the dressing room and after Everton won the F.A. Cup in 1984, he walked around the

Wembley pitch clutching onto his winners' medal, wearing the biggest pair of blue toy sunglasses and a massive Everton top hat, as he lived the dream.

A HAPPY NEW YEAR, FROM MARTIN HODGE.

"It's freezing today! I thought there would have been a few other fans here," says Cooper.

"They're all at school. It's a school day," mutters Skinny Maca.

"Well, we haven't got long to wait. I've just spotted Martin Hodge getting into his Ford Cortina," pipes up Parker.

"Hodgy from the Port," laughs Cooper.

"Why 'Hodgy from the Port'?" enquires a confused John Saidie.

"It's Hodgy because his name is Martin Hodge," replies Cooper.

"No shit, Sherlock. Are all Evertonians as clever as you?" smirks John Saidie.

"Yes, we are. It's to do with our genes. We're born Evertonians, not manufactured, like your robot, glory hunting, fans," butts in Rochey.

"Oh my, is that Sherlock's assistant? My dear Watson," laughs John Saidie.

"No, it's just me; a Scouse Evertonian, born in Liverpool," replies Rochey.

"I was just asking about the Port bit," mutters John Saidie.

"You can ask him yourself. Let's stop him to get his autograph," says Parker.

"I'm not here for autographs! I just didn't fancy double French with Miss Walsh. I support Liverpool," replies John Saidie.

Martin Hodge stops his car with a big smile.

"Happy New Year, Martin. How's Southport funfair these days?" smirks Cooper.

"I'm not sure. It's been a long time since I went there," replies Martin Hodge.

"I thought you were born in Southport?" asks Skinny Maca.

"I was born in Southport. I still live there and at the start of the season, I often train on my own on the beach near my house. It's a lovely place," replies Martin Hodge.

"See, Saidie, that's why he's Hodgy from the Port," says Parker.

"I guessed that myself, Sherlock," replies John Saidie.

Parker looks at Rochey, whispering "Wow, is he always this grumpy?"

"He supports Liverpool. What do you expect?" replies a smirking Rochey.

Martin Hodge drives away wishing all the lads a Happy New Year.

Martin Hodge, Everton's goalkeeper between 1979/83 was born in Southport on 4th of February, 1959. He signed for Everton in 1979 making twenty-five league appearances, before seeking pastures new in 1983.

He had loan spells at Preston, Oldham Athletic, and Gillingham, before returning to Preston during. His biggest games for Everton were the two F.A Cup Semi-Finals ties against West Ham United, but his most memorable game on a personal level was the F.A Cup 4th round tie the following season against Liverpool when Everton won 2-1 in front of their fans.

A HAPPY NEW YEAR FROM ASA HARTFORD.

"Look Its Asa Hartford! He's in his Rover, driving out," yells Cooper.

"Alright, calm down. It's not like it's Bob Latchford," replies Parker.

"It wouldn't matter if it was Bob Latchford. The only thing these two have in common is that they've both got Ford in their name, and neither of them drive one," pipes up Rochey.

"Yeah. Asa drives a Rover 3500, and Latchford drives a Talbot Alpine," states Skinny Maca.

"And the Rover 3500 stops at the gates to sign our books," sneers Rochey.

"Shut up, will yers. Bobby Latchford walks on water," snarls Parker.

"So do the fellas on them jet-skiers and I bet that they'd still stop to sign our books," snaps Rochey.

"Let's just concentrate on Asa Hartford. He's stopping now," utters Skinny Maca.

"Hello, Asa. Happy New Year," says Cooper.

"Aye, lads. It's a cold one today," replies Asa Hartford.

"No golf today, Asa?" asks Skinny Maca.

"No, not today. This winter weather is no good for the putting greens," replies Asa Hartford.

"Can you sign our autograph books please, Asa?" asks Cooper.

Asa Hartford signs all the autograph books, wishing the lads a Happy New Year, before driving off.

"That's a great autograph," says Skinny Maca.

Looking down at his autograph book Rochey replies "It would have been better if Cooper's pen had ink in it. I hate when they sign the books with the pen they are given. I like them to sign my book with my own pen."

"I know. It's 1981. It's been a whole twelve years since man first set foot on the moon, and still his pen has no ink in it. Unbelievable!" laughs John Saidie.

"Do you know, Asa Hartford, is quoted as saying, his career highlight so far is when Scotland beat England at Wembley in 1977," pipes up Skinny Maca.

"I thought it would have been when he signed for Everton," argues Rochey.

"Me too," says Parker.

"That England team they beat had four Liverpool players in it," pipes up Skinny Maca.

"Ray Clemence, Phil Neal, Emlyn Hughes, and Ray Kennedy, all won European Cup Winners medals for Liverpool a few weeks before," states John Saidie.

"They didn't win the 1977 Home Nations, did they?" smirks Rochey.

"No, Scotland did. Their fans invaded the Wembley pitch after the final whistle, snapped the crossbars and wrecked the Wembley pitch where Kenny Dalglish had scored that vital second goal," replies John Saidie.

"I know, I supported Scotland in the 1978 World Cup Finals after they beat England at Wembley in 1977," says Rochey.

"Well, you couldn't have supported England as they didn't qualify," pipes up Skinny Maca.

"Why Scotland? I thought you were French, with you name being Le Roche?" says Cooper.

"He's as much French as I'm Italian, in French tests in school, Le Roche always comes last," pipes up Parker.

"That's because my family are the Irish Roche, my great grandad only came over here because he ran out of spuds,"

"Ran out of spuds? Next, you'll be telling us your great grandad was King Edward," smirks Parker.

"No, don't be stupid. The royal side of the Roche family comes from my French ancestors back in the day," replies Rochey.

"Royalty my arse," snipes back Parker.

"The only royalty that Parker's clan will be connected to is through your arse when you're having a shite on your throne in your two up, two down, council houses," smirks Rochey.

"Listen to him! King Roche who hasn't got a bean. He bunks the bus wherever he goes, drinks all the lemonade in my house, and lives in the next street to me in his council house," snaps Parker.

"Well, we lost all our wealth when my great-grandad ran out of spuds," smirks Rochey.

"Someone else is on his way out! Get your pens at the ready!" shouts Skinny Maca.

Richard Asa Hartford was born in Clydebank, on 24th of October,1950. He signed for Everton in 1979 and made eighty-one league appearances, scoring six goals from midfield, before moving on in 1981. He represented Scotland fifty times, his last appearance being against Brazil in the 1982 World Cup.

HAPPY NEW YEAR, FROM JOHN BARTON.

"John Barton's on his way out," says Skinny Maca.

"Is Spit with him?" smirks Cooper.

"Who's Spit?" asks a confused Skinny Maca.

"Spit the dog. He looks the spitting image of that fella off Tiswas," replies Cooper.

"Who? Chris Tarrant?" smirks Parker.

"No. The fella with the dog, Bob Beegees," replies Cooper.

"Don't you mean Bob Carolgees?" says Rochey.

"The fella with the black hair and moustache. That's him. He's the spitting image of John Barton," replies Cooper.

"He looks nothing like him. They've both got a moustache, that's it. If he shaves off his moustache he'd look more like Sally James," laughs Rochey.

"Yeah, and if he grows a beard, we could swap him over to the other side and he'd look like Noel Edmonds. Then we could get him to ring Cheggers, to play pop," jokes Parker.

"Well, whoever he looks like, get your books out. He's stopping now," says Skinny Maca.

John Barton stops his car and smiles at the lads.

"Hello, John, Happy New Year. Can you sign our books please?" says Rochey.

John Barton signs all the autograph books and talks football with the lads for the next ten minutes, before driving off.

"It's worth sagging off school when you get to chat to players from your team isn't it?" says Parker.

"Like I said before, I'm not here for autographs. But it's good that the players stop to chat," replies John Saidie.

"The players love chatting to us just as much as we love chatting to them," says Rochey.

"It's great supporting Everton," mutters Skinny Maca.

"That's why I'm an Evertonian. It's in my blood! Once a blue always a blue. We are the famous Blue Army, *Nil Satis Nisi Optimum*," pipes up Cooper.

"Alright, Cooper, take it easy, I thought you were reading a piece out of a Shakespeare play then," says John Saidie.

"No, not a Shakespeare play, just what being an Evertonian does to you. He's an Evertonian Poet, yet he didn't even know it," laughs Parker.

John Barton was born in Birmingham on 24th of October, 1953. He joined Everton in 1979, making twenty league appearances at full-back. John left Everton in 1983 for pastures new, joining Derby County.

JOHN BAILEY

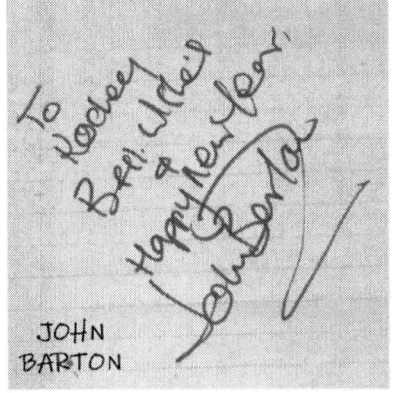

JOHN BARTON

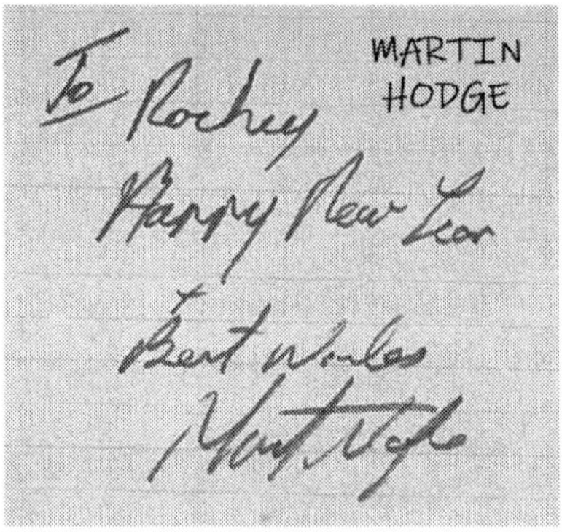

MARTIN HODGE

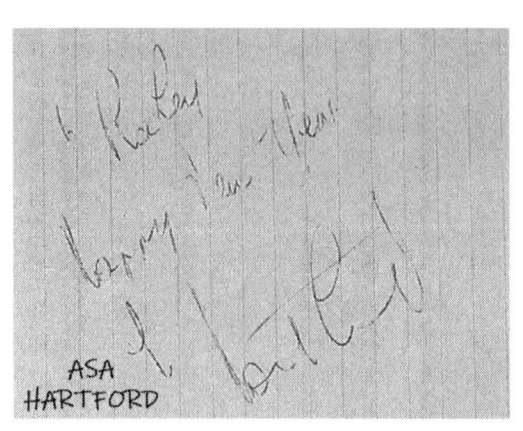

ASA HARTFORD

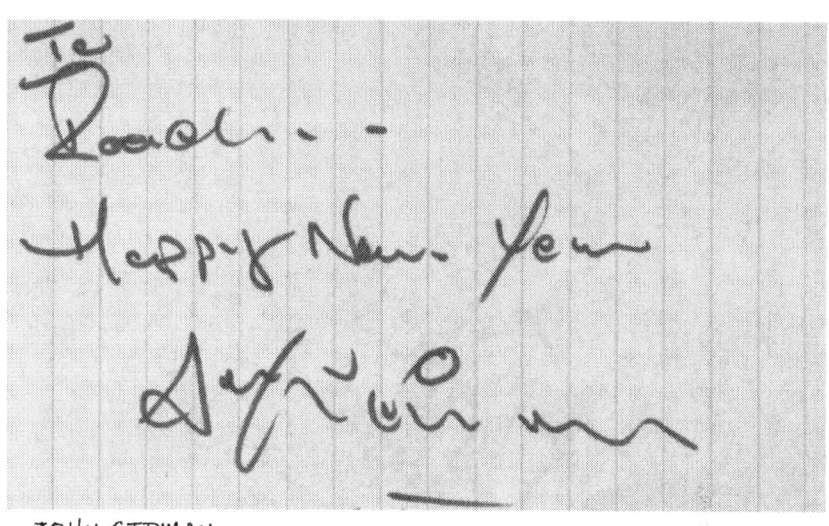

JOHN GIDMAN

PETER EASTOE

GARY MEGSON

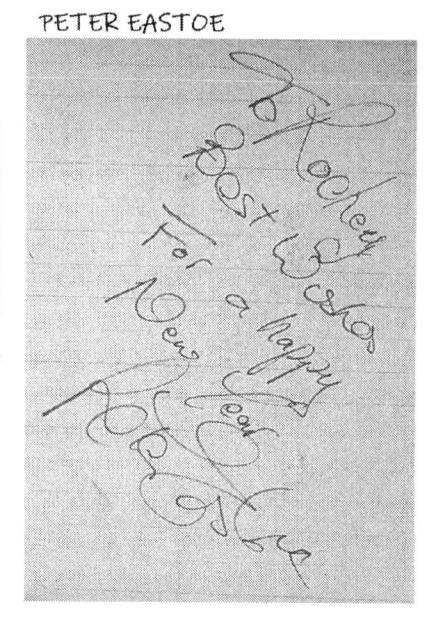

HAPPY NEW YEAR FROM – GARY MEGSON.

"Megs is on his way out," says Skinny Maca.

"Megs? Megs is what I do to you when we're playing football outside the Harvester pub," smirks Cooper.

"Oh, yeah, I forgot you were the nutmeg king," replies Skinny Maca.

"He can only nutmeg you because of your bow legs," laughs Parker.

"Ginger Megs is driving down now. Get your pens out," utters Cooper.

Gary Megson stops his car and sees the lads in their school uniforms shakes his head, a big smirk on his face, as he overhears the lads talking about nutmegging each other. A term used in football when you slide the ball through the opposing players legs.

"Hello. Can you sign our books, Megs?" requests Skinny Maca.

"Do you want me to put the books through your legs?" jokes Gary Megson.

"No, just pass me it back and save them Christmas cracker jokes for your teammates," replies Skinny Maca.

"What's up with him?" asks Gary Megson.

"Take no notice of him Gary. Someone's robbed his ruby slippers," jokes Rochey.

"No, they haven't. I'd never wear anything red. It's just everyone thinks they're a comedian. If I wanted a comedian, I would have knocked at Jackie Hamilton's house, in Harecroft. He lives in Canny Farm and he's a proper Evertonian comedian," utters Skinny Maca.

"Yeah, he's a funny man. I saw him on the telly, on the Comedians. My dad said they call him the Pele of Comedy," pipes up Parker.

"Did you have a good Christmas, Gary? Did Garry Stanley cook Christmas dinner in your bachelor pad?" asks Rochey.

"Yes, I had a great Christmas, thank you. I've just moved into my own house, so Garry had Christmas with his family. My Mother and Father are staying with me while Dad looks for another job in football. My Dad wants to go back to America, but it's better for him here at the moment as there are more clubs in the North West. So, it was a nice family Christmas dinner in my new house," replies Gary Megson.

"So, The Don served Christmas dinner then, Megs?" utters Skinny Maca.

"The Don? Has Gary Megson got mafia connections? Why was the Godfather serving Christmas dinner at his house?" whispers Cooper.

"The Don is Meg's dad, Don Megson. He was in the Sheffield Wednesday team that Everton beat 3-2 in the 1966 F.A. Cup Final.

Everton were 2-0 down after two goals from the Cornishman, Mike Trebilcock. Derek Temple then scored the winner," says Skinny Maca.

"Yeah, he played in defence. He was their captain, but I think he got a bit tired as I'm sure Eddie Kavanagh outran him that day when he did his pitch invasion onto the Wembley pitch," laughs Rochey.

"That's okay, then, because for a minute, I thought he had Mafia connections, and I always call him Ginger Megs," mutters Cooper.

Gary Megson signs the autograph books, laughing, as he listens to the carry on from the lads.

Gary Megson was born in Manchester on 2nd of May, 1959. He made twenty-two league appearances for Everton as a midfielder between 1979 and 1981, scoring two league goals. He then moved to one of his dads' former clubs, Sheffield Wednesday, where his true potential flourished.

After his playing career came to an end, that young lad went on to manage nine different football league clubs, twice guiding West Bromwich Albion into the Premier league.

His dad, Don Megson, and his brother, Simon, were both former professional footballers. Simon Megson, who was also born in Manchester, gained two international caps for the United States National Team.

IT'S A HAPPY NEW YEAR, FROM JOHN GIDMAN.

"Look who's coming out now! It's Keith Richards from the Rolling Stones," smirks John Saidie.

"Don't be daft! It's John Gidman. He's one of us, a Scouser. And he's more a Beatle than a Rolling Stone," snaps Rochey.

"You say that, but there's this other saying, 'a rolling stone gathers no moss'," laughs John Saidie.

"That's true, but there's another saying; 'a Scouser takes no shit, and they're the best of the best, so don't just talk the talk, but walk the walk, as well," utters Rochey.

"You have just made that up. I've never heard that saying," replies John Saidie.

"You have now," fires back Rochey, smirking.

"Get your books out, Giddy. is on his way down," mutters Skinny Maca.

"Giddy? Giddy-up-? Do you think you're riding a horse?" smirks Cooper.

"No. I just got a glimpse of those gums of yours and it reminded me of Red Rum chewing on a carrot," laughs Skinny Maca.

"That's not even funny. Red Rum supports Liverpool. Don't ever associate me with anything that has red in it," snaps Cooper.

"Shut up, the pair of yers and just get John Gidman's autograph," barks Rochey.

"Looks like he's got a new car. That isn't that sponsored Skoda car he had last time we got his autograph?" pipes up Parker.

"He's always changing his cars. That black BMW he's in now is my favourite," says Cooper."

"As long as he didn't buy it with his bonus from when he was playing for Aston Villa, when they beat us in the 1977 League Cup Final, then it's okay. He can drive whatever car he wants," pipes up Parker.

"That was nearly four years ago. Why would he still have his win bonus from then? Just because you still have the first ten pence your Great Gran gave yer, not everybody is as tight as you," laughs Rochey.

John Gidman stops his car wearing a big smile on his face and chats to the lads, whilst signing their autograph books. He wishes them all a Happy New Year before roaring off in his brand new, shiny BMW.

John Gidman, was born in Garston, Liverpool. On 10th of January, 1954. He made sixty-four league appearances for Everton at right-back, scoring two league goals between 1979 to 1981. He later moved to Manchester United.

Giddy Played four times for the England Under-23-side between 1974 and 1976, two caps for the England B team in 1978. His one and only full cap was against Luxembourg in 1978.

He played in the Aston Villa side that defeated Everton in the 1977 League Cup Final, and was also in the Manchester United side that defeated Everton in the 1985 F.A. Cup Final. John Gidman always gave one hundred per cent for whichever team he played for. He was a true professional.

HAPPY NEW YEAR, FROM PETER EASTOE.

"Peter Eastoe is on his way out," says Skinny Maca.

"He's in his Citroen," replies Parker.

"Eastoe's car is like what the teachers drive in our school," says Cooper.

"Well, the car suits him, then, because he reminds me of one of the teachers that's in Grange Hill," says Rochey.

"How would you know what teachers look like? You're never in school," laughs John Saidie.

"Says you, the one who's bunked off school with us to come here, who doesn't even support Everton," replies Rochey.

"Yeah, that's so we can go to Melwood afterwards," fires back John Saidie.

The other three lads look at Rochey, whispering, "We're not going to Melwood after here!"

Rochey smiles at John Saidie and replies, "We're taking you somewhere better than Melwood later."

"I don't think there's anywhere better than Melwood. So, where you taking me?" replies John Saidie.

"You'll just have to wait and see. we'll take you after we get Eastoe's autograph. As for, 'there's no better place than Melwood,' a day of Math's, French, and Science would be better than going there. And I hate all them subjects," says Rochey.

Peter Eastoe stops his car wishing all the lads a Happy New Year as he looks at Rochey, Parker, and John Saidie in their school uniform shaking his head saying, "Education is important lads."

"It's dinner time, Peter," replies Parker.

"You've been here for nearly two hours. How long do you have for dinner?" asks Peter Eastoe.

"We have to have a few hours for lunch as Rochey's a big eater so we have to go too as he won't eat alone.

But he wasn't hungry today, so we all came here to get our New Year autographs," replies Parker.

A smiling Peter Eastoe replies, "Well, don't forget school is supposed to be the happiest time of your lives" as he hands them back their books before driving off.

"I told you; he was like a school teacher. He even had his own brown felt-tip pen to sign our books," mutters Rochey, looking at his signature from Peter Eastoe.

"That wasn't his felt-tip pen! That was my felt-tip pen, that I gave him," pipes up Skinny Maca.

"I wish you would bin that pen! That's twice it's happened now. The brown felt-tip pen spoils my book," rages Rochey

"Never mind him being a teacher, and brown felt-tip pens, where you taking me now?" asks John Saidie.

"Follow me!" says Rochey, still raging, as he walks away from Bellefield.

Peter Eastoe was born in Dordon, near Tamworth, Staffordshire, on 2nd of August 1953.

He was a centre-forward during his time at Everton, playing ninety-five league games and scoring twenty-six league goals for the club between 1979 and 1982.

He left to join West Bromwich Albion.

CHAPTER 15   HAPPY NEW YEAR BILL SHANKLY

So come on, where are you taking me? Where could possibly be better than Melwood?" asks John Saidie.

"Well, you have just been at Bellefield, which is better than Melwood. But seeing as you support the red shite, we're introducing you to Bill Shankly. We're going to his house" replies Rochey.

"Don't take the piss. Shankly's house? Bill Shankly is the Messiah, he lives in a big mansion with armed guards outside, patrolling his ten-foot perimeter walls," says John Saidie.

"Well, maybe he's the Messiah to your lot, but to us, he's just a nice fella that knows a little bit about football, who lives around the corner. As for the armed guards, he's got a dog that nips at your ankles," jokes Rochey.

"That only knows a little bit about football? in the sixties Shankly was more famous than the Beatles," boasts John Saidie.

"He might have been bigger than the Beatles, but he wasn't bigger than Elvis," pipes up Parker.

"No, not many were, Shanks might only be five-foot seven, but he's a giant in status," replies John Saidie.

"We'd best get in touch with Jack then," smirks Skinny Maca.

"Jack? Who the heck is Jack?" asks a confused Cooper.

"Jack! that fella who climbed the beanstalk to visit the giant," giggles Skinny Maca.

The other four lads look at Skinny Maca, not quite believing what he has just said.

"Did you really just say that? We're taking Saidie to see his Messiah, and you're cracking a daft joke about a fella called Jack that's not even funny. And you had the cheek to have a go at Gary Megson about his Christmas cracker joke," says Rochey, shaking his head at Skinny Maca.

"I thought it was funny," replies Skinny Maca.

"I'm glad you did, because none of us did," pipes up Parker.

"Anyway, forget about the Christmas cracker jokes. Get me to Bill Shankly's house. I want to meet the great man," says John Saidie.

"He lives just down this road, number 30," says Cooper.

The lads walk down the road towards Bill Shankly's house, not noticing the cold weather, as the thought of them meeting the great man again gives them a warm glowing feeling. No matter if you are a Blue or a Red, Bill Shankly always made you feel welcome and important. Bill and Nessie never turned anyone away. Never once did he refuse to sign an autograph book.

To Liverpool supporter's he was their Messiah. To these four young Evertonians, he's a kind caring man, that has time for them, gives them advice, and treats them as human being. Bill Shankly always had a smile on his face, and he made an impression on the lads that will never leave them.

"I can't believe I'm going to meet Bill Shankly! I can't wait to tell Betty. She'll never believe me," says John Saidie.

"Who's Betty? Is Frank Spencer his brother-in-law?" whispers Cooper to Rochey.

"Betty is his mum, soft lad, 'some mothers do av' em, " laughs Rochey.

"So, when his mum found out that she was having him, did his older sisters say, 'Oh Betty, Betty's having a baby,' or something along those lines?" smirks Skinny Maca.

"No Jenette said, 'do you think my mum will name him John

or Paul, after the Popes, or Ron after big Ron Yeates?'" answers Rochey.

"So, I guess the Pope won then," replies Skinny Maca.

"The Pope always wins in our eyes. His mum named him John Paul and the pope now is John Paul the second. Plus, you never hear him answer to Ron," smirks Rochey.

The lads reach the front door of Bill Shankly's house. John Saidie looks like he's doing an impersonation of Elvis Presley, his legs are shaking that much.

"Knock on the door, not on the window, this time soft-lad," says Rochey.

"Okay, calm down. I will do," replies Cooper.

The lads wait for someone to answer. John Saidie shaking can't believe he's about to meet the great man himself. As the door opens, the lads are greeted by a smiling Bill Shankly.

"Hello, Bill, Happy New Year!" Cooper says, as Rochey, Parker, and Skinny Maca, shake their heads as he has just called him Bill again. John Saidie just gazes in awe.

"Happy New Year, Mr Shankly. We've bought our mate, John Saidie, to meet you as he's a red. He wants one of them postcards off you, with the F.A. Cup, if that's okay?" says Rochey.

"Happy New Year, lads. So, you must be John Saidie laddie. I know them four as they often knock for a chat," says Bill Shankly, looking at John Saidie

"Hello, Mr. Shankly. Yes, I'm Floor Faidie," replies John Saidie, getting his words mixed up. He struggling to grasp that Bill Shankly has just spoken to him.

"Floor Faidie?" smirks Cooper.

"Aye, are you okay, sonny?" asks Bill Shankly.

"Yes, sorry, Mr Shankly. I'm John Saidie. You're the greatest thing to ever happen to Liverpool. My mum says you're the best thing since sliced bread."

"Well, I don't know about that, sonny. Tell your Mum that sliced bread is great for making sandwiches and dipping into your soup. I'm not that tasty dipped in soup," replies Bill Shankly, with a wee smile.

"Can you sign our autograph books Mr Shankly?" Parker asks, politely.

"Can we have a signed postcard as well, Mr Shankly?" pipes up Skinny Maca.

"Hmm, the four Evertonians all want a signed picture postcard now?" replies Bill Shankly, with a smile on his face.

"Yes, if that's okay, Mr Shankly. It's for our dads," says Rochey.

"Can I have two please, Mr Shankly? One for my dad and one for my mum, Betty Saidie," asks John Saidie.

"Aye, no problem, sonny," replies Bill Shankly, as he goes back into his house.

"Wow, Bill Shankly, knows my name!" says John Saidie.

"I told you this place is better than Melwood, didn't I?" laughs Rochey.

"It certainly is. Bill Shankly, the Messiah, knows my name! and even dips his bread into his soup," mutters John Saidie.

"I bet his favourite soup is Scotch Broth," pipes up Cooper.

"Yeah, I bet he has Everton toffee mints on the sly before he's starting training at Bellefield," smirks Rochey.

Bill Shankly returns with the picture-postcards and signs them for each of the lads and then signs their autograph book. The five lads leave glowing. They feel like they're on the top of the world. Ten feet tall. Nothing was too much trouble for Bill Shankly. He was a man of the people who left a lasting impression no matter which team you supported, red or blue. The four lads thought that, as

Evertonians, they were not supposed to like Bill Shankly, but that soon changed once they met him and realised, he was a kind, caring, family man. Bill Shankly was a man with true values in life. Sadly, Bill Shankly, OBE, passed away that same year, on the 29th of September 1981. He was 68 years old. A great man gone, but one who will never be forgotten.

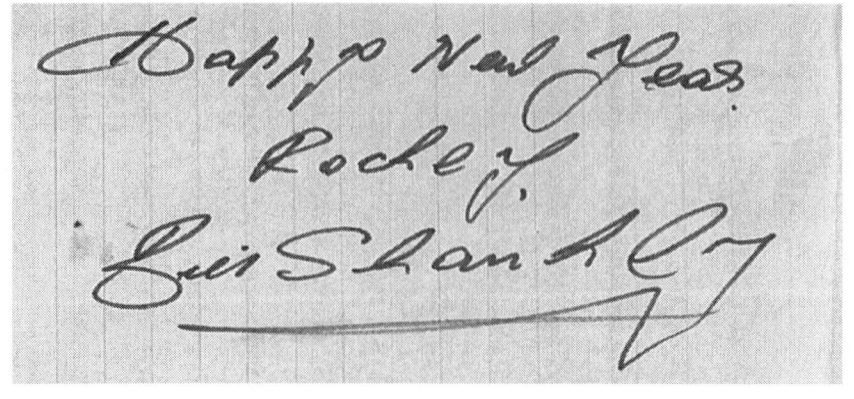

BILL SHANKLY

CHAPTER 16   IF YOU KNOW YOUR HISTORY

Tuesday 27th of January, Evertonians all around the world are still walking around with smiles on their faces, after beating their great rivals from across Stanley Park in the fourth round of the F.A. Cup.

It was a typical Merseyside derby cup tie with six bookings in the match, Steve McMahon, Peter Eastoe, and Eamon O' Keefe, got a yellow card from the blue side of the city, whilst Avi Cohen, Jimmy Case and Graeme Souness all received a yellow card on the red side.

It was a fierce cup tie fought on the Goodison turf. Ten Scouse lads' amount those on display: John Bailey, Billy Wright, Mick Lyons, and Steve McMahon were running out for the Blues, whilst Phil Thompson, Colin Irwin, Jimmy Case, Sammy Lee, David Fairclough, and Terry McDermont represented the red side.

The blues ran out winners, recording a fabulous 2-1 victory. All 53,804 supporters witnessed a great performance from an Everton team that wasn't going to leave that pitch without a victory.

It's 10am and the freezing conditions have left most schools in the area unable to stay open. The freezing conditions have taken their toll on boilers everywhere.

Rochey, Parker, Cooper, and Skinny Maca have therefore taken it upon themselves to jump the bus to get some autographs at Bellefield.

As the 12C bus stops outside Melwood, the four lads notice John Saidie with his mate, Paul Fitzpatrick, outside (the big red gates) of Liverpool's training ground. They all push the stop button then leg down the stairs, shouting, "Hey, driver! Stop the bus!"

"What's with all the commotion lads? One day off school and I get all this! It's usually a nice quiet bus ride on a Tuesday morning," says the driver, as he stops.

"Sorry, mate. We just spotted our mates outside Melwood," pipes up Skinny Maca.

"I'm a Blue myself, so I don't know what the big deal is," replies the driver.

"We're all Blues mates. We're only going to have a chat with the Liverpool players about Saturday's match," laughs Cooper.

"That's okay, then. But next time you get on my bus, can you pay your bus fare, lad?" asks the driver.

"I could, mate, especially with you being an Evertonian. But if I did, I'd lose my nickname 'Cooper the Bunker,'" says Cooper, as he jumps off the bus.

Shaking his head, Parker looks at Rochey. "When did he get the nickname, 'Cooper the Bunker'?"

Rochey shrugs his shoulders. "I haven't got a Scooby-Doo. I've never ever heard anyone call him that."

"It's official then: Cooper is full of shit," laughs Skinny Maca.

The lads join John Saidie and Paul Fitzpatrick outside Melwood.

"Why are the Everton blue brigade here?" asks John Saidie.

"We've come to discuss Saturday's cup match and your players," laughs Cooper.

"Well, don't be standing by us when we get our autographs. We're proper Reds!" fumes big Paul Fitzpatrick who, at fourteen years of age, standing six foot tall, is a bit older than John Saidie and the four lads.

"We know you're a proper Red with your ginger hair," replies Cooper, as Rochey, Parker, and Skinny Maca look at each other bewildered.

"Hey! I'm strawberry blonde, not ginger," snaps Paul Fitzpatrick.

"It looks ginger to me," replies Cooper.

"Well, it's not ginger, okay! You must need glasses, lad," snarls Paul Fitzpatrick.

"What time do the players finish training?" asks Rochey, changing the subject.

"They finish about 12:15, go to the changing rooms for ten minutes then get on the team coach to go to Anfield for their lunch," replies John Saidie.

"We can get some autographs here first, then go to Bellefield," says Parker.

"Yeah, that's okay with me. Saidie, will you and Strawberry Blonde be coming to Bellefield with us?" laughs Rochey.

"No, Fitzy, is a proper Red. We're going home after here," smirks John Saidie.

"I'm a proper Blue, but we still get autographs from both teams. We even have gingers in our team. Gary Megson is a ginger. I don't think he would get away with calling himself a strawberry blonde," smirks Rochey.

Paul Fitzpatrick looks at Rochey and John Saidie with a big grin on his face.

A few months later, after getting autographs with the four lads, John Saidie and Paul Fitzpatrick both became minor celebrities on the streets of Cantril Farm, after both of them ran onto the pitch at Anfield after Liverpool's match against CSKA Sofia on the 4th of March, 1981. Liverpool had just beaten CSKA Sofia 5-1 in the quarter-finals of their European Cup tie.

Graeme Souness bagged a hat-trick, so both John Saidie and Paul Fitzpatrick decided that they would run on the pitch to congratulate him.

They both appeared on the ITV midweek sports show that night racing after Souness with John Saidie, patting him on the shoulder. Meanwhile Paul Fitzpatrick patted Souness on his famous permed head.

In those days, Maggie Thatcher and her Tory puppets labelled anyone who went to a football match and was a bit boyish an 'Hooligan.' When, in fact these were just two lads who got caught up in the moment after a famous victory in Europe.

Many fans run onto to the pitch to embrace their team after a win. To most pitch invaders, it was their dream to be on the pitch with their heroes. It was the next best thing to playing for the team they loved and supported.

That doesn't make them hooligans.

John Saidie and Paul Fitzpatrick were far from football hooligans. In fact, both went onto represent Liverpool Football Club. John Saidie signed schoolboy forms while Paul Fitzpatrick signed professionally living the dream, turning out for Liverpool reserves alongside nine international players. He was the only outfield player in the Liverpool side that day who wasn't an international footballer. Bob Bolde, in goal was the other.

The Liverpool players start to walk out of Melwood towards the coach that will take them back to Anfield for lunch.

"There's Phil Thompson with Colin Irwin! Leg it over to them. Let's get their autographs!" yells Cooper.

"What about the groundsmen?" replies Skinny Maca.

"Don't worry about the groundsmen! Just leg it to the players. They don't call me 'Cooper the Bunker' for nothing," utters Cooper, as he legs it over to Phil Thompson.

"There's that name again! 'Cooper the Bunker,'" smirks Rochey.

"He's a legend in his own head," laughs Parker, as he runs over to the players with Rochey.

Cooper reaches Phil Thompson first, with Rochey, Parker, and Skinny Maca, just behind. John Saidie and Paul Fitzpatrick head the other way towards Kenny Dalglish.

"Hiya, Phil! Can you sign my autograph book: 'Phil

Thompson, M.B.E'?" smirks Cooper.

"I haven't got an M.B.E.," replies Phil Thompson.

"Yes, you have. You got it on Saturday against Everton. Phil Thompson M.B.E. Miles Behind Eastoe, for the first goal," laughs Cooper.

"Behind him, because he was off-bloody-side!" replies Phil Thompson, shaking his head, as he signs the autograph books.

"No Phil. If you'd watched the match on Saturday night, you'd have seen Colin Irwin being awarded an M.I.F.O.E."

"Yeah, I saw him get that award, Coops," laughs Rochey, as he hands Phil Thompson his book to sign.

"The M.I.F.O.E. award?" utters Phil Thompson, shaking his head as he boards the coach.

"Yes, the M.I.F.O.E award; Miles in Front of Eastoe, and keeping him on-side for the first goal," laughs Cooper, as he turns and legs it over to David Fairclough.

"Hello Davie. Can you sign my autograph book: David Fairclough, O.B.E.?" utters Cooper.

"Why O.B.E, Lee? How's your dad?" replies David Fairclough.

"O.B.E, because when you went out of the F.A. Cup on Saturday, you went Out Before Easter," laughs Cooper.

"Oh, not funny Lee! I know I lived in same street as you in Cremorne Hey, but here, at Liverpool, we don't like losing any game," replies David Fairclough, as he signs the autograph books.

"Don't worry, Davie lad. Me and John Saidie are proper Reds. And Cooper has just got a C.B.E. award," pipes up Paul Fitzpatrick.

"C.B.E. award?" replies David Fairclough.

"Yeah, a C.B.E. award for being the number one Cremorne

Bell End. He's won it eleven years on the trot," laughs Paul Fitzpatrick.

"Yeah, and Fitzy's ginger, not strawberry blonde," snaps Cooper.

"There's nothing wrong with being ginger, Lee," says a smiling David Fairclough, shaking his ginger locks.

"Why are you shaking your head, Davie? You're not even ginger! Your carrot, Red Rum would chew your head to bits," smirks Cooper.

David Fairclough looks over at Paul Fitzpatrick smiling. "I know what you mean now, mate."

"Davie, me, and Parker have a O.B.E. as we live in the next street to Cremorne! Over, Brandearth, End," laughs Skinny Maca.

The other lads all look at each other, not quite believing what has just come out of Skinny Maca's mouth.

"Did, he really just say that?" utters a stunned Parker.

"I didn't think his jokes could get any worse, but that one has just topped the lot of them," says a shocked John Saidie.

"Never mind his bad jokes. There's David Johnson in his football kit. Let's get his autograph. He once played for Everton," says Rochey.

"Every player is in their training kit. They get changed at Anfield. His nickname is The Doc. He might be able to treat Skinny Maca for them sick jokes," laughs John Saidie.

"Hello, Dave. Can you sign my book?" asks Parker, as he shoves his book into David Johnson's hand.

"You should never have left Everton, Dave. You would have still been in the F.A. Cup," smirks Cooper, as David Johnson signs all the autograph books.

David Johnson gets on the team coach with a little smile on his face as the lad's head towards Terry McDermott, Ray Kennedy, and Alan Kennedy.

"Don't mention to Terry McDermott about us beating them in the cup. He's John Caldwell's cousin, and we go to school with him," Rochey says to Cooper.

"I'm okay, then, as I don't go to your school," replies Cooper.

"It doesn't matter if you do or don't. Just get his autograph and don't mention Saturday's match to him," snaps Rochey.

First Terry McDermott and Ray Kennedy sign the autograph books, leaving Alan Kennedy with the lads. Behind them the coach driver revs up his engine ready to move.

"Can you sign my book please, Alan?" asks John Saidie.

"Hey, Alan! Did you play in the third round of the F.A. Cup? Cos you didn't play on Saturday and, if you're not cup-tied, you can play for us," utters Skinny Maca.

"I don't want him playing for us! John Bailey is our left back and he's a Scouser. Alan Kennedy is a Geordie. Why aye man!" utters Cooper.

"You don't always win with Scousers in your team. Liverpool had six Scousers, on Saturday compared to Everton's four, yet we still won," recalls Parker.

"He's not a Geordie! He was born in Penshaw in the City of Sunderland, so he's a Mackem!" mutters Skinny Maca.

"How does he know all that?" asks a puzzled Paul Fitzpatrick.

"They know everything about football, Fitzy. They even know where Bill Shankly lives," replies John Saidie.

Alan Kennedy boards the departing Liverpool team bus, giggling to himself, as the lads have a conversation about him.

"They don't know everything. Cooper just said Alan Kennedy was a Geordie! And isn't it common knowledge, Bill

Shankly lives in a big fuck-off mansion in Southport?" smirks Paul Fitzpatrick.

"Hey, Fitzy. We sleep, eat, and breathe football. Cooper just got himself a bit confused because Liverpool signed Alan Kennedy from Newcastle in 1978, and the mansion in Southport, where Shankly is supposed to live, is just a myth. Bill Shankly is a man of the people who gives out more than he receives," pipes up Rochey.

"I'm not confused now! Here's the groundsmen. Get on your toes and let's get out of here," says a bolting Cooper, as he legs it past the departing Liverpool coach, closely followed by the rest of the lads, who start banging on the team bus as they pass it.

"Everton, Everton, Everton!" chant Rochey, Parker, and Skinny Maca, whilst Cooper sings, "And If You Know Your History," at the Liverpool team bus, whilst John Saidie and Paul Fitzpatrick chant, "Liverpool, Liverpool, Liverpool!"

Once the Liverpool team bus is out of sight, Rochey, Parker, Cooper, and Skinny Maca head towards Bellefield, knowing that most of the Everton players will surely be gone. John Saidie and Paul Fitzpatrick have had enough and cross the road to get the bus back to Canny Farm.

It's a ten-minute walk to Bellefield so the lads walk at pace hoping to catch a few players before the day's end. The four lads reach Bellefield at 1pm and catch Imre Varadi as he's driving out.

"Imre, great goal on Saturday! What's it like to score the winner in a derby match in the F.A. Cup?" asks Cooper.

"It's an unbelievable feeling. It felt good."

"Can you sign my autograph book and underline it please, Imre? It's so I will always remember you signed my book after scoring the winning goal against Liverpool in the F.A. Cup," says Rochey.

"Yes, of course I will. No problem."

"Are there any players left in Bellefield Imre?" asks Parker.

"No, they have all gone, I stayed behind for some treatment, but I do know Geoff Nulty is on his way out."

Imre Varadi drives away and the lads wait for Geoff Nulty whose career was prematurely ended the previous season in the 1980 Merseyside Derby, when after challenging for the ball, he came out second best in a tackle that caused him severe ligament damage.

"Geoff Nulty is driving down in his car! Get your pens at the ready!" yells Cooper.

Geoff Nulty stops his car and gives all the lads a thumbs up.

"Hello, Geoff. What a great result on Saturday against Liverpool," says Parker.

"Yes, it was a great win. Especially with it being against Liverpool. I would have loved to have been out there on the pitch," replies Geoff Nulty.

"What are you doing now, Geoff?" asks Skinny Maca.

"He's sitting in his car talking to us, soft lad," mutters Parker under his breath.

"I'm just helping out now, doing a bit of coaching," replies Geoff Nulty.

"Well, your coaching must be something special, Geoff. That was a special victory over Liverpool on Saturday," says Rochey.

"Yes, that win, and the performance, were a bit special!" replies Geoff Nulty, as he signs Rochey's autograph book.

Geoff Nulty chats to the lads for the next ten minutes before saying goodbye and driving off. That's what it was like in the 80's, the players loved chatting to the fans, just as much as the fans loved chatting to the players.

"Oh, my word, look at what Geoff Nulty signed in my autograph book!" beams Rochey.

"That is brilliant," says Cooper.

"No, that is extra special," smirks Parker.

"Imre Varadi has underlined his signature in your autograph book like you asked him," says Skinny Maca.

"I know! That's why I love Everton, and why I love coming to Bellefield. Nothing is too much trouble for the players," replies Rochey.

"And that's why, if you know your history, it's enough to make your heart go worrrrrrrr, because we don't care what the red shite says, what the fuck do we care?" chants Cooper, as the four lads make their way home.

TO GEOFF THANK YOU

Extra Special Wishes
to Rochey from

GEOFF
NULTY

PHIL
THOMPSON

RAY
KENNEDY

DAVID
FAIRCLOUGH

ALAN
KENNEDY

DAVID
JOHNSON

TERRY
McDERMOTT

CHAPTER 17   ENGLAND COME TO BELLEFIELD

Tuesday 24th of February, 1981. Today, Rochey, Parker, Cooper, and Skinny Maca are in for a surprise when they turn up at Bellefield. It's 11am and there isn't a single car in the Bellefield car park. The Everton players have been given a day off, and the lads are just about to head home, when a coach pulls up, with an England emblem in the front window.

"Who's this?" says Skinny Maca.

"Well, it says England Under-21 on that sign, so I'm guessing that's a bit of a giveaway," smirks Cooper.

"That means nothing. There was a picture of Stork margarine on the side of our bus this morning but I didn't see the driver selling!" comes back the reply from Skinny Maca, pleased with himself.

"Does it really matter? Let's just get their autographs!" yells Parker.

First off, the coach are the coaching staff.

"Hello, mate. Can you sign my book for me. By the way, who are you?" asks Cooper.

"I'm Dave Sexton," comes back the reply.

"Ain't you the Manchester United manager?" mutters Skinny Maca.

"Yes, that I am. I'm also Head Coach of the England Under 21 team," replies Dave Sexton, as he signs the book.

Dave Sexton was sacked as the Manchester United manager (on the 30th of April 1981) Just over eight weeks after signing the lads' autograph books. He continued to coach the England Under-21 team and enjoyed success with them, winning the UEFA Under 21s Championship twice in 1982 and 1984.

The four lads move on from Dave Sexton and push their autograph books into the gentlemen next to him.

"Alright, mate. Can you sign my book?" asks Rochey.

"Can you sign my book as well, mate? And can you tell me who you are?" mutters Cooper.

Parker nudges Cooper in the back. "It's Terry Venables, knobhead! He co-wrote that program on ITV."

"What program?" asks Cooper.

"Hazel, the TV program! It's about a wise cracking detective, played by Nicholas Ball. Me and my dad use to watch it every week," replies Parker.

"So, are you saying he doesn't even have anything to do with football? And who is Nicholas Ball?"

"Shut up, soft lad. He's one of the England under 21 coaches. And he's the manager of Crystal Palace. Nicholas Ball is the main actor in it!" snaps Parker, interrupting Cooper mid-sentence.

"He's not the manager of Crystal Palace no more. He left them in October. He's the manager of QPR now. But, yes, Hazel was a great programme," mutters Skinny Maca, as he gets a growl from Parker. Meanwhile Terry Venables is signing books with tears of laughter rolling down his cheeks.

Terry Venables held the distinction of being the only player to represent England at Youth, amateur, Under 23 level and senior levels. He also represented the Football League XI.

As well as being a coach under Dave Sexton for the England Under-21 team. Terry Venables also became the manager of the England national team.

The England players get off the coach and make their way into Bellefield, as the lads scramble to get more autographs.

"Hey, mate, can you sign my autograph book? What's your name? Who do you play for?" asks Cooper.

"My name is Justin Fashanu. I play for Norwich City."

"Didn't you score that wonder-goal last season against the red shite?" asks Cooper.

A smiling Justin Fashanu nods as he signs his autograph.

Justin Fashanu became the first £1m black footballer in the August of 1981 when he left Norwich City to join Nottingham Forest. The wonder-goal that Cooper asked him about, was the goal he scored for Norwich City against Liverpool in a 5-3 win on the 9th of February, 1980. The goal he scored in that match was later voted' BBC Goal of the Season.'

"Steve McMahon is over there! Shall we get his autograph?" asks Skinny Maca.

"No, don't be soft. We get his autograph every time we come here. Let's get another player before they disappear into Bellefield," says Rochey.

"I'm only asking because the last three have all been Cockneys. I know it's England, but there are also great English footballers and coaches outside of London. At least Steve McMahon is a Scouser," replies Skinny Maca.

"Let's get that fella over there. He doesn't look like a Cockney," utters Cooper.

Rochey, Parker and Skinny Maca, all look at each other bewildered at Cooper's last comment about what a Cockney looks like.

"Hey, lad. Can you sign my autograph book for me?" asks Cooper.

"Yeah, no problem, mate," comes back the reply.

The four lads look at each other and start whispering amongst themselves;

"Did you hear his accent? He sounded Australian," mutters Rochey.

"He sounded South African to me," whispers Parker.

"I bet he's a Cockney trying to wind us up," says Skinny Maca, as quietly as he can.

"No, he's definitely not a Cockney. Or Australian. Or South African. He plays for England. He's wearing an England tracksuit," pipes up Cooper.

"He definitely didn't sound English," replies Parker.

"Hey, mate. What's your name? And where do you come from?" asks Cooper.

"I come from the team hotel! I'm Craig Johnston. I play for Middlesbrough."

"See! I told you he was English. He even speaks English," says Cooper, as he walks away from Craig Johnston, who, in turn, looks at Rochey, Parker, and Skinny Maca and winks at them as he makes his way into Bellefield.

Craig Johnston was born in Johannesburg, South Africa, to Australian parents. His parents returned home to Australia when he was a small child. He left Middlesbrough to join Liverpool for £650,000 in 1981. He enjoyed a successful career with Liverpool, although his biggest success came once his playing days were over when he designed the Predator football boot as a prototype for Adidas.

The next evening, 25th of February, the England Under-21 team beat the Republic of Ireland's Under-21 side, 1-0 at Anfield. There was a crowd of 5,882. The referee for the match was Ronald Bridges. Gary Shaw, who played for Aston Villa, scored the only goal of the match in the 2nd minute.

Steve McMahon led by example, winning the midfield battle against two Irish lads who would go on to enjoy illustrious careers. Ronnie Whelan, who went onto win many trophies with Liverpool. And a lad named Kevin Sheedy, who went on to play for the greatest Everton team ever, winning many trophies.

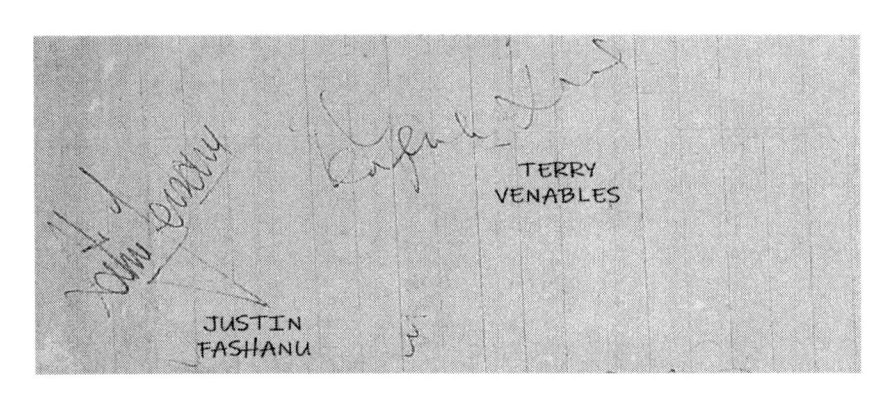

JUSTIN
FASHANU

TERRY
VENABLES

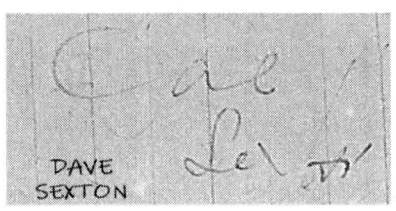

DAVE
SEXTON

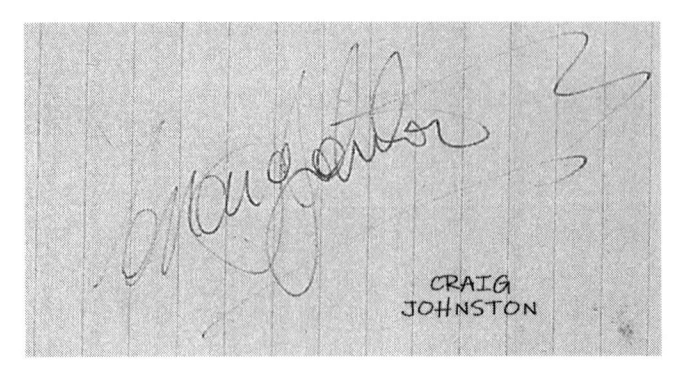

CRAIG
JOHNSTON

CHAPTER 18   ROYALTY RETURNS

It's Saturday, 11th of April 1981, and Everton are welcoming Norwich City to Goodison Park. Everton have been on a bad run their last win being a 3-2 victory away to Crystal Palace. Since, they have drawn two and lost six.

Despite the side's lack of form the four lads still get themselves to the ground early, win, lose, or draw their love for Everton never changes.

Rochey, Parker, Cooper, and Skinny Maca have got to Goodison Park just in time to see the Norwich City team bus pull up. The lads have little Lee Murray with them today who, at seven years of age, has been nicknamed 'Infant Blue!'

"Look over there! It's big Joe Royle. Let's get his autograph!" yells Cooper, as the lads leg it over to the Norwich City coach.

"Joe, can we have your autograph?" yells Skinny Maca, getting Joe Royle's attention.

"Yeah, no problem lads. Have you got a pen and paper?" Joe Royle, asks.

"No, we haven't Joe. We've just got off the bus. We only have pen and paper on school days," replies Cooper.

"When has your school ever had pens and paper? You and Skinny Maca don't even wear a school uniform!" says Rochey.

Joe Royle goes back onto the team bus and emerges with a pen and paper, handing each of the lads a signed autograph.

"Thank you, Joe. Take it easy on us today. We haven't won since February," says Parker.

"That's eight games, Joe. Please don't make it nine. Remember Joe, you once wore the famous number 9 royal blue, jersey," pleads Rochey.

"Lads, as professional footballers, we always go out onto the pitch to do our best, no matter who we play for," replies Joe Royle.

"We know that, Joe. You scored against us in November, in your home fixture," laughs Skinny Maca.

"You've also scored against us when you played for Manchester City," says Rochey.

"That's my job lads! Enjoy the game!" replies a smiling Joe Royle, as he gives the lads a wink and goes into Goodison Park.

When Joe Royle's name was announced over the tannoy as the Norwich City number 9, a huge show of appreciation rang out around the ground. Every Evertonian stood up and applauded Joe Royle. In the 24th minute, Joe Royle put Norwich City ahead with a fine. the whole of Goodison Park clapped, as Joe Royle made his way back to his own half.

Everton had three Scousers in their team that day: John Gidman, Billy Wright, and Mick Lyons. But it was the two Scousers of Norwich City that ran out winners in a 2-0 win. As a young Dave Watson shut up shop at centre-back, helping Norwich City keep a clean sheet, whilst Joe Royle won the battle of Norris Green against Billy Wright. The attendance for the game that day was 16,254.

After the game, the Norwich City manager, Ken Brown, said to Joe Royle, "Joe, I'm gob smacked. Most players get booed when they return to their former clubs. You get a standing ovation. They even clapped when you scored."

Joe replied with a big smile. "Today, was a very emotional day for me. It gave me goosebumps all over. When the fans clapped when I scored, it took me back to those days of wearing the royal blue jersey."

The four lads, and Lee Murray Walk home after the match. They're a little upset but take with them something that they might never see again at Goodison Park.

"Can I ask you four something?" requests a confused looking Lee Murray.

"Sure can," replied the four lads.

"Who is Joe Royle, that fella who gave us his autograph?"

"Joe Royle is an Everton legend, who wore the famous number 9 jersey, and made his Everton debut in 1966, aged just sixteen" replies Skinny Maca.

"He played centre-forward in Everton's 1970 League winning team," says Parker.

"He's also a Scouser from Norris Green," pipes up Cooper.

"He's all of these things but more importantly than that, he's Everton royalty. He's part of the Royle family," says Rochey.

A few years down the line, Joe Royle returned to Everton once again, this time as Everton's manager. He led his team out in the 1995 F.A. Cup Final against Manchester United making sure all his Everton players met and shook hands with, Royalty before the match. Everton won the match 1-0. When Everton scored, Joe Royle could be seen winking to one of his background staff. That same wink that the four lads witnessed all those years ago outside Goodison Park.

The young Scouse centre-back, Dave Watson, who had played for Norwich City all those years ago, was now Everton captain. That day, Dave was the one who went up to receive the F.A. Cup Prince Charles. Last to receive his medal from the future King was Joe Royle.

That was the day the Royle family got to meet a Royle from Liverpool, who the City of Liverpool, could call one of its own.

Best Wishes Lads

JOE ROYLE

CHAPTER 19   END OF THE 80-81 SEASON

It's Friday 1st of May, 1981. Everton sit 17th in the League table with two away games against Birmingham City on the 2ND at St Andrews, and Wolverhampton Wanderers at Molineux on the 4th left to play. The game at Wolves will be Everton's 3,200TH league match.

Rochey, Parker, Cooper, and Skinny Maca, accompanied by Rochey's younger brother, Mick, who is also another big Evertonian.

The lads have turned up late and the Bellefield training ground seems a bit empty. The lads are wondering, as it's 1pm if the players have already begun their journey down south for their Midlands double header. All of a sudden, Cooper and Skinny Maca spot the Everton manager, Gordon Lee, walk out of the Bellefield building and get into his car.

"That's Gordon Lee! Let's get his autograph!" yells Skinny Maca.

"Okay, stop shouting! Wait till he drives out," says Cooper.

"Don't let him drive straight past us," replies Skinny Maca.

"He won't drive past. He's one of us," says Cooper.

Gordon Lee drives towards the lads and stops for a chat as he signs their autograph books. After spending twenty minutes with the lads, Gordon Lee says his goodbyes, wishing them all the best.

"How good was that! Gordon Lee, the Everton manager, stopping to chat to us. And signing our autograph books," beams Skinny Maca.

"It's not that good. Look what he signed in my book!" moans Rochey.

Parker, Cooper, Skinny Maca, and his younger brother Mick, look at Rochey's autograph book.

"Why are you moaning? He's put 'Everton are magic on it. That's brilliant," replies Parker.

"He's even signed it 'best wishes Gordon Lee.' That

autograph is class," says Skinny Maca.

"Look closely. He's signed it to 'Rochey and Mick,' it should just say, Rochey," moans Rochey.

"I think that's brilliant! I've only been to Bellefield once and the Everton manager knows my name," smirks Rochey's younger brother Mick.

"It's not brilliant! He's ruined my autograph book," utters Rochey.

"Just scribble out Mick's name," mutters Cooper.

"I can't, 'cos he'll tell my dad, and then my dad will tell my mum not to give me a roast dinner on Sunday."

"Hmmm, now that's a hard one because your mum's roast dinners are out of this world," replies Cooper.

"Yeah, your mum's roast dinner is one of the best I've eaten," pipes up Parker.

"You'd betta just leave Mick's name in the book. You can't miss out on your mums' roast dinners," says Skinny Maca.

The lads walk towards the bus stop; heading home after adding another name into their books.

The next day on the Saturday away to Birmingham City, Everton drew 1-1. Then two days later Everton drew again, this time 0-0 against Wolves, finishing the season in 15th place, three points above the relegation places.

Everton had won just one from their previous twelve league games, losing eight and drawing three. Two days later on the 6th of May 1981, Everton parted company with their manager Gordon Lee.

Gordon Lee had become Everton manager in the January of 1977, replacing the sacked Billy Bingham. A few months later, Everton reached the League Cup Final, narrowly losing 3-2 against Aston Villa, following two replays. In the league they finished the season in ninth place. Everton also reached the semi-finals of the

F.A. Cup in that first season, losing 3-0 to Liverpool in a replay, after drawing the first-game 2-2, in what is still labelled to this day as the Clive Thomas show.

In football matches a good referee is one that goes through the whole match unnoticed. Except Clive Thomas had other ideas that day. The Welsh referee had always wanted to be the centre of attention.

After that semi-final he walked off the pitch leaving football with one of the greatest mysteries never explained, when he controversially denied Everton a late winner with the match level at two a-piece. Bryan Hamilton had come off the bench to score, what looked like to the rest of the world, a perfect winning goal.

The following season, 1977-78, Everton finished in 3rd place. In the 1978-79 season, Andy King scored a memorable winner against Liverpool at Goodison Park. Everton finished 4th that season. In the 1979-1980 season they finished 19th in the league. To finish so low in the league was down to a lack of confidence in the team.

Everton reached the semi-finals of F.A. Cup yet again that season and, in the first game were leading 1-0, only for Brian Kidd to be sent off in the 63rd minute, allowing Stuart Pearson to snatch an equalizer to take the tie to a replay, which Everton lost 2-1.

Under Gordon Lee Everton were becoming the 'nearly men' of football. But, for Everton Football Club, with its motto: Nil Satis Nisi Optimum, which means (nothing but the best is good enough) being 'nearly men' wasn't good enough.

To this day, Rochey still regards meeting Gordon Lee as an amazing day and tells everyone how warm a person he was, and how it would have been a perfect day if only he had got the autograph spot on. but he didn't, did he? He signed it to 'Rochey and Mick.'

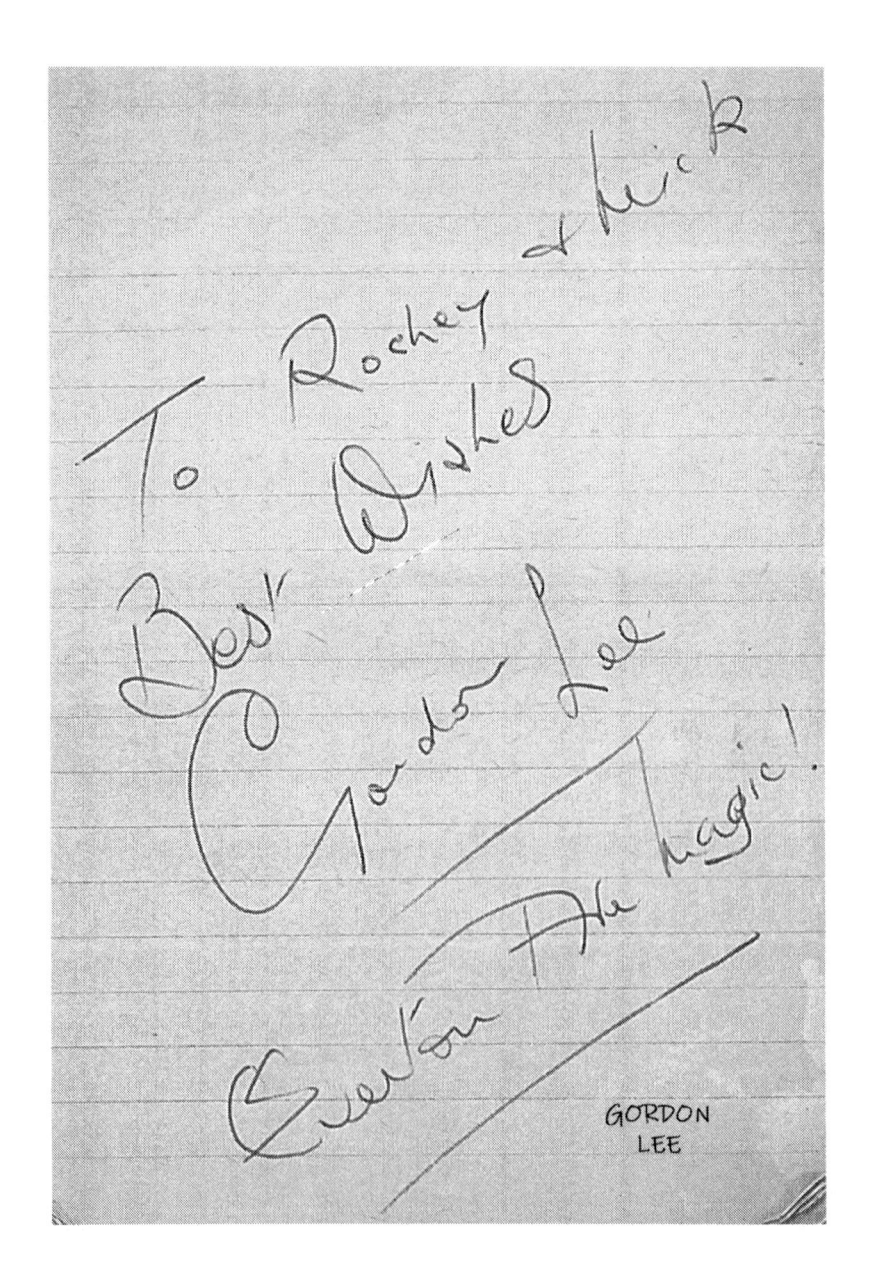

To Rockey & Mick
Best Wishes
Gordon Lee
Everton the magic!

GORDON
LEE

CHAPTER 20   THE MAGNIFICENT SEVEN

There is a lot of excitement around Bellefield, as there's a new manager calling the shots, who goes by the name of Howard Kendall. How will he do? Only time will tell.

During the summer of 1981. The first pre-season of the Howard Kendall reign. There were lots of coming and going at Bellefield, as Howard was trying to make his mark.

That summer saw quite a few players leave; young Brian Quinn signed for the Los Angeles Aztecs on the 22nd of May on a free transfer.

Next to leave on the 1st of July, were three players out of contract: George Telfer, Mark Ward and Ray Deakin.

Next to go on the 15th of July was Bob Latchford. He signed for Swansea City for £125,000. Parker and Rochey were in shock. Parker, couldn't believe Everton had sold his idol, the man who he looked up to and copied when he was playing football himself.

Rochey was in shock as he couldn't see how he could have signed for Swansea City as he was always so reluctant to put his signature onto a piece of paper. As he never stopped to sign their autograph books! Other players to leave Everton, were John Gidman to Manchester United, Gary Megson to Sheffield Wednesday. Jim McDonagh to Bolton Wanderers and Imre Varadi to Newcastle United. They were all sold before a ball had been kicked in the 1981-82 season.

Rochey, Parker, Cooper, and Skinny Maca, who have moved up a school year at their comprehensive schools. Have chosen to visit their favourite place, Bellefield, today instead of going to school.

It's three games into the new season. Howard Kendall registered his first win as Everton manager, in a 3-1 win against Birmingham City at Goodison Park. This was followed by an 1-1 away draw against Leeds United, before they suffered their first loss in a 1-0 defeat away from home to Southampton.

With three games already played in the new football season, the lads want to get a few autographs 'cos during the summer break there has been a lot of transfer activity.

Howard Kendall has come in and signed seven new players. The local papers have named these players 'The Magnificent Seven.'

"It's a new season. So today with-it being September. I'm going to use my green pen," declares Rochey.

"Is that because we have signed two new goalkeepers?" asks Cooper.

"No, it's the only pen I've got," laughs Rochey.

It was still early days in the Howard Kendall reign, and in the coming months there would be lots of departures as he built his team and stamp it with the Kendall signature.

First out of the dressing rooms is Paul Lodge, who was part of the first team under Gordon Lee, the previous season.

"Hello, Paul. Can you sign our autograph books please?" asks Parker.

"New season, new beginning, Paul!" says Skinny Maca.

"Yeah, it certainly is. We're all working hard to impress the new manager," says a smiling Paul Lodge, as he drives away.

Paul Lodge went on to make sixteen first team appearances under Howard Kendall before he was sent out on loan to Wigan Athletic then Rotherham United in the 1982-83 season, before moving permanently to Preston North End.

Next out is Kevin Ratcliffe, who is all smiles as he stops to sign the books for the lads.

"Hello, Kevin. Can you sign our autograph books please?" asks Rochey.

"You're doing great under the new manager, Kevin. Two starts out of three," says Cooper, as Kevin Ratcliffe signs the books smiling before driving off.

Kevin Ratcliffe had become be part of Howard Kendall's plans and in time becoming his Captain Marvel. As well as becoming part of the furniture at Bellefield.

Next out was Mark Higgins who hadn't started any of the games yet.

"Hello, Mark. Can you sign my book?" utters Skinny Maca.

Mark Higgins signed the autograph books for the lads and drove off.

Mark Higgins, had a severe injury during Kendall's reign at Everton and was forced to temporarily retire from playing football in May 1984. Defying all the odds and expectations eighteen months later he joined Manchester United. However, he was unable to recover the form that had made him a stand out centre- half at Everton. He played eight games for Manchester United. He was sent out on loan to Bury where the loan was made permanent in February.

Next out of Bellefield was the cheerful Scottish winger, young Joe McBride.

"Hello, Joe. How was training? Can you sign on the dotted line?" says a smiling Cooper.

"It was a hard training session. But saying that it enjoyable at the same time," replies Joe McBride.

"Keep working hard, fight for your place Joe. You're one of our favourite players," says Parker.

"I will do," replies a smiling Joe McBride signing the autograph books, before driving away.

Joe McBride figured in eight games in Howard Kendall's first season in charge. He left Everton to sign for Rotherham United.

"Trevor Ross, has just got in his car!" shouts Skinny Maca.

"Let's stop him. I'm getting him to sign my book!" says Copper.

Trevor Ross, chats to the lads for five minutes talking about the new season under Howard Kendall.

Trevor Ross was named in the first game of the season under Howard Kendall. In the second game he was named as the substitute. He missed the third game. He went on to play twenty-eight games for Everton during Howard Kendall's first season.

During the 1982-83 season is game time was limited to just two games. He was loaned out to Portsmouth then Sheffield United. He left permanently to join Greek side A.E.K. Athens, who play their football in Greece.

Peter Eastoe followed next. He had started in the first three games of Howard Kendall's reign, scoring in the first game in their 3-1 win against Birmingham City.

"Hello, Peter. I see you've got off to a flyer. In the first game you scored. Impressing the new manager, I'm guessing?" says Skinny Maca.

"I would be impressed, if you went to school a bit more. You spend more time here at Bellefield, than at school," replies Peter Eastoe.

"We learn everything we need to learn here, Peter. Our specialist subject is Everton F.C," replies Skinny Maca.

"Plus, the truancy officer knows where we are. If he really wants to find us," says Cooper.

"He knows we will always be hanging out around the Bellefield gates, waiting for the players to come out after training. I think he is an Evertonian," smirks Parker.

"I think Peter Eastoe is after a job as a truancy officer when he hangs up his boots. I'm sure on his back seat are school-board forms to join up," whispers Rochey to Parker, as Peter Eastoe signs their autograph books.

Peter Eastoe, went on to play nineteen times scoring five times for Everton, in the 1981-82, season under Howard Kendall. He was sold to West Bromwich Albion in the August of 1982.

Next out of Bellefield was Asa Hartford.

"The players are coming out thick and fast," says Cooper.

Rochey looks at Parker and Skinny Maca, smiling, "Just, like you, hey Coop."

"It's not like, Cooper, then. He's not that fast," smirks Skinny Maca.

"Hey, I'm fast! I could beat you in a race!" snarls Cooper.

"Okay, you win. Your thick and fast, like the players, coming out," says Skinny Maca, grinning.

Asa Hartford stopped and signed all the books.

Asa Hartford had started in all three games of Howard Kendall reign, but unfortunately, he was living on borrowed time during that time as he was sold less than two months later to Manchester City.

The next two players out of Bellefield were two scouse lads, Mick Lyons and John Bailey, who had travelled together in John Bailey's car.

Mick Lyons, often gets called, Mr Everton. He's an Everton legend. Mick played twenty- seven games, scoring three goals in the 1981-82 season. He was sold to Sheffield Wednesday in the March of 1982.

John Bailey, become part of Howard Kendall's team for the next four seasons. He was a great character to have in the dressing room. He made everybody laugh with his scouse humour.

"Who's this on his way out! Is that Rod Stewart?" queries Skinny Maca.

"Rod Stewart? It looks more like Joe Brown!" says Cooper.

"It's Alan Biley. Yer pair of muppets! He's one of our new signings," replies Parker.

"He just scored two goals in his first two games, he's one of Howard Kendall's 'Magnificent Seven'," says Rochey.

"Look at the head on him. He's got some haircut," smirks Cooper.

Alan Biley drives up towards the lads, stopping to sign their autograph books.

"Can you sign our autograph books please, Alan?" requests Skinny Maca.

"Two goals, in three games, Alan. Well done," says Parker, handing him his autograph book.

"Is your nickname Spike?" asks Cooper, as he passes him his autograph book.

Alan Biley, who was one of the new signings scored two in the first three games, against Birmingham City and Leeds United.

Rochey, Parker, and Skinny Maca, all look at each other shaking their heads in disbelief. In football, managers come and go, new players are bought and others are sold. But with Cooper, some things never change.

Next out is another one of the new signings, Mickey Thomas. The little winger Everton signed from Manchester United.

Mickey Thomas stops to sign the books and Cooper does a little dance as he sings, "Mickey Thomas, might be Welsh, but he runs down that wing like Mighty Mouse, Mickey for England."

Mickey Thomas, looks at the other three lads, not knowing what to say.

"Don't worry, Mickey. You'll take to him after five years," laughs Skinny Maca.

Last out of Bellefield was Imre Varadi. He was wearing a pair of Jeans and a Jumper. He left Everton a few weeks earlier to join Newcastle United.

Imre Varadi, was at Bellefield picking up the rest of his belongings before heading back up to Newcastle. The four lads wished him all the best. They told him that his goal that knocked Liverpool out of the F.A. Cup the previous season would be remembered forever and that in years to come he would go down in Everton folklore.

This was the start of the Howard Kendall revolution. The papers named the new signing The Magnificent Seven:

THE MAGNIFCENT SEVEN

ALAN BILEY:

Alan Biley who was a centre- forward who was signed from Derby County. Alan scored on his Everton debut and followed that up with another goal the following game. The Everton fans thought they had found the new Bob Latchford. But things went a bit pear-shaped after the first two games. Alan scored just one more time. His dream start didn't last and after a frustrating spell of three goals in twenty-one appearances. Howard Kendall loaned him out to Stoke City in the March of that same season. Permanently selling him to Portsmouth at the start of the 1982-83 season.

MICKEY THOMAS:

Mickey Thomas, a winger, signed from Manchester United, in a part exchange deal, that saw John Gidman go the other way to Manchester United. Mickey Thomas spoke about being an Everton fan as a kid. His dream move ended with Everton after ten league appearances. Howard Kendall terminated his contract after he refused to play in the reserves. There was only ever going to be one winner in that stand-off. Howard Kendall showed his class as Everton manager. Mickey Thomas went to the seaside signing for Brighton and Hove Albion. Three months after he signed for Everton. People say they do love a day at the seaside, but that wasn't the case for Mickey Thomas, as his wife struggled to settle in Brighton. He moved to Stoke City the following season in 1982.

Howard Kendall showed leadership that day. He made a statement by terminating Mickey Thomas contract, showing he's the man in charge that no player is bigger than Everton Football Club. Rochey, Parker, Cooper, and Skinny Maca, still to this day can't understand how a footballer who supported the club as a boy would refuse to wear the royal blue jersey at any level. The four lads would have run through brick walls with no pay for Everton, such is their love for *EVERTON F.C.*

ALAN AINSCOW:

Alan Ainscow, a midfielder who could play on either flank was signed from Birmingham City. He scored on his Everton debut. He played twenty-eight league games for Everton scoring three goals. But he soon fell out of favour and in the 1982 season he was loaned out to Barnsley. Being sold permanently to Eastern AA who played their football in Hong Kong.

That was another one of the so called Magnificent Seven to bite the dust; that was three down four to go.

MICK FERGUSON:

Mick Ferguson, a centre-forward, Howard signed him from Coventry City. Less than a year after signing Ferguson he moved to Birmingham City, initially on loan before the move was made permanently. Mick Ferguson's record at Everton was quite good, scoring six goals in ten games. If you think Mickey Thomas was sold by Howard Kendall for being too big for his boots, you'd be entitled to think that as he really was sold because it came across as thought he was too big for his boots. The thing with Ferguson was that he only had little feet. He was a size 7 football boot. He only had small ankles that had to support his 6ft 3inch frame. which resulted in him always picking up injuries, not allowing him to play. Howard Kendall thought it would be best to move him on.

JIM ARNOLD

Jim Arnold, was one of two goal-keepers signed that summer who was part of the so-called 'Magnificent Seven.' He signed from Blackburn Rovers, at the age of 29. He started the 1981-82 season in pole position in front of the young goalkeeper Neville Southall that

Everton had also bought that summer. Jim spent four years at Everton mainly as understudy goalkeeper. He never let anyone down when he was called upon. In1982-83, he was loaned out to Preston North End then was sold to Port Vale, in the 1985-86 season.

MIKE WALSH

Mike Walsh was a no-nonsense centre-half that Everton signed from Bolton Wanderers. In the 1981-82 season he played eighteen league games for Everton. He was another one who fell out of favour. In the 82-83 season he was loaned out to Norwich City. He then went to Burnley, was recalled, making another two appearances for Everton. He left permanently when he signed for Fort Lauderdale Strikers in 1983.

NEVILLE SOUTHALL

Neville Southall who was the youngest out of the seven signing was signed from Bury. Out of the Magnificent Seven, he was the one that truly was Magnificent.

He spent seventeen years at Everton, and for quite a number of those years in his prime, he was considered to be the best goalkeeper in the world.

One out of seven is not bad. But to sign a player that would become the best in the world was some achievement.

So that's the so-called 'Magnificent Seven'.

There were two other players that signed for Everton during that period, that are often forgotten. One was Alan Irvine who was signed from Queen's Park on the 15th of May 1981.

Many would argue that he wasn't one of Howard Kendall's signings as Howard had only become the Everton manager a week earlier on the 8th of May 1981.

But there was another signing who should have been regarded as one of the Magnificent Eight, that everyone forgets about.

The player that should have been part of the Magnificent Eight was Howard Kendall himself.

He registered himself as player that season even though he was the manager. He played four league games that season before hanging up his football boots.

In the first two seasons of Howard Kendall's reign, he chopped and changed and wasn't scared to move a player on if he didn't think he was good enough for the Everton cause. Not many managers taste instant success. Managers who inherit a winning team may do. But a lot of the time it's finding the right balance and that is what Howard Kendall was doing in his first three seasons at Everton. He was finding the balance. Howard Kendall had his ups and downs in his first three seasons. He knew what had to be done to make Everton great again but had to be given time. As the saying goes, 'Rome wasn't built in a day.' When you become a manager, you automatically inherit the previous manager's team. It takes time to put your stamp on your team. When Howard Kendall did that results spoke for themselves when his players started to believe in themselves.

The rest after that is history that Evertonians will never forget.

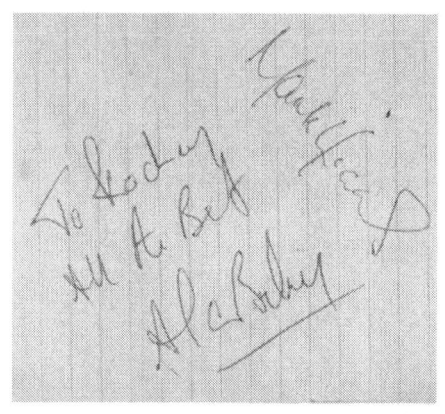

MARK HIGGINS

ALAN BILEY

TREVOR ROSS

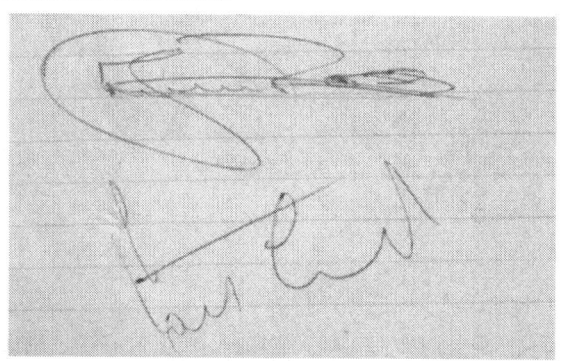

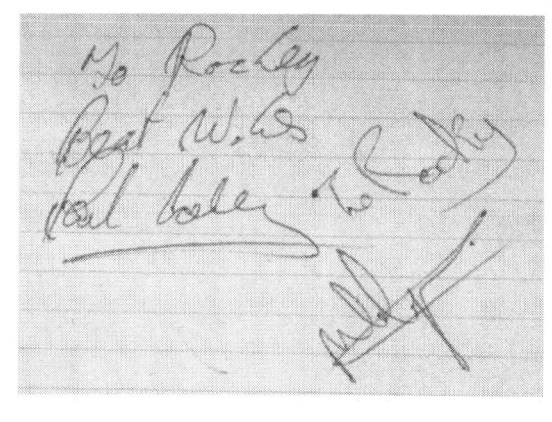

ASA HARTFORD

PAUL LODGE

MICK LYONS

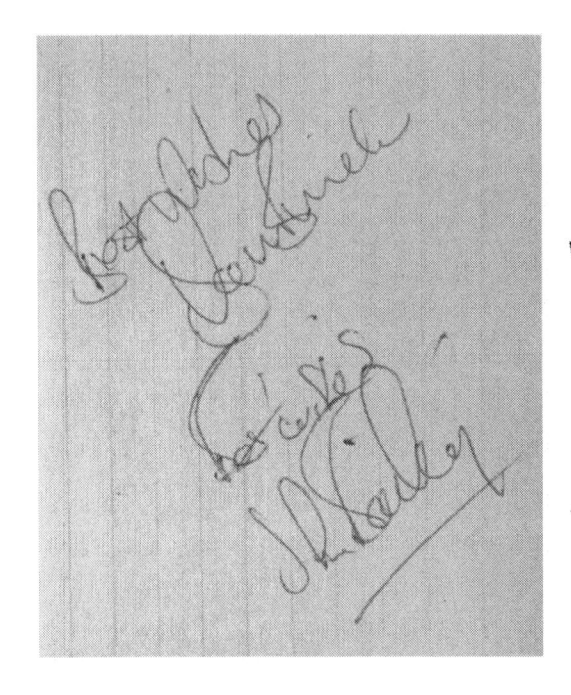

JOE
McBRIDE

JOHN
BAILEY

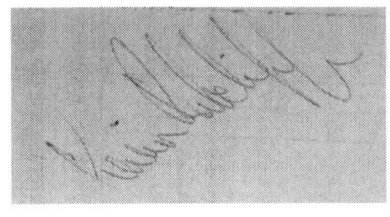

MICKEY
THOMAS

KEVIN
RATCLIFFE

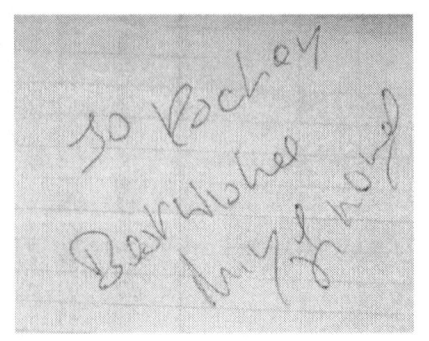

CHAPTER 21   TALES FROM WITHIN

KEVIN RATCLIFFE 1977-1992:

Kevin Ratcliffe spent 15 years at Bellefield. He started as a young lad who would become the most successful captain in the history of EVERTON FOOTBALL CLUB. Training every day at Bellefield became part of his life. Kevin shares a few stories of his time at Bellefield:

"I started my Everton career as an apprentice in 1977. The first time I walked into Bellefield I was a bag of nerves. I had been an Evertonian growing up in Mancot, Wales, and here I was walking into Bellefield to wear that famous blue jersey. I started off in the Everton A and B teams, playing in the Lancashire league. I remember playing in the reserves alongside Roger Kenyon, who was coming to the end of his Everton career at that time. I learned so much from him, it stood me in good stead for later on in my career.

Inside Bellefield there were four changing rooms. Two were for the first team players, another was for the young pros making their way up the ladder, and the other changing room was for us apprentices When I first signed, my job was to clean the dressing room of the first team; you weren't allowed just to walk into the changing rooms, you had to knock on the door and wait until you got the shout to enter. I shared these duties with another apprentice, George Tulloch, who was an apprentice goalkeeper. As the years passed, I moved up the ladder to different rooms. When I got into the first team dressing room, I was like, 'Wow! Have I hit the jackpot?' It was a great feeling, coming into work and heading into the first team rooms. I felt like shouting out, 'Top of world, Ma, top of the world,' I knew what James Cagney was talking about in that movie (White Heat) the day I got promoted to the first team changing room at Bellefield. I felt like I was on top of the world.

During my time at Bellefield, six managers sat in the manager's office, either as caretaker, or permanent. Billy Bingham, Steve Burtenshaw, Gordon Lee, Howard Kendall, (twice), Colin Harvey, and Jimmy Gabriel. As well as these six managers I would often bump into Bill Shankly who would pop in to give advice to the young pros. The first time I saw Bill Shankly at Bellefield was when

I was in the sauna. The door opened and in he popped. I was a young pro then. He just smiled at me saying, "Hi laddie, it's hot in here today." Many a time I would bump into him around Bellefield. Each time he would ask how I was, always ready to offer advice.

Bellefield was one of the best training grounds around back in the day. It was state- of -the -art, years ahead of its time. But saying that, you couldn't close the doors in the toilets! If you did, you could guarantee that a cold bucket of water would be thrown over the locked doors. Every Friday, players from the first team, down to the A and B teams, would gather around the glass cabinet where the team sheets were put up. There you would read if you were in the team for the game the following day. You weren't told if you were playing or not. I remember some players being over the moon, whilst others were ready to hammer on (or knock down) the manager's door, after reading those team sheets.

We would often play indoors. The pitch was made from a substance that was orange dust. You would come out of there with your sock's bright orange. There would be dust everywhere, although back then orange dust was considered state of the art. Nowadays in the modern training grounds, it's all artificial grass or astroturf. When you leave Everton, it's a very sad day. Not only do you miss the players; you miss everyone; the ground staff, kitchen staff, the tea lady, it's one big happy family.

Like the late great Andy King once told me:

"The biggest thing you miss when you leave Everton is Bellefield."

KEVIN RATCLIFFE.

MARK WARD 1977-1981:

Mark Ward had two spells at Everton. He signed schoolboy forms in 1977 and the club went on to offer him an apprenticeship in 1979. Gordon Lee released Mark in 1981. But like Arnie once said, "I WILL BE BACK." And Mark Ward did come back, ten years later, in 1991. this time to work under Howard Kendall. He loved his time at Everton and shares some stories of his experiences at Bellefield:

"My first memory of walking into Bellefield was as a twelve-year-old young lad playing for Whiston Juniors in a specially arranged game against an Everton Under- 12 team that had been picked from their best kids from around the country. It was like walking onto hallowed ground.

The facilities were second to none and the football pitches were like Wembley. I couldn't sleep the night before the game which, in reality, was a farce, as we got battered six nil.

My dad, Billy, was a massive Evertonian. He stood on the touchlines at Bellefield, proud as a dad can be. He was standing there with all the other dads.

After the match, Graham Smith, the youth team coach pulled my dad to one side and asked him if it would be okay for me to come and train with Everton on a Tuesday and Thursday night after school. Obviously, he said yes.

For the next two years, Bellefield became my training ground, with all the other local lads at hoping to become professional footballers.

I became a schoolboy, then an apprentice. Bellefield became my place of work. Cleaning boots was not a chore for me. Being around the first-team was amazing and Andy King made me his personal apprentice. He saw something in me and I looked after him in more ways than one.

Kingy was a legend. He sent me errands that some of the other lads would refused do, but I never once said no. He'd look after me with a tenner here and there, and if one of his bets came up it was a few quid more.

I ended up as a sixteen-year-old apprentice putting bets on at the Scofield's bookies outside Goodison before kick-off. I looked about twelve. I was there so often that I had an arrangement with the manager.

The day I was released by Everton was a horrendous day. Gordon Lee told me I'd never be big enough or strong enough, or quick enough, to make it at the top level.

I cried like a baby when I got home and told my dad. He was positive though and told me that as I got stronger, my pace would come and I'd be a player one day.

Hours later Everton sacked Gordon Lee. I often wondered if only they had sacked him a week earlier, maybe I wouldn't have waited ten years to make my first team debut!

A year previous, I'd won the 'Player of the Tournament' in Groningen with some big clubs competing.

We had the likes of Steve McMahon, Kevin Richardson, and Gary Stevens in our team and playing against the legendary Ronald Koeman.

I knew I had the ability, but it was still sad to be leaving the club I adored. Little did I know I would return ten years later, after a long career away to sign for the club, I loved."

MARK WARD: 1991-1994.

"Re-signing back for Everton was always my dream. It took ten years. My journey, after I left Everton at first took me to Northwich Victoria. Then, the big man himself, Everton legend Joe Royle, signed me for Oldham Athletic for £9,500. After that West Ham United signed me, before Howard Kendall, took me to Manchester City.

Walking into Bellefield brought all my memories back from my schoolboy and apprentice days. It was just the same. Immaculate from the walls to the grass. But this time I was a seasoned player who was still not big enough, but who was a lot stronger and so much quicker.

This was the second time Howard had signed me. He told me it was a mistake for the club to have let me go the first time. But it had been Gordon Lee's decision. The pain of leaving Everton the first time around never left me. I think that fueled the fire inside me to prove Gordon Lee was wrong.

My first day back training with the lads was one I'll never forget. We had shooting practice against Big Nev. Snods (Ian Snodin) betted me I couldn't chip him. I took the tenner bet. In my eyes, it was money for old rope. I dinked the ball with accuracy and precision, then watched the ball floating over Neville Southall's head and into the top corner.

BIG MISTAKE. I turned to Snods all smug with myself, but he had this big smirk on his face. It was at that moment that I sensed that something was not right. Then out of the corner of my eye I saw Big Nev sprinting towards me. I wasn't waiting around for him to congratulate me on a great goal, so I shot off up the pitch with him running behind me, shouting that he's going to rip my head off and kill me.

After four laps of Bellefield and with Big Nev still chasing me, telling me he was going to follow me home, I decided to take my punishment. He picked me up like a rag doll. He threw me on the grass, put his big boot on my chest, pushing me into the turf with his Welsh eyes glaring at me with that 'how dare you chip me?' look. Howard was screaming 'don't hurt him. He's got a game Saturday!' Big Nev was shouting at everyone, "Nobody chips Nev"" His moustache was flaring as he walked back towards his goal. Snods was on the floor pissing himself laughing. I had bright red stud marks all across my chest. I learnt a lesson that day. Nev and I eventually became very close and would often arrive early to play head tennis. For a goalkeeper, he had amazing skill and footwork. It was an honour to have played with the best keeper in the world at the time.

When Mike Walker was in charge, I drove into Bellefield and in the parking bay there was a parking space with MW written on it, so I thought 'Nice one, happy days. I'm in the big league with the big boys,' so I parked in that bay. Mike Waker drove up two minutes later and as I was getting out of my car, beeped saying that it was his parking space so could I move my car? I said, 'I can't boss. My car's broken down.' He wasn't happy! In fact, he was fuming, but I wasn't arsed; it made my day! It still makes me laugh thinking about that.

During my footballing career, I had three Everton legends manage me. And when I say that word. I'm not using it lightly. These three were proper Everton legends: Joe Royle, at Oldham; Peter Reid, briefly at Man City; and the greatest Everton manager of all time, Howard Kendall. I played for a lot of clubs during my footballing career but, as Howie once famously said (when he left Manchester City to rejoin Everton), 'With the other clubs it's just a love affair, but with Everton it's a marriage.'

I'm so grateful I got to play for my club, EFC."

MARK WARD.

TOMMY WHEELDON EVERTON 1976-1978:

Tommy Wheeldon signed for Everton in 1976 when he was eighteen years old, spending two years in the Reserve team. He never managed to break into the first team but, to this day he says those two years training at Bellefield were the best times in his footballing career. He recalls his first day at Bellefield:

"See you later, Tommy. Have a good one lad," were the wise words I heard from my dad as he left for work.

"Do you want a sarnie son?" asked my mum, with a smile as long as the river Mersey.

"No, thanks Mum. I'm signing for one of the biggest football clubs in the whole wide world today. I can't eat."

"You have to eat something, Tommy. You're training with the elite today."

"Don't you worry, mum. I will be okay. They'll most probably feed me after training."

"I'm not worried son, I'm the proudest mum in Huyton."

My parents left for work that morning, beaming with pride, their glow lighting up Liverpool. My mum walked into her workplace, Huntley & Palmers, feeling ten feet tall, whilst My dad couldn't hide his smile as he walked into Dunlop's in Walton.

I floated to the bus stop to get the number 76 Crossville bus up to Huyton Village, then jumped on the number 75 Corpy bus to Sandforth Road in West Derby. Sitting on the bus my head was spinning because I would be signing for Everton Football Club.

Could life get any better? Was this the greatest day of my life? All these thoughts whizz around inside my head. I got off the bus and walked down Eaton Road where I was passed by my boyhood heroes in their posh cars, Martin Dobson whizzed past, followed by Big Bob Latchford, then Steve Sargeant, who passed was giving a lift to Mick Buckley and Terry Darracott.

When I arrived, I climbed over the Big Blue entrance gates but, on doing so, I encountered a huge Alsatian dog, that had its eyes like black saucers, bounding towards me.

"Shit!" I yelled, as I jumped and scrambled back over the gates to escape the jaws of Everton's finest guard dog. Fortunately for me the head groundsman, Syd McGuiness, contained the excitable dog, with a treat after some soothing words. In the background Sarge, (Steve Sargeant) Mick Buck and Herbie (aka Terry Darracott) were laughing their heads off.

I overheard one of them remark, "If he can jump like that in the box when we get a corner, he'll be a great asset to the team."

I chuckled at that. Here I was, nearly eaten alive, yet the lads were thinking that I'd be 'good at corners.' That's how the pros must think, was my first thought as I reached the entrance doors of Bellefield. Mick Buckley smiled at me saying, "When he gets to know ya, he'll lick you to death. He's soft as shite."

I entered the Bellefield building for the very first time, where I was greeted by Colin Harvey who introduced me to the two Everton apprentices who would be looking after me: Ged Stenson and Paul Lodge. I got my kit off Lodgey and the number 19 spec next to big Mark Higgins, who played center-half.

My first training session was an 11 v 11, reserves v first team match. It was arranged so that the Everton coaching staff could get a good look at the new signings, namely Duncan McKenzie, Bruce Rioch and myself. I looked around Bellefield. It was unbelievable. You couldn't make this up in a fairy tale, yet this was now my life. After training, the boss, Billy Bingham took us, the three new signing over to Goodison Park to sign our contracts with the Club Secretary Jim Greenwood.

During the 1977/78 season, the Everton Reserve squad was joined by the legendary Bill Shankly, the former Liverpool F C manager. Before I'd met him, I'd hated him with a vengeance. My family were die-hard Evertonians. After meeting Mr Shankly, spending time with him on the training pitch, and listening to the advice he gave to all around him, my perspective towards him changed completely.

On the football pitches at Bellefield, I saw how Shanks would kick any player that tried to go past him, then bollock any player that didn't give him the ball. He would moan if you were on his team and conceded a goal, but would celebrate like it was a Wembley Cup Final when the tables were turned. When Shanks was involved, training was never boring.

I remember Shankly's passion for the game being incredible. In the changing rooms, all the players listened to his every word. He would tell stories about Jesus Christ, but not the Jesus Christ taught in Sunday school. No, the man he referred to as Jesus Christ was the Liverpool player, Ian Callaghan.

Daily, Shanks would give the players advice on how to progress in the game and, more often than not, Ian Callaghan would pop into the conversation. Shanks would tell them how Cally would do things. How he was the ultimate professional footballer, and the ultimate human being. According to the Gospel of Shanks, Ian Callaghan he was the player to be.

Shanks often told the players footballing stories after training. He'd stand there in the dressing room, wearing his Stan Ogden white vest and baggy undies. Shanks was a caring human being and regularly invited the players around to his home where we'd be treated to soup, prepared by his wife, Nessie, and then a session of 'Fetch' with their dog, Scamp.

Those memories of Bellefield will live with me Forever."

TOMMY WHEELDON.

JOHN BAILEY 1979 -1985:

John Bailey a local lad from the Four Squares, signed for Everon in 1979 from Blackburn Rovers. He played at left back and won a League title, an F.A. Cup, and a European Cup Winners' Cup during his time at Everton. He recalls his time at Bellefield:

"It was Gordon Lee that signed me for Everton. I remember my first day at Bellefield. I was a bag of nerves. It was like the first day at school all over again. I drove through the Bellefield gates and saw Yogi, the dog that belonged to Dougie Rose. Yogi was dribbling the ball around the Mini Wembley pitch at the front of Bellefield. Even dogs were was good on the ball at Bellefield. I was thinking of telling Gordon Lee to throw him into the midfield for the next game. I was hoping I would do well and fit in at Everton.

As I got out of my car, my legs were shaking. I walked towards the entrance and could hear shouting. My stomach was turning. I was greeted by Andy King who gave me the biggest welcome you could imagine. What a man! A legend in my eyes. Andy took me into the changing room and introduced me to all of the team. I just sat down in the corner starstruck. In the opposite corner was thunder-thighs Bob Latchford, Brian Kidd, and Mick Lyons. The place was full of international footballers.

The training ground was the best I had ever seen. It was state -of -the- art. Bellefield was a fabulous place. I couldn't wait to get into the dressing room each morning. There was always great banter at Bellefield. I was surrounded by a great set of lads. A few of us (John Gidman, Garry Stanley, Andy King and Gary Megson) would often go to the Pembroke Sports Club in London Road for a game of snooker after training if we had the Wednesday off. I remember a story Mick Lyons told all the lads one morning about the lads from Everton's 1970 title winning team. The older members of the team including Gordon West and Brian Labone, always had people reporting back to them if any of the younger players were spotted in nightclubs, buying jewellery for their girlfriends, or holding hands in public. Every Monday, after training, the senior players would hold council against those young footballers who were spotted. Those youngsters were led into a room to face the charges, the unfortunate youngsters of crimes such as, or simply just getting too big for their boots.

Gordon West would exert his authority as Judge by carefully placing a grey cleaning mop over his head. Only then were punishments handed out. He told us, the point of the council was all in a day's fun, that it was in our best interests to keep us on the right track, so none of the younger lads went off the rails. When Howard Kendall replaced Gordon Lee, the place got even better I began to witness a winning team evolve.

The 'judge' in my playing days was Big Nev, who usually took the law into his own hands if anyone chipped him during training. In Nev's world, chipping him was outlawed. Oh, and he didn't like it when I used to cut his socks in half either which in hindsight was a bit stupid as I sat next to him in the dressing room.

In 1982 I scored against Luton Town from inside my own half in a 5-0 home win, so, on the Monday morning in training at Bellefield, I warned Big Nev that he better be on his toes, reminding him I had done something not even Pele had done. Being a former altar boy, I can't repeat the words he said back to me. The deal to transfer me out of Everton was done on the motorway. When completed, I was asked if I wanted to be taken up to Newcastle that day. I said no as I needed to go to Bellefield to pick up my football boots and some other bits. The following day I was in Bellefield and Richard Keys asked if he could interview me. Half way through the interview and I asked him to stop. I was too upset to continue.

I left Bellefield that day with tears in my eyes. I knew i was leaving something special behind."

JOHN BAILEY.

PAUL BRACEWELL 1984-1989:

Paul Bracewell signed for Everton in 1984. He went on to win two league titles with the club. The first time he walked into Bellefield as an Everton player he was in awe of the place. He started to think of all the former Everton players that had graced the pitches at this training ground. When we asked him about his time at Bellefield, he give his insight:

"Bellefield was a working environment. The will to win was immense. The training there was a daily lesson in honesty and hard work. It didn't matter how much the club paid for you everyone was treated as an equal.

It was a great place to work, everyone played their part, from the ground staff to the kitchen staff. Howard made sure there weren't any superstars. Every day, the black bin liners worn by the players during training covered their kits in sweat.

No one wanted to get beat in training. It didn't matter the drill, whether it be small-sided games or head tennis, winning was in our DNA.

The big challenge during my time at the club was that once you win the first trophy you switch your attention to win the next one. Howard would always be looking to bring in new players. No one could rest on their laurels.

It kept everyone on their toes. The social side was a big thing with the gaffer. He made us go out together to form a great team spirit. There were no superstars at Everton during my time at the club. We were just a bunch of hard-working professionals that played as a team.

It was a great club to play for. Once you have put on that blue jersey, and run out onto the pitch in front of 50,000 Evertonians, you get a feeling that never leaves you.

Once a Blue always a Blue."

PAUL BRACEWELL.

ALAN HARPER 1983-1988:

Alan Harper had three spells at Everton, playing under the guidance of two of the Holy Trinity masters: Howard Kendall and Colin Harvey. His nickname at the club was 'Bertie Bassett' as he could play in all sorts of positions. He won two League titles, the F.A. Cup, and the European Cup Winners Cup during his time at

Everton. He recalls his time at Bellefield during those happy days:

"I remember my first day at Bellefield. It was pre-season and, being a local lad from Netherley, finding it should not have been a problem.

But with it being well hidden between all the houses, I kept driving past. I knew a lot of the players quite well as I had been playing against them for years in the A and B teams. I was quite lucky in that respect. It was like going from home to home.

The day I signed for Everton was one of the best days of my life. I loved going into work. I didn't class it as a job. It was a joy to train at Bellefield every day.

Everton was my extended family. It wasn't just the players but also the office staff, kitchen staff, ground staff, everyone connected with the place.

We're all one happy family. Every day was fun. It was a great set of lads. At the front entrance of Bellefield was the main door.

Above the main entrance door, on the first floor, was an open window from where the players would pour pints of water down onto victims who tried to enter the complex.

Nobody was safe! Especially the journalists that had given us a bad write up in the local papers. The poor postman got wet daily. We ended up calling him the 'wise postman' as, after a few soakings, he would deliver the mail under an umbrella.

One memory that sticks out to me at involved my great mate, Neville Southall, who was also my roommate. After training, the players would get a shower. Nev had a two-litre bottle of shampoo that would last a normal person a year. Then one day after training John Bailey, never one to be backwards coming forward, took it upon himself to sample Nev's shampoo. Bails was in the shower, happy as Larry, whistling Dixie, when Big Nev picked him up, turned him upside-down, and dropped him head first into the cold bath.

Bails didn't know, at the time but one of the apprentices had tipped Big Nev off. Even the apprentices knew not to mess with Big

Nev's shampoo!

Another memory again involved the man that you just didn't mess with. Big Nev that day drove into Bellefield, parked his car, (his pride and joy, silver Volvo) and went to train as usual. One of the players took it upon himself to take Nev's car keys and hide his car.

By the time Nev had finished training, his car keys were back, but his car was not in sight. Not particularly amused, he turned the air blue. No one was safe. He checked every corner of Bellefield. Even checking the indoor sports hall.

Thinking the joker had parked it outside the training complex. Nev legged it outside Bellefield checking every street as far as Queens Drive. No luck. Back at Bellefield with Nev bouncing around West Derby, the lads dared to laugh.

By chance, Nev noticed that the blue tractor that cut the football pitches was parked funny, so he checked the garage that it was supposed to be in and found his silver Volvo.

To this day the player who hid it never owned up. A clever move with hindsight as many players would testify to.

You never messed with Nevile Southall if you wanted to live and tell the tale. Those were the days. Great memories."

ALAN HARPER -THE RETURN OF BERTIE: 1991-1993:

"I signed for Everton for the second time in 1991. Howard signed both myself me and Mark Ward on the same day.

A few weeks earlier we had been under his guidance at Manchester City. Now we were both reunited with him at Everton. It was a homecoming for all three of us.

Bellefield was still that homely place with the same kitchen staff, same office staff, same ground staff. It was like I had never been away!

Straight away I was chatting with the kitchen staff with a cup of tea in hand, catching up. It was one big happy family.

After training I would drive out of Bellefield and stop for the young Evertonians like the four heroes of this novel to sign their books, or their football jerseys. I loved having a chat with them.

Those fans looked up to us and we needed to set them the right example. They were the bread and butter of the club!

Without fans, clubs don't exist. We got to know a lot of those kids who waited outside Bellefield. To us players, they were like family.

It was another two fabulous years back at Bellefield.

They're memories that I will never forget."

ALAN HARPER -The Coach: 2000 – 2005:

"The third, and final, time I returned to Everton was as the Under-18-team-coach. I had been at Burnley, coaching their youth team, when I got a call from Colin Harvey, who had been Everton's head of Youth Development at the time.

The young lads would change at Bellefield then get on the minibus and head towards our academy in Litherland. That felt a bit strange because, when I was an Everton player, all the players trained at Bellefield.

All the young lads in the A and B teams would play their matches at Bellefield, but now the young lads were shipped out to the academy complex. This was new to me. It didn't feel the same.

Walter Smith was the manager of the first team with his trusted lieutenant Archie Knox alongside him; two great guys that loved the game. I hardly ever saw Walter, but, when I did, he always stopped for a chat. I remember when I first returned, and he passed me as I was walking out of the Bellefield canteen.

With a smirk he said, "You've had more comebacks at Bellefield than Frank Sinatra."

The knowledge I absorbed from having Howard Kendall and Colin Harvey as my managers during my time as a player helped me provide a great foundation of knowledge for my journey as an

Everton coach.

'I did it my way', just like the great man Howard Kendall, used to sing. Howie also did it his way and led by example.

I left Bellefield for the third, and final time, in 2005. It was a place that, first time around, I couldn't even find; now it was a place I will never forget. Bellefield left me with so many wonderful memories."

ALAN HARPER.

JOHN GIDMAN EVERTON 1979- 1981:

John Gidman spent two seasons at Everton. He was a local lad from Liverpool, who an attacking full back. He made sixty-four league appearances for the first team scoring two goals. John took time out from his Spanish lifestyle in Marbella to recall his time at Bellefield:

"Gordon Lee, the then Everton manager signed me in 1979 as an attacking full-back.

When Gordon left in 1981, Everton appointed a new manager, Howard Kendall, who had plans of his own. Shortly after, I also left to join Manchester United in part-exchange for Mickey Thomas.

The first time I went to Bellefield, I looked around the dressing room and saw some big names all laughing and joking. Scottish internationals, George Wood, and Asa Hartford were sharing a joke.

My fellow Scouse, full back John Bailey, was cracking jokes too. Brian Kidd and Bob Latchford looked like giants, two great footballers. I trained every day with a great set of lads. I loved the club.

I started my career at Liverpool as an apprentice winger, before for Everton, via Aston Villa.

The day that Ronnie Moran took charge of the Liverpool youth team changed my life for the better.

He took me to one side and told me, 'Your new position is full back! I want you to do the same as you do as a winger but defend a bit more,'

I progressed to the Liverpool reserve side alongside, Tommy Smith, and several other famous Liverpool names. I was getting good reviews, but then my heart was broken when Bill Shankly released me at the end of that season.

I signed for Aston Villa and, the following season, won the F.A. Youth Cup, beating Liverpool in the final.

I loved the set up at Liverpool's Melwood but, Bellefield was years ahead of its time. Bill Shankly and I crossed paths many times after I left Liverpool. I held no malice towards him. How could you dislike Bill Shankly?

One lasting memory of Bellefield I have includes Bill Shankly, who lived around the corner and would often come in to train with the young lads. On this particular day I was on the treatment. As Shanks walked past, he popped his head through the doorway and looked me in the eye saying, "Giddy, I was wrong to let you go when I did all them years ago." It was short and sweet but I felt about ten feet tall. They were words I would never forget.

I loved driving out of Bellefield to sign the autographs for the young Evertonians milling about the Big Blue Gates. We were one big happy family.

I loved my cars and would park up my black BMW every day in Bellefield. A local garage heard of my passion for cars and asked me would I like a sponsored car.

I jumped at the chance. The day I picked it up, Ginger McCain was at the garage alongside Red Rum, his former racehorse, getting their picture taken. I looked for my car and was in shock! The car that had my name plastered all over it, in Everton blue, was a Skoda car! I didn't know whether to laugh or cry. I opted to laugh and took the keys. To be fair, it wasn't a bad drive.

The next day, the car was the butt of every joke across Bellefield. Bails was having a field day, taking the piss out of me and the car.

After training, Bails asked did anyone fancy going into town for a game of snooker as in those days, we had quite a bit of free time after training. So, myself, Gary Stanley and Gary Megson, said yes. John Bailey, who was still taking the piss, said, 'You three follow me in the tank. I'll lead the way.' Bails stopped at the first set of traffic lights and we smashed into the back of his Ford Capri 2000, his pride and joy.

He got out fuming shouting 'What are you doing?' Gary Stanley and Gary Megson were in shock. I turned to Bails, keeping a straight face and said "You said it was a tank, so I'm trying to wreck it so they take it back!" The four of us burst into laughter. John Bailey didn't take the piss out of it after that and we remained one happy family.

For my first six months at Everton, I stayed at the Holiday Inn Hotel. After training, Gary Stanley and Gary Megson who were also staying at the Holiday Inn would sit in my hotel room playing records. Whilst I sat nearby, playing along with my guitar.

In training the lads would take the piss after it Bails; leaked that myself, Gary Stanley and Gary Megson were retiring from football to form a boyband.

There was never a dull moment at Bellefield. I have some great memories of the place but, in football, things change and players move on. I never got to say goodbye to Bellefield.

On the way home, from a pre-season in Tokyo we stopped off in Los Angeles. In the hotel, I got a phone call from Ron Atkinson. I was joining Manchester United.

I boarded a plane that same day and, the next day I was a Manchester United player.

I had some great times at Bellefield with a great set of players. I loved Everton but in hindsight it was time to move on but I will never Bellefield.

It was a place that never left you, no matter what other clubs you signed for. It training ground that was years ahead of its time."

JOHN GIDMAN.

PAT VAN DEN HAUWE 1984-1989:

Pat Van Den Hauwe was a no-nonsense attacking full back. He signed for Everton in 1984 from Birmingham City. He made 135 appearances for the first team scoring two goals. One of two goals he scored, clinched the title for Everton in 1987, away at Carrow Road. He won 13 caps for Wales. Pat won two league titles and the European Cup Winners Cup during his time at Everton. He recalls those happy times at Bellefield:

"Howard Kendall was the Everton manager who signed me. The day I signed for Everton was like a dream come true. On the morning of the day I signed, I reported for training with Birmingham City.

The then Birmingham City manager was Ron Saunders, who had himself played for Everton. He gathered all the players into a circle before training and said five of us were leaving that day. He pointed at me and said, "Pat, go and get dressed. You're signing for Everton. Drive up to Liverpool. Howard Kendall is waiting for you!"

I was in shock. A few months earlier, I had watched Everton win the F.A. Cup, beating Watford 2-0. I didn't even know how to get to Liverpool but I somehow managed to find It. Howard sat me down and ordered a pot of tea.

We discussed the terms of the deal, including me how much I wanted per week in wages. I told him I'm not interested in money; just show me the forms and I will sign.

Howard looked me in the eye and said, "You will do for me, you're the type of player I want in my team!" With that he said 'Forget that cup of tea. Let's have a couple of pints of lager.' I was over the moon to sign for Everton.

My first day at Bellefield was daunting. The place was years ahead of its time. It was a lot different to what I was used to at Birmingham City. I looked around the changing room and I saw a team of winners. Howard set us up to all be focused, and he set up a defensive system for the back four to master. Every training session at Bellefield was a mission

Bellefield was our workplace; a place where Howard would work us hard, prepare us for the war that lay ahead. Matchdays, we would go out and battle as a team, every player working hard for each other. We never came back into that the changing room, without having giving one hundred percent. All the work we did during the week at Bellefield prepared us for the matchdays.

During my time at Bellefield, I don't think I ever took a penalty against the greatest goalkeeper in the world, Neville Southall. I would always stay in the background, away from the penalties, just in case I got lucky and scored one past him. Nev hated anyone scoring against him.

When we won the league title in 1987 at Carrow Road, against Norwich City, the journey back to Bellefield was the longest journey I had ever been on. Howard stopped the coach three times to fill it up with booze.

It was a great trip home with great teammates. Passing the Everton supporters on their way home from that match, in their coaches, dancing and singing, is something I still remember today. I work match days at Everton and also work for Everton in the Community and I'm proud to call myself an Evertonian."

Alan Ball once famously said, "Once Everton has touched you, nothing will be the same. These words came from a World Cup Winner. I understand the words he spoke, and the passion with which he said them. I love Everton. I love the fans. I was blessed to be part of a great Everton team.

The day Howard Kendall signed me was the day Everton touched me. Alan Ball was right. That feeling has never left me."

PAT VAN DEN HAUWE.

ANDY GRAY 1983-1985:

Andy Gray signed for Everton in 1983. He won the League Title, The F.A. Cup, The European Cup Winners Cup and the Charity Shield during his time at Everton. The Canny Farm Four nicknamed him 'Winalot'. Standing tall at 5 foot 11 inches, the

Canny Farm Four said he was the modern-day William Wallace. Both were Scottish; both leaders that led by example, myth had it that people who had never been in a battle alongside William Wallace thought he was seven foot tall.

In the years to come, people would hear tales about the aerial duels that Andy Gray was involved in. Those hearing the stories would think he was also seven-foot tall. Evertonians would be told all about the goals he scored with his head. Especially when he out-jumped Watford's Steve Sherwood in the F.A. Cup Final in 1984. Steve Sherwood was six foot four! And a goalkeeper!

Andy Gray made 49 appearances for Everton scoring fourteen crucial goals in matches such as the F.A. Cup Final and European Cup Winner's Cup Final. Andy Gray got twenty full caps for Scotland, scoring seven international goals. Now he recalls those happy days at Bellefield, alongside Everton's most successful team ever.

"I always remember my first day at Bellefield. I turned the corner on Eaton Road towards a row of houses, seeing the Big Blue Bellefield Gates for the very first time. I drove into Bellefield thinking I was driving into a housing estate.

At the gates I noticed, a few young supporters collecting autographs so I stopped my car, and signed their books, and had a little chat with them. Straight away I could feel the passion that they had for the club. I came to love this part of the job, signing autographs, taking about all things Everton.

That first day after I signed their books, I drove ten yards into Bellefield and all I could see were two football pitches either side of a car park. I was shocked because Aston Villa (the club I played for before I signed for Wolverhampton Wanderers) had a big open complex with lots of pitches. It was very open but, on the downside, it could get very windy.

I walked into the changing rooms in my blue jeans that I'd turned up at the bottom because they were a bit long, and I'm greeted by the lads. I noticed Peter Reid nudging all the players and them all laughing. I asked Reidy what was the joke? He burst out laughing, pointed at the turn ups in my jeans and said, 'You be careful you don't get a tug off the fashion police in them jeans!' The other lads all pissed themselves laughing. I thought to myself, 'The cheeky bastards.' I realised from that first day that I had made the right move and that these lads would do for me. I was surrounded by a great bunch.

I changed into my training kit and was shown around the back of Bellefield. There, I saw all the other pitches, the sports hall, all the other facilities. It was hidden away but the place opened up the more you walked around it. I was impressed. When I first drove through the Big Blue Gates, I was thinking I was driving into a housing estate but, in reality, I was driving into a state-of-the-art training complex. I loved how it was all enclosed and there was hardly any wind during practice matches. I loved the closeness of the place.

A few weeks before the 1985 F.A. Cup Final, the BBC asked me to give them a tour of Bellefield while they filmed build-up material for the day itself.

Everything was going great until it was time to take them into the changing rooms. Off camera, I told all the lads I would be bringing the BBC camera crew into the changing rooms so they could show the nation how we prepare and bond during the week at Bellefield. So, it was lights, camera, action. I walked into the changing room with the camera crew. There was not a soul in sight. No one. I just looked at the camera crew and shrugged my shoulders and said the place was full a minute ago.

The cameras stopped rolling when twenty players, who had all been hiding in the showers ran past me laughing their heads off. As they legged it and sang, 'Here we go, here we go, here we go.' I looked at Sharpie and Reidy, who had the biggest mischievous smiles on their faces. I myself couldn't hold my laughter in. Even in this moment of madness, I felt so proud of the togetherness of my teammates. The team spirit inside Bellefield was second to none.

On a Friday, in training, Neville Southall would have us all taking shots at him with his hands behind his back. he would head our shots clear. That or use his chest, or his knees or his feet. Even without using his hands he would still save most. As a striker, he didn't do much for your confidence.

No one could score past him. I think that comes with having the best goalkeeper in the world in your team.

Howard Kendall signed me for Everton giving me my most successful time as a footballer. I had two amazing years at Everton with a great bunch of lads and fans. I played in a team that would become the most successful in Everton's history. I will be forever grateful to Howie for giving me that pleasure.

Howie also sold me during the summer of 1985 which ranks as one of my saddest times as a footballer.

I never got to say goodbye to anyone at Bellefield. I would have loved to have one more day to say goodbye to my teammates, and all the amazing staff at Bellefield. I wasn't given that chance as I was sold during the summer break.

I also never got the chance to say goodbye to the amazing Everton fans, or to the young kids that stood outside the Big Blue Bellefield Gates in all types of weather.

I loved my time at Everton. At Bellefield we were one big happy family."

ANDY GRAY.

IAN SNODIN 1987-1995:

Ian Snodin, or Snods as he was known, signed in the January of 1987 and, in his first season with the club, he helped Everton win the League Title. His never-say-die attitude was well received by Evertonians, especially as he chose Everton over Liverpool. He added class and bite to the team whether that be from midfield or as a tough tackling full back. Snods made 148 appearances for Everton, scoring 3 goals. He recalls his time at Bellefield:

"The day before I signed for Everton, I had a choice between Everton and Liverpool. I met Kenny Dalglish in Burnley. Shortly after I met Howard Kendall in Blackburn with my then Leeds United manager, Billy Bremmer. I went home after the two meetings and, even before I got through my front door, I had made my mind up to sign for Everton. They were the team that had impressed me most. To this day I have never regretted that decision.

Everton is a top club. In most workplaces, including football, you're just a number. But at Everton it felt different. It felt like it was one big happy family and that everybody cared. I needed that belonging when I was on the sidelines injured for two seasons. At Everton they looked after me. I was made to feel that I was more than a number. That's why I was pleased to later return to the club to as an ambassador. Blue blood runs through my veins.

The first time I set foot in Bellefield, I was amazed with how good the set up was. At Doncaster Rovers and Leeds United, my two previous clubs, I had never witnessed anything what I saw Bellefield. Training in private grounds was new to me. I was impressed. The first time I put on an Everton training top, I felt so proud. From that day my love of Everton never left me. I always arrived at Bellefield early for training. and never wanted to leave the place after training. There we would eat together as a squad. We would go to the canteen where Mary and Lyn would make us cheese-on-toast, or a ham sandwich with a cup of tea. These were happy days.

It was one big family. When the squad finally did leave Bellefield to go home, we would be greeted by the best football fans I have ever come across. At the gates they would wait, wanting to chat us, or sign their autograph books. It showed me what a great club I had signed for. Each day I drove out and felt a million dollars. I loved Yogi. That was Dougie Rose's dog. Sometimes he would go for the players. Most of the time we would get away from him but, pre-season, after a big session, the last thing you would want was Yogi trying to bite a chunk out of your backside.

People often ask me about the funny times at Bellefield. I recall one particular time when the Everton A-team were playing a game on the B-team's pitch. It was 1988. Colin Harvey was the manager. I was out injured, and was pottering around Bellefield, when out of nowhere I heard someone shout, "Snods, get in here!" I looked up and it was Colin Harvey. I was thinking, 'What have I done?' as I walked into his office.

He was stuttering around his office like Norman Wisdom and grabbed me by the arm. Colin was fuming. He took me to a window that looked out onto the pitches. Then shouted down my ear, "What can't you see on that pitch? The one that the A-team are playing on?" I just shrugged my shoulders and muttered, "I don't know gaffer." (To be honest, I was just glad he wasn't gunning for me, for something I had done.

"Look closer! There are no white line markings on the pitch! Go and find Plug! Tell him I want him in my office, now!" Plug was our young groundsman, aka nineteen-year-old Jimmy Ryan, who was a cracking lad. I walked around to the front pitches and asked Terry Darracott if he had seen Plug.

I explained to Terry what the gaffer wanted Plug for. Terry, laughed saying, 'Don't tell him.' Before shouting Plug over.

Instead of the real reason, we told Plug that the gaffer wanted him in his office, right away, for some advice on the A-team match. We told him that when the gaffer tells him to look out onto the pitch and asks him what he can't see, to reply that he couldn't see any runs from the midfielders into the away team's box. Plug, smiling away, thinking he's up for a coaching job, marches into the gaffer's office nodding at Colin who, at this point, is about to explode.

"Plug! What can't you see on that pitch?"

With that, 'Plug, cool as you like, replies "I can't see any of our midfielders' making runs into their box."

Colin, who was already in a bad mood, looked at him disbelieving what he had just heard. 'What?!' Just as he was about to tear a strip off young Plug, he spotted me and Terry Darracott curled up laughing out of the window. He went from a raging bull into a laughing policeman in a split second. Luckily, Colin, saw the funny side. It put a smile on his face and ours for the rest of the day. I had great times at Bellefield; special memories that will be with me forever.

Across my eight years at Everton, I got to work under five managers; Howard Kendall, Colin Harvey, Jimmy Gabriel (who was caretaker manager) and Joe Royle. Four legendary former Everton players who understood what it meant to wear the famous royal blue jersey. The other was Mike Walker.

I spent eight happy years at Bellefield. Being out on the

training pitch, watching Neville Southall, (between the sticks,) making save after save, was a joy to watch.

I left Everton aged 32. I knew my best playing days were behind me. So, when I left for Oldham, it was with no regrets but at Oldham it wasn't the same. I did still miss playing for Everton, missed the set-up, the happy times I had at Bellefield. No other club ever came close. You leave may Everton but Everon never leaves you."

IAN SNODIN.

GRAHAM STUART EVERTON 1993 –1997.

Graham Stuart signed for Everton in 1993. He will be forever remembered for the two goals he scored against Wimbledon on the last day of the 1994 season. Those two goals cemented his place in Everton's folklore history, although people often forget about his goal line clearance that kept us up that day. Without it, Wimbledon would have got at least a point and changed Everton's course of history. Everton's kit man, Jimmy Martin, nicknamed Graham, Diamond Geezer. When Everton won the F.A. Cup in 1995 Graham Stuart's shot hit the crossbar that led to Paul Rideout scoring the winning goal. Graham talks about his time at Bellefield:

"I signed for Everton on a Sunday, at Bellefield. It became my workplace for the next five years. Harry the gateman opened the big entrance gates and said, "Welcome to Everton!" From that instant, I was drawn to Everton. It only got better as Harry escorted me to the manager's office.

The late, great, Howard Kendall welcomed me with a can of Heineken saying, "Get that down your neck, lad!"

He then took me for a bite to eat and told me all about Everton and how I would love the place.

He wasn't wrong. I still love Everton now. It's my club and always will be.

When I was at Chelsea, the training ground was huge and very open. It was always freezing out there. At Bellefield, I loved how compact and private it was.

On a Friday we got to play on the side pitch, by the front entrance that we called Wembley.

After training we'd sometimes meet the fans at the gates. Some had been there hours, waiting for us to sign their autograph books and chat to them. The Everton fans are magical people. I felt it an honour to be associated with them.

Howard Kendall signed me for Everton, then, during his last spell at the club, sold me which filled me with great sadness. I had no ill-feeling towards him as it was out of his hands.

The club were having financial problems and I was a sellable asset. I loved Howard Kendall. I would have run through a brick wall for that man.

Howard had two spells as manager during my time at Everton. Jimmy Gabriel enjoyed a brief period as caretaker manager, during the hiatus as did Dave Watson. Big Joe Royle was another manager I played under.

All great Evertonians. (Mike Walker also managed Everton during my time.

Every Christmas at Bellefield, each player would have to sing a Christmas song and whoever got voted the worst singer would have to dress up and do a lap of the entire complex.

Sounds easy enough? Except, Yogi, the groundman's dog, never seemed to appreciate fancy dress and would give chase, nipping away at their heels as they did their lap.

The rest of us cheering on Yogi from the safety of inside the building. It was great festival fun. There was never a dull moment during my time at Bellefield.

During the shooting drills there was one person who refused to get beat; the big man himself, Nevile Southall.

Nev was a perfectionist, the best goalkeeper I have ever played with. Once, during training, we were practicing set pieces and Nev got bored. The session was long and he wasn't particularly active for the majority of the drill, so he decided to amuse himself by laying down across the top of the crossbar at the other end of the pitch.

When the players saw what he was doing, it stopped the training session for a full ten minutes, we stood in wonder at the miracle. As a squad, we tried to figure out how had he managed to get up there? How was he able to balance and not fall off?

My last day at Everton was a bit of a shock to me. Howard rang me. On this occasion instead of offering me a Heineken. He asked me to meet him at the Logwood Mill Hotel, just off the M57.

As soon as I got there, Howard sat me down. I noticed he was sipping a cup of coffee. I realised then that something was not right. He turned to me and said, 'The club is selling you to Sheffield United, son. It's out of my hands. You'll leave today. You have been a great servant to the club and you'll be missed.'

With that he opened a bottle of Champagne, gave me a glass, reflecting on my time at Everton.

I left Everton with great sadness although, I was making a fresh start and enjoyed my time at my next clubs. After Everton I played for Sheffield United, Charlton Athletic and Norwich City.

But it was Everton that left something in my heart which has never left me. It's hard to explain the feeling. I guess only an Evertonian can understand.

All I can say is that my time at Everton was extra special and that Everton will always be my club."

GRAHAM STUART.

TERRY CURRAN 1982-1983. 1983-1985:

Terry Curran had two spells at Everton. The first spell in 1983 he was on loan. He could do no wrong on the pitch during that initial seven game loan spell. Everton were 2nd to bottom in the league table. Cooper still to this day says Terry Curran drove into the City of Liverpool cleared up the mess and steadied the ship at Everton Football Club. The following season he signed permanently for Everton, he recalls his time at Bellefield.

"Howard Kendall first signed me for Everton on loan during the 1982-83 season. The first time I walked into Bellefield I was amazed at the place. It had everything; full length pitches, ice baths, saunas, a massive indoor football pitch. The facilities there were second to none.

In my first training session, I looked at the players and thought to myself, 'I'm surrounded by all these fabulous football players. Why are they second to bottom?' I soon realized they were low on confidence.

During my seven-game loan spell, we moved up the table and confidence at the club was restored. I was happy at Everton.

John Bailey was one of the main characters at Everton, he would make people laugh all the time. It was a fantastic club.

I was ready to sign permanently but the transfer hit a few snags when Manchester United and Arsenal came in for me. The extra interest pushed the transfer fee beyond Everton's budget at the time. I was sent back to Sheffield United

The following season I finally did get to sign for Everton. Just before I signed permanently, Brian Clough tried to sign me for a second time at Nottingham Forest.

I thanked him, but declined his offer, telling him "Brian, I'm signing for Everton. There is something special about this team. This Everton team is going to win the league." He looked at me, puzzled.

It was great to be back at Bellefield, surrounded by a great bunch of young lads who were all winners. Peter Reid joined the club and what a character he was to have around Bellefield! The whole atmosphere around the training ground was a joy to be part of.

During one training session, Jim Arnold, the goalkeeper walked into the dressing room wearing the loudest tie you could imagine. Inchy, aka Adrian Heath commented that you could make a pair of bell-bottoms out of it. so, for a laugh, I cut it up into tiny pieces. Well, when big Jim Arnold found out, he legged me all around Bellefield shouting, "I'm going to kill you, Curran!" Luckily,

I was pacey and outran him. I was lucky enough to get to train every day with Neville Southall. He was elite. He was the best goalkeeper I have ever seen on a football training ground.

Those were great days although not all my time at Bellefield was out on the training pitch. I had a bad time with injuries during my time there and I felt those injuries held me back from unleashing my true potential.

During those dark days, our great Everton fans often lifted my spirits. When I first joined Everton, I drove out to sign some autographs and to have a chinwag with the fans.

I was presented with an Everton Plaque from an Everton fan engraved with the words *Nil Satis Nisi Optimum*. I still have it to this day.

Evertonians are great fans to play for. They know their football.

When I left Everton and drove out the Bellefield gates for the last time, I was filled with sadness.

But I also drove out with a wry smile on my face, knowing that the team that I joined, struggling second to bottom of the league, were now League Champions."

TERRY CURRAN.

JOE ROYLE 1962 –1974:

Joe Royle was the 'boy who became a man' during his time at Everton. Joe signed as a schoolboy for Everton in 1962. He made his Everton debut aged just sixteen, becoming the youngest player in Everton's history to do so. That day, a dream came true for the local lad from Norris Green. He won the league title in 1970, scoring goals for fun in that great Everton team. Later, he returned as manager and won the F.A. Cup. Joe recalls those golden times at Bellefield with a big smile on his face:

"My first memory of Bellefield was as an eleven-year-old lad collecting autographs. I grew up an Evertonian and lived the dream as a player and as a manager. When I was just ten years of age, my headmaster at Ranworth Square, Primary School, used to send me up to Goodison Park once a fortnight to pick up complimentary tickets of the then Everton manager Johnny Carey.

The Everton manager who gave me my debut at Everton, aged just sixteen was Harry Catterick. He was a strict no-nonsense type of manager who was great at his job and who was good to me.

I made my debut away at Blackpool in 1966. We were beaten 2-0 and a certain young red-haired lad bossed the game. It will always be a game I remember for two reasons: the first was because I got to wear that famous number nine royal blue jersey, and the second was that I got to witness the talents of that young red-haired lad, then Blackpool player, Alan Ball.

Alan seemed to dance around that frozen pitch, whilst the rest of us struggled to stay upright.

In my next training session at Bellefield, after I made my Everton debut, I was still on cloud nine. I was soon brought back down to earth after we finished training at Bellefield. I was sent back to Goodison Park with the rest of the Everton apprentices to do my chores.

I remember my great mate and fellow apprentice, Roger Kenyon, smiling at me saying, "Bins first? Or the mop?" We would often finish about four in the afternoon and, after we had emptied the bins, we would mop the floors, get the kits hung out, clean the boots, as well as many other chores. It was hard work. But the chores were always forgotten as soon as you got to put on that famous blue jersey, whether it was in training at Bellefield, or in a full-scale match.

There were four changing rooms at Bellefield: one for the first-team, one for the reserves, one for the young pros; and one for the apprentices.

There were strict rules and guidelines to follow during my time at Everton. We were told to report to training early, before the pros, who would roll in later at about nine-thirty to start their drills at ten. The Everton fans always sat on the back wall at Bellefield, alongside the press as we trained.

Back then Bellefield was the best training ground in the country, it was top notch, when I was a player.

When I got to train regularly with the first-team, Brian Labone a great captain in his own right, took me under his wing and looked after me, going so far as to give me a pair of Puma football boots. That made my week. I remember Brian once telling me, 'Never forget your roots, Joe. You're never bigger than the fans' I took that advice to every team I played for and it worked. Jimmy Gabriel was another who made sure I was looked after every day, giving me advice. I would look around the changing room seeing the Golden Vision, (Alex Young) and pinch myself, thinking (I'm really sharing a football pitch with these Everton greats.) even getting t to train daily with the Holy Trinity: Kendall, Harvey, Ball.

When I first met Howard Kendall, he said, "Hiya, you're promising, you, son. You have a great future in the game!" I couldn't believe it. I didn't even know that he knew who I was, never mind him thinking I was a good player. I went home to Norris Green that day happy as Larry. Colin Harvey was young man from Liverpool, who led by example. Alan Ball was the best player I have ever shared a pitch with. Watching him in training was a treat.

During my time on the pitches at Bellefield, I watched Tommy Wright being moulded from a midfield player into one of best right-backs I have seen. He went onto play for England in the 1970 World Cup finals, playing against that mighty Brazil team which went on to lift the World Cup. I became great friends with John Hurst, who I still meet up with most weeks! (Sadly, John Hurst passed away as I (The Author) was writing this book. Rest in peace, John)

I left Everton, and Bellefield, on Christmas Eve 1974. It was one of the saddest moments of my career. I loved Everton and always will. I didn't want to leave but it was out of my hands. At that time of the year most people get gifts off Father Christmas. I got Billy Bingham telling me I was getting sold.

Billy wanted to sell me to Birmingham City in a deal that would see myself, Archie Styles, Howard Kendall and Gary Jones all leave in exchange for Bob Latchford. Instead, I learned that Manchester City wanted me and that's where I told him I was going. I left Everton with a burning desire inside me. I was determined to prove to Billy Bingham that he was wrong to sell me. In hindsight I think I did just that by returning to the England squad under Don Revie and later scoring for Manchester City in a 3-0 win against Bingham's Everton side.

In one respect, I left the pitch happy that day. I'd shown Billy Bingham there was still goals in my locker. On another note, it wasn't a nice feeling, scoring against the club I loved. Everton were, and always will be, my club. But as a player when you're on that pitch, you're a professional and must always give one hundred percent, no matter who you're playing for, or playing against. You may leave Everton but you never stop loving the club."

JOE ROYLE THE EVERTON MANAGER. 1994-1997:

"I returned to Everton Football Club in 1994 as first-team manager. The Oldham Athletic chairman, who I had a great working relationship with, had given me permission to chat with Everton.

I met Cliff Finch at Goodison Park and was ushered into the press room my eyes were immediately blinded by camera flashes, the press eager to take their first pictures of the new Everton manager.

Before I knew it, I was led out that room, having been unveiled as the new boss.

I walked out of the press conference and returned back to Oldham, to clear my office and to say my goodbyes.

I knew Everton weren't in a very good league position with only 8 points.

I switched on the car radio and the Celine Dion song Think Twice came on but I didn't have to think twice. I was back at the club I loved.

I didn't sign a contract until two months later, but I didn't really care. I was back at Everton, the club that I joined as a young lad.

I was back as manager! I was living the dream.

The manager's office was fourteen feet long and fourteen

feet wide. It was the smallest office you could imagine, but, again, I didn't care.

I was back at the place I loved so much: my beloved Everton.

I think I only ever went into that office twice in all my time as a player. Now I was sitting in it as the manager.

During my time as manager, Ray Minshull, who was the Youth Development officer, at the time asked me could I be present at Bellefield for the signing of a particular schoolboy.

He thought this young lad was a bit special, so he thought it would be a good idea for me to meet him and his parents.

The schoolboy's name was Wayne Rooney. (I often wondered what became of that young lad when I left Everton.)

When we won the F.A. Cup, the feeling I had was one I will never forget.

I felt like shouting out the office window.

Everton! the 1995 F. A. Cup winners!

I sat in my office in Bellefield thinking of ways to improve the team to take us to even greater heights.

When I left Everton for the second time, it was again with great sadness.

I had a meeting with the chairmen, Peter Johnson, and found that we had a difference of an opinion over a player I wanted to sign.

I felt I had no choice but to leave the club with immediate effect.

I headed back to Bellefield and I explained my decision to my good friend, and club physio, Les Helm. Les said, 'Joe if you go, I go with you.'

I walked out of the Bellefield gates and never looked back. The sadness was huge. As much as I was hurting, my love for

Everton never left me and never will.

    Once a blue always a blue."

JOE ROYLE.

SIMON KENDALL:

Simon Kendall is the son of one of the greatest players to wear the famous royal blue jersey. His dad was also a bit special as Everton's manager. As a young lad, Simon grew up an Evertonian and, to this day, even living in the USA, he still loves the club. Simon crosses the pond to watch Everton a few times a season. Every time he returns to Goodison Park, the famous Kendall smile returns with him. His dad once famously said, 'With other teams it was a love affair but with Everton it was a marriage.' Simon was part of that marriage and in many ways is still married to Everton. Simon, recalls his days growing up as a young schoolboy at Bellefield:

"I don't think I need to convince you that Bellefield was a little bit special. To a kid growing up in the '80's, I can tell you, the place was nothing short of magical. I will keep the memories of my time there with me forever. That's not to say, as the son of the manager of Everton Football Club, I spent a lot of time there, but then who gets to spend countless days at their parent's place of work? Perhaps that's what makes the memories even more precious!

I moved to the US in 2015 and started to enjoy an annual tradition, allowing us to 'bring our kids to work' for the day. That involved bringing my 3 boys to a technology campus, where my colleagues entertained and educated them with science experiments and technology demonstrations. They always left with beaming smiles and, more than likely, the opinion that Dad doesn't do any real work! The next day the kids return to their school classrooms to share their experiences with their schoolmates. If I cast my mind back 35 to 40 years, I can't help but think that I would have had the coolest stories to share about my parent's workplace!

Although the points were being put on the board at Goodison Park, it was the hard slog on the training pitches at Bellefield that laid the foundation for the most successful period in the history of Everton Football Club. Of course, I'm immensely proud of everything dad achieved, with the most vivid memories coming from those magical mid-80's.

Although my visits to Bellefield were not frequent by any means, they followed a similar routine each time. Shortly after arriving, Dad would get to work, overseeing the morning training session. That would leave me with a few hours to kill and there was nowhere better to do that than the huge indoor artificial pitch, which with all the players outside, I would often have to myself, I'd spend hours smashing balls against the walls, until my legs practically fell off.

The only interruption to this routine would come from random security checks. "What are you doing in here?" was the usual question that would come echoing across the open space. I'm pretty sure they thought I'd scaled the Bellefield perimeter wall and come in for a kick-around. "Dad told me to play in here!" was the usual retort. "Oh yeah, and who's your dad then?" was the natural progression of the interrogation. The response of, 'Howard Kendall,' would quickly put an end to the questioning and they'd let me get back to my business! It's fair to say Dad commanded respect but equally seemed to have fantastic relationships with everyone at the club.

A visit to the changing rooms would follow the kick-around. It was a chance to enjoy the huge baths. It also meant braving the cold plunge. I distinctly remember hovering over the edge, dipping my young toes into the icy cold water, debating whether to 'man-up' and take the plunge, only for Terry Curran to run up behind me and push me in.

Later in the day, Dad would often be working out of his Bellefield office. It had large windows and was positioned on the front floor as to have a great view of the outdoor pitches. While he worked through a sizeable stack of letters, took calls, held meetings, I would make my way to the pool table in the dining area. The uninitiated would have to keep feeding the table coins with each game. Those of us lucky enough to know the players' secret would locate the stash of socks and stuff them into the pockets to stop the balls from being swallowed. Hard to imagine players being asked to pay to play pool in the current era!

You didn't get to leave Bellefield without a flash of Sid McGuinness' smile and a few words. I used to love bumping into Sid while he went about his duties, tending to the numerous pitches as one of Bellefield's groundsmen.

Those pitches always looked immaculate! I was very sad to hear of his passing in 2020, and that of Dougie Rose, Bellefield's Head Groundsman, who passed away in April 2023.

As we drove out of Bellefield, there would often be a handful of fans looking for a word, an autograph, or a picture with Dad. In fact, in Anthony's last book, 'Having a Ball with Kendall and Harvey, 84-85', he captured this nicely.

He tells the story of Dad's car being stopped by the Canny Farm Four while I was with him, the lads asking Dad questions, keen to find out if his son would also be travelling to Rotterdam for the upcoming European Cup Winners' Cup final back in '85!

Being the only visitor to Bellefield on days like those described above, will leave me with memories to cherish for life. But it was equally exciting to be part of those Bellefield Open Days when the doors were opened up to supporters.

The atmosphere on those days is hard to put into words. To see so many people getting close to the team, to see what it meant to them, it only created a stronger bond between the club and the fans.

I stumbled across a Twitter post recently where someone had posted a picture of themselves alongside Dad at one of the Open Days.

There I was, next to him, clinging onto one of those orange Wembley Trophy balls that some of you may be old enough to remember from your own childhoods. Of course, times change and the world of football today seems so far removed from the game I fell in love with as a child.

There is an unprecedented level of investment, often through foreign ownership.

The need for clubs to increase revenues to remain competitive especially with the restrictions of Financial Fair Play has seen many clubs invest in new stadiums. Everton are no different and it's so exciting to see the plans for our own at Bramley Moore Dock.

Behind the scenes, the finest state-of-the-art training facilities have become essential to help clubs continue to grow and remain competitive.

For that reason, our own move from Bellefield to Finch Farm in 2007 was not a surprise and represented a new chapter for the club, just as the move to Bramley Moore Dock will.

The current generation will, of course, create their own lifelong memories at Finch Farm and we were so proud of my niece, Holly, who was so excited to train with the first team there, during her time with the Everton Women U-21's.

Knowing the story of Bellefield has come to an end only makes the memories even more precious. I'm sure you will enjoy this book, as Anthony paints a picture of life at Bellefield, during those great days."

SIMON KENDALL.

CHRIS RYAN EVERTON HEAD- CHEF 1984 – 1989.

Chris Ryan was Head Chef at Bellefield serving breakfast and lunch to the Everton playing staff. Chris first began his journey working at Goodison Park as matchday Chef. Before being poached to cook for the whole squad at Bellefield. Chris recalls of his time as head chef at Bellefield:

"I worked under two managers at Bellefield; Howard Kendall and Colin Harvey, both great managers who made my time there so enjoyable. I would start work at eight in the morning getting the breakfast ready for the players before they started training at ten.

Most days, I would leave around 3pm, unless there was a midweek match when, on occasion, I would travel with the team. My job on those long-distance coach journeys was to the microwave the meals on the way home.

My first day at Bellefield was a real mix of emotions. Walking into the main entrance, aged just twenty-one. I was nervous but excited, proud that I was going to Bellefield as Head Chef.
As an Evertonian I would get to meet my heroes. The nerves soon vanished when I was introduced to the management team and the players. They made me feel at home straight away and I was made to feel like one of them.

Howard Kendall always said Bellefield was one big happy family, from the tea-lady up to the management team. Him saying that always made me nervously laugh, as it was me who made the pots of tea for the tea lady to pour out for the players. I had to be on the ball every day.

When I was Head Chef, my kitchen area was tiny and, hygiene wise the regulators weren't as strict as in today's football. Also, the diets of the players weren't as strict as in today's modern football.

For example, jacket potatoes were on our menu. Kevin Ratcliffe and David Unsworth loved them. Adrian Heath, aka Inchy, liked bacon on toast.

Neville Southall, who was a true professional, always popped his head into my serving hatch and would shout, "Shoey, do me one of your special cheese toasties!" Shoey referred to Shughie McFee who was cook in the long running soap *Crossroads*.

Pat Van Den Hauwe loved his chicken and ham salads. Scrambled eggs were a favourite dish of the management team. All the dishes were washed down with a big pot of tea.

Whenever there was a live a live F.A. Cup, draw, all the

players would gather in the kitchen area and listen to a little radio we had in the kitchen. The noise was frightening when Everton's name got pulled out the hat

It wasn't just the Everton team who came in to eat; lots of former players would pop in too, Jim Pearson loved a bowl of chicken soup, whilst Gordon Banks, who was doing a bit of coaching at the time, loved a jacket spud with chicken.

I would look out my hatch and see Gordon Banks and Neville Southall in the same room, eating what I had made for them. Two goalkeepers who, in their day, were the best in the world.

I remember the occasion when Big Ron from the Swan, aka Ron Atkinson, walked into the canteen wearing a trench coat down to his ankles, a pair of football socks tucked into his tracksuit bottoms, and a pair of football boots. He'd been watching a match outside on the Bellefield pitches.

Simon O' Brien, aka Damon Grant from Brookside, would also often pop in and chat with the players.

One of the funniest men to pop in was Howards Kendall's mate, local comedian, Jackie Hamilton, aka Johnny Kearns.
It was non-stop laughter when he was there.

I remember one story he told about being a television extra in the drama Tenko. He said he had just been for lunch and had downed a couple of pints of lager with his food. When he returned to the film set, he was playing a prisoner of war, when all of a sudden, the director stopped the filming and shouted over to Jackie, "Hey, lad! This is supposed to be a Japanese Prisoner of War camp where the prisoners are under nourished and under fed. You're in the line up with two rosy cheeks and an ale gut!" Quick as a flash, Jackie Hamilton replied, "I know that! I only got caught this morning!"
Filming had to be halted for half an hour as everyone couldn't stop laughing including the director. Everybody at Bellefield loved Jackie's stories. They were great for team morale.

After I finished my work duties, I would often use the facilities at Bellefield. It was an amazing place. Sometimes, if a team was a man short in the head tennis games, Howard, or one of the coaching team, would ask me if I fancied joining in. I never once refused. I was living the dream! After these games I would often get a lift into town off Sharpie, Gary Stevens, or Peter Reid in his little black Fiesta.

In 1989, the year I walked out of Bellefield. I left with great sadness! I was gutted. But I had to move on in order to further my career as a chef. I left with a letter of recommendation from Colin Harvey, such was the greatness of the man."

CHRIS RYAN

TERRY ANDERSON EVERTON SUPPORTER FOR OVER 50 YEARS

Terry Anderson had the pleasure of playing at Bellefield with his football team, Kensington Fields. Lots of teams down the years have graced the Bellefield pitches, but, for Terry and his mates, this was a special occasion because after winning a cup tournament they got invited to play against Howard Kendall and his back-room staff. Here Terry Anderson recalls that special day, one he will never forget:

"I remember the day as if it was yesterday, when in fact it was in 1985. I was only nineteen. I was part of the open-aged Kensington Fields football team which had won the Radio City Cup a few weeks earlier.

First prize ended up being the right to play an Everton select team at Bellefield training ground.

The whole team was in shock. We all thought we were playing for a winner's medal.

On the morning of the game, we were all excited. Everyone's football boots were spit polished.

My mate, Gavin, who was a big Evertonian like myself, was speculating over who we might be playing against.

Most of the lads were either from the Bully, known as St Andrews Gardens or from Kenny, aka Kensington.

We had some great players in the team besides me and Gavin we had a mixture of ages. Maney, Gavin, Brownie and Brick, kept the midfield solid.

John Packi, Nicky Holt, Harnick, and Big Gilbo, sorted out the back four, with me and my other mate, Gerald up front, with Balla between the sticks, in goal.

We walked into the dressing rooms and it was unbelievable. Everton legends, past and present, had got changed in these very rooms.

Whilst we're getting changed, it was confirmed that we would be playing an 11 a-side match against Howard Kendall and his back-room team. The venue would be in the sports centre, on the indoor pitch. Thirty minutes each way.

The smiles on the faces of the players in our dressing room could have lit up Blackpool. Most in the team were Evertonians but even the Liverpool supporters were on cloud nine. This was a dream come true for everyone in our team.

We got changed into our kit then we walked out the dressing room towards the indoor pitch, we noticed that Howie and his team were wearing the full Everton strip. Just seeing those royal blue jerseys sent shivers down my spine.

I whispered to Gerald about swapping shirts with them after the match, but our manager, Jeff, shook his head reminding me that we didn't have megabucks like Everton and that we only had two full kits to our name. That idea soon went out the window!

When we took to the pitch. Balla our goal-keeper noticed the goals weren't full size. They were more in line with five- a-side pitch goals, which pleased him. "Nothing's getting past me today!" he yelled at the top of his voice. My mate, Gavin was in awe as he saw Colin Harvey and Howard Kendall take their positions.

Terry Darracott, Mick Heaton, (who was the first team coach at the time) John Clinkard, (physio) and Graham Smith, (Youth coach) also wore the royal blue jersey that day.

The match itself will live in my memory forever, as I came close to scoring with an effort that hit the goalpost.

Even though we got beat 1-0 courtesy of a Howard Kendall goal. He and Colin Harvey had us chasing shadows.

It was men against boys. We were up against two thirds of the Holy Trinity, that, in their day, were the best midfielders in the country.

At the end of the match as we walked of the pitch Howard Kendall and Colin Harvey were full of praise saying we were a good team and had played well.

The then Everton player, Alan Harper, who had watched the match, from the sidelines was grinning, taking the piss out of us saying "You let a team of old men beat you!"

I responded "old men? We couldn't get near them." Gavin, came back with, "old men lose a bit of pace, but never lose their knowledge of the game.

They didn't need to run around. Their footballing brains had us running around in circles." We left the pitch full of smiles. We had such a laugh out there on that pitch.

It was an unbelievable memory, one that will never leave any of our team that day. What a day that was at Bellefield!"

TERRY ANDERSON.

SUE ENGLAND EVERTON CLEANER 1998 – 1999.

Sue England was a cleaner at Bellefield during Walter Smith rein as Everton manager. Like previous managers before Walter, and many after him, the one thing that all the managers had in common with each other was it didn't matter what job or pay-scale that you were on from the tea lady to the cleaner to the caretaker, right up to the management team - the manager always treated everyone the same. Each role that each person did was just as important as the next person, as this is what made the team tick. It became one happy family and everyone was happy. which helped create a bond of togetherness and helped to create a successful team. Sue recalls her time working at Bellefield:

"I remember my first day as if it was yesterday. I walked into Bellefield, a bag of nerves. I was only supposed to stay there for a few weeks as cover for a woman who was off sick. In total, I stayed there for over 8 months.

When I walked through those Bellefield entrance gates the first time, I was amazed at how big the training ground was, hidden behind rows of houses.

On my first day, I was taken into the building and straight away was made to feel welcome. I was given my duties as a cleaner.

I would mop the stairwell, the dining area, and some of the upstairs offices which would also require get a spring clean and hoovering.

There were parts of the building that were no-go areas, such as like the manager's office and the changing rooms. One of the first things that struck me were the four hoovers. They were all the colour blue!

I was introduced to Jimmy Martin, the Everton kit-man, on my first day. He helped me settle in, a true gentleman. He told me if I wasn't sure about anything to just ask him. He was like a big brother to me. After a few weeks in the job, I was mopping the stairwell as the players walked into the building after a hard session.

Jimmy Martin stopped the players and told them to wait at the bottom of the stairs until I had finishing mopping the stairs.

Every player waited patiently until I had finished then smiled saying, "Thank you, Sue," as they passed.

There were no airs or graces about any of them. They were all lovely young lads who made my stay working at Bellefield so memorable. It was such a lovely place to work. It really was one big happy family. All the staff that worked at Bellefield were lovely people.

Walter Smith, who was the Everton manager at the time, would often pass me with the biggest smile as I was hoovering the floors. He treated all his staff with the utmost respect; it was a pleasure being part of his team.

The Everton players were all true gentlemen who couldn't do enough for the Bellefield staff regardless of their station.

One day I left a birthday card at the front desk to get signed by the players. It was my daughter's birthday and I couldn't think of a better gift.

As they arrived, one by one, every last one of them stopped at the front desk and signed the card. They handed me it saying, "Say Happy Birthday to your daughter, Sue!" I couldn't believe that they knew my name;

When I got home that night I was still in shock. And the look on my daughter's face the next morning when she opened her birthday card! Priceless!

A few weeks into my job, I was mopping the dining area and in walked David Unsworth. He shouted over to me saying, "Sue, put that mop down and have some toast with your cup of tea!" I went to drink my cup of tea, but it was spilling everywhere. My hands were shaking that much! I was starstruck!

The day I was told that the woman I had covered for was coming back to work, I was devastated.

I didn't want to leave. All I could think of was that I was

never going to see my adopted Everton family again. That very same day as I left the building, the Everton players wished me all the best and thanked me for keeping the place so clean.

I walked out of Bellefield and didn't look back. I had tears rolling down my cheeks.

I had walked through the gates eight months earlier, a red. Now I was leaving with so much love for Everton Football Club.

That love has never left me. I will never forget my time working at Bellefield.

I often pass the site where Bellefield once stood and reminisce about my time there.

The leadership of Walter Smith, the kindness of Jimmy Martin and the caring side of David Unsworth. Those memories can never be taken away from me.

I was so proud to have worked at Bellefield."

SUE ENGLAND.

DEREK WALSH 1983 – 1987:

Derek Walsh signed for Everton as an apprentice in 1983. A year later, he was in the Everton youth team that won the F.A. Youth Cup. He also represented Scotland at youth level. He made his Everton debut in 1985, in the title winning team. He recalls his time at Bellefield:

"I signed for Everton when I was just fifteen years old. I was a Scottish schoolboy international and I signed for them on the same day as Andy Gray.

I'd had trials at other English clubs before then at places like Nottingham Forest and Aston Villa. In Scotland I'd had trials with teams like Celtic, Motherwell, Dundee United and St Johnstone.

Back in Scotland, teams were training in public parks. At Forest, even though they'd been European Champions and had won the English First Division, their training facilities weren't much better: about a pitch and half of grass.

But Everton were always ahead of the game and they were one of the first clubs to have their own training ground and facilities. Bellefield was just miles and miles ahead.

At Bellefield, we had two good pitches; we had an indoor area with astroturf; a gymnasium, sauna, treatment rooms; we had the lot! There was also a dining area where we were provided with a three-course meal after training, every day.

I was the last apprentice at the club. After me, it was a batch of Youth Training Scheme players. Along with me there were two other apprentices. We trained a lot with the young pros and mixed with the first-team as well.

Obviously, Howard Kendall was the manager at the time and you knew he was the boss! He ruled the roost. He was a great guy and he could talk to anyone.

He was great with people. I used to think he could have been like the CEO of a multi-national corporation. He was that sharp and professional.

A measure of Howard's charisma came when Everton were hosting Watford at Goodison and Elton John came to the game. He was one of the biggest stars in the world and, yet, he was the one asking Howard to come for a drink after the game.

Bellefield was where Howard built his teams. I remember he said he always liked to watch the first half of a match from up in the stands. He said he could see things more clearly from the evaluated vantage point.

At Bellefield there was a flat roof and Howard would have one of the apprentices put a chair up there so he could climb out of his office window so he could sit there, watching. It was always on your mind. In your peripheral vision, you would always be checking for the gaffer up there.

Bellefield was also where he prepared for games. Training was very regimented. Howard developed your skills by making you a better footballer. The pitches at Bellefield were like a carpet, perfect for skills work. There were lots of five-a-side games, head tennis, that kind of thing.

I remember one day, there was a pool competition and Howard played Stuey Rimmer. Howard potted the black from the break. Stuey should have won because of that. But Howard ripped the rules off the wall, took them to his office, then came back to insist the frame had to be replayed. Stuey was such a nice guy that he allowed it and Howard won the frame.

When I arrived at Everton, Howard was under a bit of pressure. But, over the next few years, we won the FA Cup, the League, twice, and the European Cup Winners Cup. Everton had fantastic players at the time, including the likes of Andy Gray, Gary Lineker, Neville Southall, Gary Stevens, Trevor Steven and Derek Mountfield.

Howard was meticulous about preparing for individual teams. For example, Wimbledon were in the First Division at the time. You knew that fixture would be a huge physical battle. Howard's training would reflect that.

Howard once brought in Gordon Banks as a specialist goalkeeping coach for Neville Southall. My uncle had played with Gordon at Leicester City, so I had spoken to him before training.

During shooting practice, because Nev was so good, you would feel like doing a lap of honour if you managed to score. Well, I scored and ran away shouting, 'Don't watch my eyes Nev!' (Referring to giving a goalkeeper a clue where you're going to hit it.) The thing is, I ran straight into Gordon who shouted back, 'Don't watch my eye.' A bit of a faux pas with one of the world's best goalkeepers!

It wasn't all work, work, work, though. There were lots of laughs and lots of great characters around Bellefield. The likes of the groundsmen (Dougie Rose, Sid McGuinness, and the dog Yogi) chef (Chris Ryan), and so many more.

My favourite person who worked at Bellefield was a lad called Dave Ash. Everyone loved him. He was a doorman and amateur boxer. We had the physio, John Clinkard, and a doctor who drove a Porsche.

I remember John Bailey nicked the spark plugs one day and the doc couldn't work out why his car wouldn't start. That was the atmosphere around Bellefield.

It was where Howard Kendall made Everton a great club in the 1980s! It was a really special place."

DEREK WALSH.

PETER REID 1982 – 1989:

Peter Reid, the lad from Huyton, signed for Everton in 1982. One word summed him up, WINNER. During his time at Everton, he was the General; if you were in a hard-fought contest out on the pitch, he would be in the middle of the pitch leading by example. Peter recalls his time at Bellefield:

"Howard Kendall, signed me in 1982. For me to sign for Everton was a dream come true. A year earlier, Everton had tried to buy me but, for one reason or another it hadn't materialized. It was a bit upsetting at the time, but I just gritted my teeth and kept playing to the best of my ability. So, the day I did sign, I went home and rang my old mate from Bolton Wanderers, Neil Whatmore. We ended up having a bevvy, but one led to another one, to another, then a few brandies for a night cap.

The next day I took my football boots to Bellefield but, in all honesty, I felt that rough I should have worn a pair of workie boots. I was awful! During the warm up, the gaffer called me over saying, 'Reidy you will pair up with me, we can run together,' I thought, nice one, I have got a chance here to hide my hangover. How wrong I was. The gaffer lapped me!

The practice match didn't go any better. On that first training session, I would have struggled to trap a bag of cement, so maybe I should have worn those workie boots. The players were looking at each other thinking. Is he a footballer or has the gaffer just dragged him of the street to make the numbers up!

After training, I was summoned to the Gaffer's office. I was thinking, 'Oh here we go, I'm getting sent back to Bolton.' I walked in, and, before he could say anything, I held out my hands and said, 'Gaffer I need to explain something. Last night I was so overjoyed at signing for Everton that I had a few beers to celebrate. But I think I might have overdone it a bit. It will never happen again.'

The Gaffer looked at me saying, 'So, you like a drink son? I replied, 'Yes, I like a drink'.

He looked at me with a big smile on his face, and said, "You will do for me, son. You will have a great career at this club." I walked out of his office feeling ten-foot-tall.
I would have run through a brick wall for that man. Training was a pleasure. After that first day, I knew that I was surrounded by a great set of lads who could all play football. And there were some characters at Bellefield.

In the pre-season of '86. I had been in Mexico with England at the World Cup Finals. In my first training session back at Bellefield, the Gaffer was watching from his chair on the roof-top, outside his office window. After training he asked me to come up to his office.

I was walking up those stairs thinking, what does he want me for? I was thinking, did he watch that game against Argentina? Does he think I've lost a bit of pace after that Maradona wonder goal? Surely, he must have known we were playing at high altitude.

Never mind sprinting, it was hard enough putting your boots on. I knocked at his door. 'Come in son,' I went in. You had a great World Cup, son. You did yourself proud. But I have noticed you have lost a bit of weight. On your way out, by the door, is a crate of Guinness for you. Take it home and drink it. Put some iron back into your body.'

That was it. I walked out of that office thinking. That is man management at its finest'.

The day I left Bellefield was a day I will never forget. It was filled with sadness, but I left with amazing memories. And a few crates of Guinness."

PETER REID.

CHAPTER 22   A NEW BEGININING

Everton moved to Finch Farm on the 9th October, 2007. It was a new beginning for the club. In football you have to move with the times or you will get left behind and, as good as Bellefield was, it was essential Everton moved to a new base.

Seventeen- years later after it was first opened, Rochey and Parker were invited to visit Finch Farm by the Everton Media and Publications manager, Darren Griffiths, who kindly arranged to give them a guided tour. It was a far cry from their days at Bellefield some forty years previously when they would've done anything possible to meet their heroes.

It's six pm on a Tuesday night, mid-March. The dark nights are still lingering as Rochey and Parker drive down isolated country lanes towards floodlights that signal the new home of EFC.

The lights light up the pitch-black sky. There are two entrances into Finch Farm. We are greeted at the front gates by two security guards, who took our names, then allowed us to pass through the security gates. Another forty metres drive we were met by two Everton stewards who pointed us towards the car park and told us that Darren was expecting us. This was all a far cry from their days at Bellefield when Yogi the dog would 'greet' them by trying to take chunks out of their backsides.

I (Rochey) came with the mindset to nitpick at the tiniest thing. I loved everything about Bellefield all those years ago. I left disappointed! Finch Farm was out of this world. The first thing that I noticed was that everything was blue; even the cones in the car park.

Darren Griffiths met us at reception and greeted us with a smile. First, we were shown the Family Room which has a little shop serving tea and coffee. It's quite cozy.

Then we slipped through a side door to the laundry room, which was huge. At Bellefield, Jimmy Martin usually sent a few of the young lads to the local laundry in West Derby, to get the kits washed.

Here, at Finch Farm, everything is cleaned in one huge

laundry room.

Walking down the long corridor, either side had a changing room for each age group from the under 6's up to the under 16's. They all had showers with toilets, and lockers.

On the walls were pictures of all the previous academy players that have gone on to play in the first- team for Everton. It was a well thought out plan to give the young lads an incentive to work hard, as one day it could be one of them on the walls. The walls and floors in the corridor were long, bright and spotless.

Walking down the corridor I chatted to Kevin O' Brien, who works at Everton as a goalkeeping coach.

As we left that part of the building, Darren pointed over to the section where Everton Ladies team train. The pitches outside that part of Finch Farm were arranged especially for goalkeepers' drills. Whilst the school-boys were training on the pitches facing. Darren pointed over to the main pitch where the first-team trained. The excitement was huge! It had under-soil heating and was the same size to the millimeter as the Goodison Park playing surface. Finch Farm is about twenty times longer than Bellefield.

The coaching staff have a buggy that takes the training stuff from pitch to pitch; cones, balls, bibs, and other bits. Just past the pitches is a twenty foot-bench attached to a sink with running water to clean their football boots after training.

In the corner were two back-to-back five-a-side pitches. named the 'Sid Benson' and the 'Bob Pendleton.' I remarked that was a great touch as both of these men were great Evertonians who scouted for Everton. These two men didn't need an introduction. With those two, if you know, you know what their all about.

Darren then took us inside to show us the indoor pitch. It was twice the size of the indoor Bellefield pitch, with an astroturf surface, smooth as carpet. We were both blown away! Inside, Darren introduced us to former Everton player, James Vaughan, who was coaching and supervising the Everton Under six, seven, eight, nine, and ten teams. The pitch was divided into areas so the kids could train without any interference from their parents, who viewed the training session from up above on the balcony.

We were then taken into another part of the building. It was like a never-ending corridor, with rooms coming at us from all angles. The whole scale of the place was huge. We passed the state-of-the-art treatment room and a doctor's surgery was situated next to the treatment room. A bit further down was an indoor pool with a jacuzzi.

We carried on walking and both of us were astonished with the high-performance gym. The kit rooms and store rooms were twice the size of the kit and store rooms that were in Bellefield. You couldn't help but be impressed with the place. It was immaculately clean and well-lit up. It was like being in another world, ahead of our time.

Next, Darren, took us through a doorway which led us into the under 21's dressing room. Two baths in the shape of a number 8, showers, full size lockers, a television on the wall with Sky Sports news on and a darts board in the dressing room was what we got to see. Unbelievable!

Going outside the building were the first-team training pitches. They were set out with drills and goals here and there and everywhere. The pitches were next to each other, with trolleys full of energy drinks with individual players' names on them.

We weren't allowed into first team building but as they were away on a team bonding training camp in Portugal. It hardly mattered, as what we had been shown was out of this world. And that was just what the kids used. We ventured back inside up to the first team dining area that had on-site chefs working there. The room was set up, fruit and drinks; all healthy options, it was like eating inside a five-star hotel.

Everton take their recycling very seriously using colour coded bins for their different types of waste, helping the environment any way they can.

Moving out of the first team dining area we walked a few feet down the corridor into the under 21's dining area which they share with the women's team, the staff, and the under 18's team.

There was a Rota on the noticeboard that showed each team when it was their time to eat.

Darren Griffiths, was the perfect host.

He smiled at Tony Bellew, as he walked through the dining area. The former W.B.C. cruiserweight World Champion, is a great Evertonian himself.

Parker ended up having a flashback, much to the embarrassment of me.

In his head Parker was thinking, how did Tony Bellew, only come second in I'm a Celebrity.

He was his winner of I'm a Celebrity…. Get Me Out of Here!

Parker went back to being that 11-year-old kid who collected autographs all those years ago.

He asked Tony Bellew for a picture with him and he duly obliged like a true gentleman he is. I stayed cool (well one of us had to) and restrained myself from asking for a pic and I just chatted to Tony about football.

The tour ended after a visit to the media room.

Darren Griffiths was the perfect host. One of his jobs at Everton is helping to build bridges with the supporters.

Lots of his work goes unnoticed but what he does for the club is phenomenal. He's a true blue. A top Evertonian.

I have seen Darren's work first-hand in the Everton Hub for Everton in the Community and I was very impressed with his enthusiasm and management skills.

As me and Parker were thanking Darren after a great tour we bumped into Lawrence Wilson, at the Main Entrance.

He was a former Everton player who was on the Everton bench for the first team in a European Cup tie.

He stopped to chat. I was glad Parker didn't get another flashback and ask Lawrence for his autograph, which would have been really odd, as they're cousins!

Me and Parker were impressed by Finch Farm, it's out of this world.

if Richard Masters, the managing director of the Premier League has ever visited Finch Farm and still called Everton a 'small club,' it would answer a lot of questions that have been unanswered. (as small clubs don't train in a complex so advanced as Finch farm)

One thing Finch Farm didn't have that Bellefield did, was the closeness and the bond that the players had with the supporters that turned up day in day out for autographs. The kids of today will never have what the kids of yesterday did all those years ago standing outside Bellefield.

I hope everyone who has read this book has enjoyed the tales of Bellefield and that it has bought back a few memories from those that grew up during those times. For those that didn't experience those days I hope it has shown them what it was like before the Premier League was formed, because at times you'd think (with all the coverage and stats on the footballing channels) that football didn't exist until 1992!

The End

Printed in Great Britain
by Amazon